THE LONG REFRAIN

SWEET SOUTHERN
BOOK 4

MAYA JEAN

Alpha read by JJ and Hannah

Beta read by Amber, Lexi, Gabi, Devin, Donatella, and Jenni.

Edited by L.C. Valentine

Proofread by Judy's Proofreading

Cover by Black Jazz Design

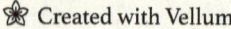 Created with Vellum

For Kristen and Lauren,
thank you for talking me down from the balcony ledge.

DEAR READER,

Thank you for joining me on this journey. Benji and Nolan are probably the rawest story I'll ever write. Unfortunately, it took me a while to learn as an author how to write characters that aren't born from my soul. I learned that after finishing this particular story. That also means this book left me flayed open and vulnerable.

Nolan's journey is personal to me because his journey is my own. Benji is a beautiful mix of every person who has ever looked at me and thought that I was worth loving. Because of many Benjis in my life, I'm still here today.

If you're struggling, there are many places to contact for help. Please call 988 if you're in crisis or visit thetrevorproject.org if you're in the queer community and seeking help. The best thing I ever did was say, "I need help." My journey is far from over, but I take solace in sharing a journey with one of my favorite characters. I hope that maybe Nolan can help the right person at the right time, as that's always my only wish for any of my characters.

On that note, this book is the end of the journey for now. I can't write Joey and Lee in the mental state I'm in and do their story justice. One day, I'll return, but for now, I must write stories that take me away somewhere else. Clay Springs will always be there to welcome you (and me) home, but for now, I must travel elsewhere. I hope you will come along for the ride.

All my love,

MJ

TRIGGER AND CONTENT WARNINGS

- Rough sex (biting/slapping/marking)
- Suicidal ideation
- Self-hate
- Breathplay / consensual choking
- CNC
- On-page suicide attempt (NOT GRAPHIC)
- Past abuse in the foster care system (not sexual abuse)
- Death of a grandparent
- Attempted suicide of a parent
- Parents with addiction
- Parental abandonment
- Disassociation as a coping mechanism
- Past self-harm
- Depression

PLAYLIST

- Nothing Else Matters by Metallica
- Closer by NIN
- November Rain by Guns N' Roses
- Black Hole Sun by Soundgarden
- Cryin' by Aerosmith
- Only Happy When It Rains by Garbage
- Alive by Pearl Jam
- Down with the Sickness by Disturbed
- Simple Man - Rock Version by Shinedown
- Black by Pearl Jam
- House of the Rising Sun by Ramin Djawadi
- It's Been Awhile by Staind
- Turn The Page by Metallica
- Daylight by Davind Kushner
- THE DEATH OF PEACE AND MIND by Bad Omens
- Drive by Incubus
- One Last Breath by Creed
- Running Up That Hill by Placebo

Playlist

- Jenny by NOTHINGMORE
- Push by Matchbox Twenty
- Behind Blue Eyes by Limp Bizkit
- Broken by Seether (Ft. Amy Lee)
- Not Strong Enough by Apolcalyptica
- Battle Born by Five Finger Death Punch
- Breath by Breaking Benjamin
- Iris by The Goo Goo Dolls
- Here Without You by Three Doors Down
- Between the Bars by Elliot Smith
- All I Wanted by Paramore
- Black Velvet by Leo
- Hate Me by Blue October
- House of the rising Sun by Red Leather
- Time in a Bottle by Jim Croce
- Stay by Rihanna
- Nothing Else Matters by Apocalyptica
- Come Home by OneRepublic
- Colorblind by Counting Crows
- Shine by Collective Soul
- Angel Baby - Acoustic by Troye Sivan
- Eight by Sleeping At Last
- Times Like These by Foo Fighters
- Square One by Tom Petty
- I Don't Want To Miss A Thing by Aerosmith

PART ONE

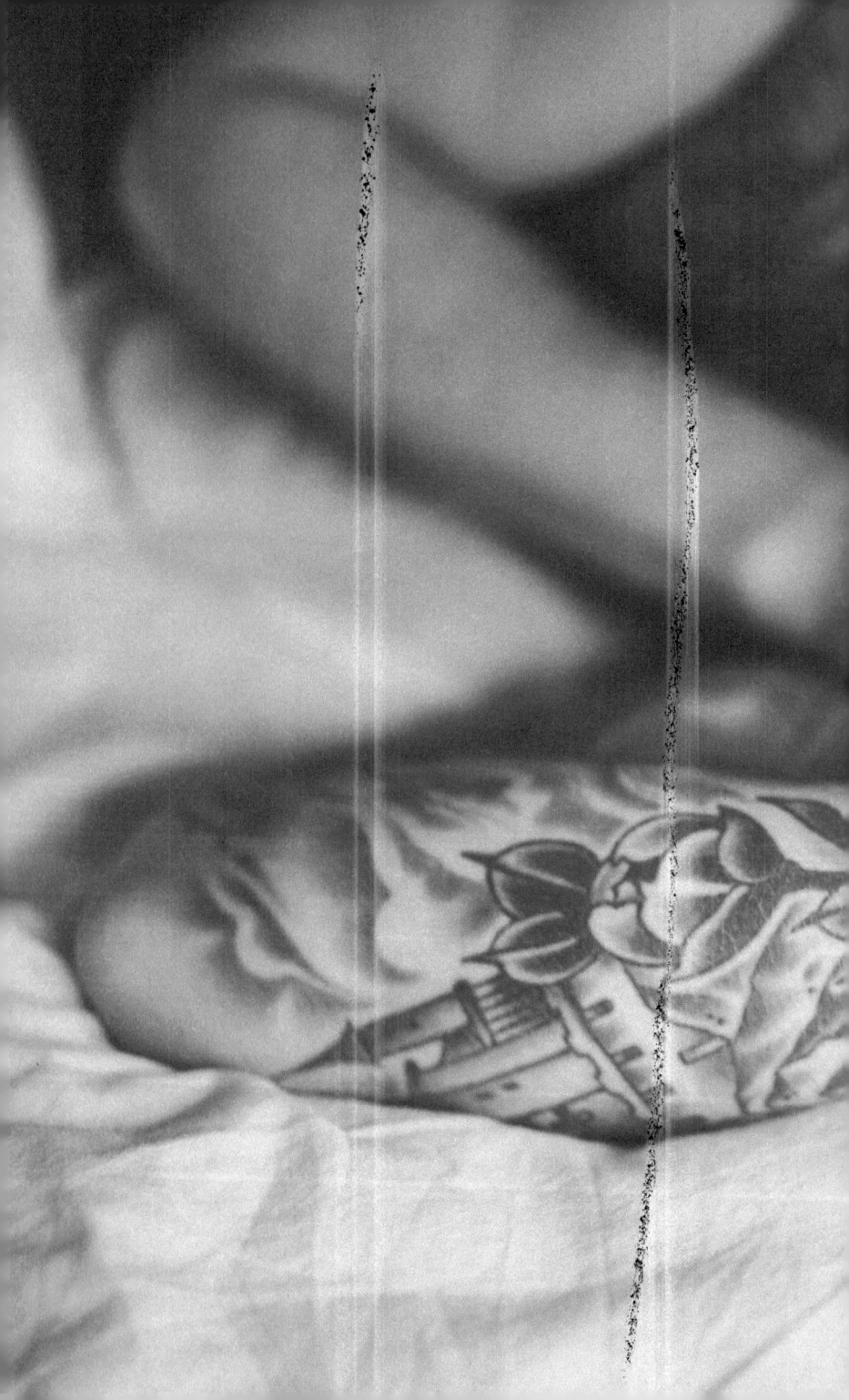

1

BENJI

OCTOBER 2026

Nothing is more exhilarating than a good hike. Even the hour-long drive out of Atlanta doesn't faze me. Fresh air in my face, compacted dirt beneath my feet, yeah, this is heaven. The burn of my muscles is a pleasant bonus when I finally reach the scenic overview.

Taking a deep breath, I let the serenity of nature instill me with peace—calm, quiet, and the absolute placidity of being one with nature.

Until my phone fucking buzzes in my pocket.

Jesus Christ.

Taking another deep, relaxing breath, I pull my phone out of my pocket. The damn thing slips in my sweaty palm for a second, almost falling over the cliff, but I grip tightly as I swipe at the screen. All that for an email from Davis. *Will—*

My heart pounds as I open the email.

Benji,

Claire is asking if you can take over the Nolan account for Trevor due to a last-minute emergency on his behalf. She asks that you do not reach out to Trevor at this time. Plea—

you're available for this weekend in Chicago. Standard rate, standard session, with a flight paid for by Nolan.

Please reply if you're available.

Davis

FIRST OFF, what the fuck is wrong with Trevor? Second... The options must be down to zero if they're asking *me* to spend a night with Nolan, the rockstar who likes to bite. I mean, we all talk, none of us are very secretive about the johns we end up with. Well, except for Trevor. That man would rather drown than admit anything remotely personal about his life.

There promptly goes the blessed high of a good hike. Might as well turn around and head back down. With my headphones snug in my ears, I dial Eli's number and slip my phone back into my pocket as I carefully pick my way back down the trail.

"Benji!" Eli says enthusiastically.

"Why are they contracting me to Nolan?" I ask, cutting through the pleasantries.

"What?" Eli whispers, voice going scarily low in disbelief.

"I just got an email from Davis that they're contracting me with Nolan because Trevor's had a last-minute thing come up."

"That's odd."

Sweat prickles at my hairline as I hurry down the trail. Nervously wiping at my wet forehead, I clear my throat to ask the question I really want to ask. Eli knows everything about all of us, the sensitive ear when we all need someone to talk it out with.

"Do you think I can do it? Trevor's always said... well. I'm not much into pain play. Receiving it at least."

Eli sighs thoughtfully. A car horn beeps through his end of the phone and Eli swears softly. I bite my lip to contain my sarcastic quip about Eli's very bad driving. The fact he still has a license is astounding. He's got to be one ticket away from attending driving school at this point.

"I think you can do it," Eli says confidently, although his tone is anything but confident. "If you're comfortable with it. I'd take him if I could but... he's a bottom..."

"Right," I say quickly.

"Also, Trevor told me that he likes it wicked rough. Like to the point that sometimes Trevor gets a little scared by it, but he's a really nice guy. Just the only way he can get off, I guess. Plus you know... closeted rockstar and all that."

I listen to Eli ramble as he drives. His points aren't helping my racing mind at all. Being a fake boyfriend is chill for me. I like to fuck and I like getting paid for it, what's not to enjoy? But I usually cater to the older guys that want someone sweet, just a boy for the weekend or on their arm. The gentle older guys are my specialty, not the borderline violent rockstars. Those are definitely Trevor's territory.

But I can take one for the team like anyone else.

"Yeah, I'll do it. Can't guarantee how it'll go if he bites me, though. My little cousin bit me when she was three and I still have war flashbacks."

"I think it'll be very different from *that*," Eli says around a loud laugh. "Plus, Nolan is hot as hell. I'm a little jealous. Maybe I could try being a top just for him."

Mocking laughter bubbles out of me before I can hold it back. I can practically feel Eli's narrowed eyes sliding through my earbuds. The bottom of the trail swims into my vision, despite the sweat dripping from my hair and down my face.

How is Georgia still so fucking hot even in October? I need to move to somewhere freezing. Penguins!

"Are you listening?" Eli all but yells into the phone.

"Sorry, I got caught up thinking about penguins."

"Of course."

"They're cute!"

Eli laughs, but it's forced. "Of course, sweetheart. Are you going to contract with Nolan? When is it?"

"This weekend. I'm going to let Davis know that it's fine. I'll do it."

"You'll let me know if you need me?"

I jump from the gravel trail to the concrete of the parking lot with a grin. "Yeah, bestie. Don't worry about it. I've got it."

Eli makes a questioning sound in the back of his throat. We hang up just as I reach my Jeep. Lifting up the back panel, I grab a towel out of my duffel bag. The sun beats down on me as I wipe the sweat off. Thankfully, I had the forethought to place a towel on the driver's seat before even starting my hike.

I forgot to pack a clean T-shirt... again. I never learn. Oh well, I'm just driving home, I don't need a shirt. Hopping into the driver's seat, heavy rock music drifts through the speakers as the Jeep rumbles to life. Before pulling out of the parking lot, I shoot Davis an email back letting him know I'll take the contract with Nolan. A weekend in Chicago doesn't sound too bad.

THE WEEKEND STARTS off great since I'm treated to first-class seats. Wow, this Nolan guy spares no expense for his escorts. Now I get why Trevor usually gives the guy whatever he wants. I have my fair share of johns that dote on me, but usually, it's in the form of fancy hotel rooms, sometimes even lavish gifts. I have a drawer of Rolexes in my apartment back at the high-rise. I've never worn them, but the thought is nice.

Departing the plane takes the least amount of time ever since I'm already at the front. An older gentleman in a suit stands at the bottom of the escalator by baggage claim with a sign that says, *Benji White.*

I skip up to him with a charming smile. "I'm Benji!"

The man takes one look at me and snorts in apparent disbelief. That's kind of mean. I'm one second away from telling him such when he takes my bag from my shoulder, leading me out of the airport.

"Is the hotel far away?"

The man shakes his head. "Just downtown. Not far." He peeks at me with his eyebrows furrowed. "The agency sent you? I knew Trevor wasn't coming, but I expected something a little more... like him."

"Blond?" I ask, confused.

The man snorts yet again, adding to my rising irritation. "When's your return flight?"

"Sunday morning."

"We'll see about that," the man utters under his breath as we make our way towards the parking garage.

Obviously, I'm not getting anywhere with this guy. He loads me into a giant blacked-out SUV and starts driving without another word. Awkward silences are worse than dental cleanings. I'd honestly rather have a hygienist all up in my mouth than sit through an awkward silence that I can't fill, which is probably why I talk through my dental cleanings.

We pull up in front of a lavish-looking hotel. I probably should've dressed better, but being dressed up on a flight is yet another thing that I hate, so jeans and a ratty T-shirt it was. I'll just change when I get into the room.

The old man turns around, hand on the passenger side headrest. He fixes me with a very hard look, but I just stare back, uncaring about whatever his problem with me seems to be.

"Let me know if you need me to pick you up early."

I grin with all my teeth. "I'll see you on Sunday morning."

Grabbing my bag from the seat beside me, I slam the door of the SUV with enough force that it rattles my teeth. The porter opens the door for me with a small snarl of his lip. All these people can suck it.

"Benji!"

The sound of my name freezes me halfway to the reception desk. Glancing around the fancy first floor, a man in a pristine suit with a sweet smile wanders towards me.

"Chris, Nolan's manager." He holds his hand out to me as his gaze sweeps over me.

We shake hands firmly, both of us sizing each other up by our grip. "Shouldn't you be at his show?"

"Show's not far. I'll get you up into the room, go over some of the rules, then I'll bring Nolan back here for you."

Rules? What rules? Chris promptly turns on his heel and heads towards the expanse of elevators at the other side of the sparkling marble lobby. He swipes a card over a reader that allows him to press PH on the pad. I assume that means penthouse. Nice. Chris taps away at his phone the entire ride up.

Sliding my duffel bag higher up my shoulder, I follow

along behind him like a good little escort. Chris unlocks the door, opening it with his shoulder so that I can walk in first. The room is dark except for the glittering lights of the Chicago skyline through the windows.

"Alright, first things first, I assume you were made aware of what Nolan expects?" Chris asks, still typing away at his phone screen.

"I signed a nondisclosure agreement with Claire."

Chris glances up at me with a deep frown. "That's not what I asked."

I tuck my hands into my jeans pockets to stop from fidgeting. "I'm aware of what Nolan expects."

"Good. There are only two penthouses on this floor, we've rented out both. Nolan has his show tonight, off tomorrow, and then he leaves on Sunday. So, you're his for the weekend."

I always hate getting spoken about this way, like because I'm being paid for sex, that takes away every ounce of *me* in my body. Like I'm just for them to use, to discard when they're done. Maybe that's true for some, but that's never what I seek out as an escort.

"I'm aware. I'm an escort," I say with as little bite as I can.

Chris glances up from the screen at my tone, approval written all over his face. He pockets his phone with a soft smile. "You'll do great. I'll be back here with him around midnight if the meet and greets don't go too long. Get settled in."

He disappears out the front door, leaving me standing alone in the marble foyer. I shake out the restless energy that accumulated throughout my travels and decide to show myself around. After a quick tour of the penthouse, I drop my bag off at what I assume is the master suite. With a couple of hours until Nolan arrives, maybe I can squeeze in a run at the penthouse gym, a long shower, and maybe even a small dinner.

2

NOLAN

OCTOBER 2026

Wretched noise. Claps. Screams. Drums. The loud sounds strike me as if I'm sand and they're lightning. A perfect storm that sends my brain into a rolling fit of anxiety until air is hard to come by. Until my fingers twitch, mouth goes dry, and the world blurs. In the earlier years of touring, the cure-all for this was to get blackout drunk after a show. But I can't do that anymore because of *sobriety*. Most days I feel like I'm sober against my will, just sober to keep my team happy, to keep the shows coming. A cash cow.

So I have to settle for the next best thing.

Fucking my brains out until the world slips away, until everything is quiet, until I'm no longer Nolan. Just any other man on this miserable floating rock of pain.

My team quietly hustles me back to the hotel nestled just a few blocks from the arena. The bodyguards rotate so often that I don't even know their names. Only Chris remains constant in my life. The perfect manager who got us number one hits and gets to spend his life babysitting me.

Chris types away on his phone as he guides me to the hotel elevators. All of the lights are too bright. I just barely resist the urge to rub at my temples, knowing that if I do, it'll send Chris on high alert. Everyone's just always waiting for me to fuck up. The odds are always high, so I don't blame them.

The elevator doors slide closed, but Chris keeps his attention off me. Probably because he knows if he asks me one single, solitary question, this entire house of cards is going to collapse. I'll never get used to the ostentatious hotels I get to stay in now that I'm filthy rich. So different from my modest childhood in a double-wide with my grandma.

It takes fifteen steps to get from the elevator to the doors of the penthouse. Chris knocks once, swipes the card over the card reader, then tucks it into the back pocket of my too-expensive jeans. He disappears down the hall with a wave over his shoulder. The perfect manager.

Darkness permeates the hotel room, only the light from the hallway cutting through it. The night skyline of Chicago shimmers outside the hotel windows. My eyes glance around for Trevor, the escort I've been contracting with for the past few months. But instead, my eyes land on an unfamiliar shape standing at the hotel windows. The man has his thumbs hooked into the belt loops of his pressed pants. At the sound of my sharp inhale, the man turns around to appraise me with piercing eyes.

He's beautiful in a way that kind of hurts. My lip instantly curls at the sight of him. This man is so beautiful, there's no way I can cause him pain like I need to. The way that'll shut off all the fucking noise in my brain. The merciless noise that whispers words to me, that makes me want to shrink into myself, curl into a tight ball until I disappear off the face of this miserable planet. This wretched, haunting place.

The man blinks light blue eyes at me in the unlit room. He swallows loudly, throat bobbing with the movement.

"Where's Trevor?" I ask abruptly, shattering the perfect silence of the hotel room.

"Busy. I'm your new boyfriend."

I snort and take a few steps towards him. "You've already lost the plot, dude. I hire escorts, not the fake boyfriend shit Claire offers. We're here to fuck. I assume Claire told you what I like?"

The man tilts his head to the side as he takes me in from the tips of my toes to the top of my head. I cross my arms over my chest, knowing that I look the picture of a rockstar after a grueling concert.

"I know what you like, but do you know what you like?"

What the hell kind of psychoanalyzing shit is that? "I know exactly what I like. Take off your clothes and get on the bed."

The man doesn't even bristle, I'll give him that. Instead, he stands there and slowly begins to undress. Over the years I've perfected my poker face, mostly for interviews when they ask benign, annoying questions that make me want to punch something. Preferably the person asking the question. Every inch of tanned skin that is slowly revealed makes me question my ability to keep that poker face, though.

Where does this fucking agency get these men? Because they're all hot to the point of absurdity. This one is no different. Trevor was hot as sin and willing to put up with whatever I threw at him. A fun time. But this one, he's radiating hostility, which is oddly kind of a turn-on. He carefully slips off his button-up, folds it, and then sets it on the chair in the corner of the room.

"My name is Benji, by the way," Benji says as he slowly unbuttons his pants.

The name takes a few moments to register in my brain since I'm too focused on the inches of skin that are slowly being revealed. He has a swimmer's build. Broad shoulders that taper to a thin waist, a splash of freckles across his cheeks, and disheveled light brown hair. My fingers twitch with the need to touch him, bruise him, toss him around like a rag doll despite him having more weight on me. We're almost evenly matched, but I'm just slightly shorter.

"I don't care about your name," I snarl.

Benji laughs once he's in only his boxer briefs. He gestures towards his body, lips twitching with a barely constrained smirk. So it's like that.

"I believe for us to fuck you need to get undressed as well."

I gesture at my own body, clearly mocking him. "That's your job."

Benji steps closer, smelling like aftershave and expensive sweet cologne. I try to keep my breathing even as he works his fingers under my shirt, slowly trailing it up over my head until I'm shirtless. Instead of moving on to my pants, Benji splays his hot hands over my chest, then curves them around to grip my ribs. The noises in my head slowly quiet under his touch, until I can only hear the gentle inhale-exhale of his slow breathing.

He tugs me to him, until I can feel the hardness of his cock against my hip. My eyes dip to his mouth, the gentle curve of his plush lips. His top lip is a little plumper than the bottom, and a freckle sitting at the corner of his mouth stands out from the rest dotting his cheeks.

"Is kissing allowed?" Benji asks quietly.

"If you're a good kisser," I reply.

Benji's lips twitch again in obvious amusement. "I'm a great kisser."

Before I can reply with something caustic and bitingly sarcastic, his lips come down on mine. My brain shuts off under the onslaught of his kiss. It's too gentle though, so the quiet doesn't last long. I curl my fingers in the hairs at the nape of his neck, using the hair to tilt his head to the side so I can kiss him harder, shoving my tongue into his mouth so he gets the idea of how tonight is going to go.

He's a good boy because he doesn't fight me. Just lets me kiss him like I'm fucking him. Licking into his mouth, biting at his lip, everything and anything until my cock is so hard that I'm afraid I'll lose my practiced stamina and come right in my pants. I back him up towards the bed until he falls, and I follow him down with our mouths still fused together. His hands never leave my torso, holding on tight, fingers digging into the spaces between my ribs.

I pull away from his mouth to bite at his neck. When my teeth press into his skin, his fingers curl painfully into my sides. Nails bite at my skin and I grin into the crook of his neck. One of Benji's hands tangles in my hair, tugging my head back until he can aim his narrow-eyed gaze at me.

"That hurts, asshole."

I blink slowly at him in the darkness. "That's the point."

"Your turn," Benji says slowly before flipping us over.

Benji takes my wrists in a tight grip, holding them over my head against the mattress. My pulse thunders at the touch, like I'm a rabbit caught by a wolf in a shadowy forest. His gaze is dark even in the pitch black of the bedroom. His fingers squeeze my wrist once, making my brain focus on the pressure of his grip instead of the sudden flip in the dynamic.

"What are you doing?" I ask quietly but firmly.

Benji's grin is infectious with its beauty. Like pure fucking sunshine.

"Giving you a taste of your own medicine."

And then Benji dips down to bite my shoulder. The pain slides through me, slowly, like lava inching down the side of a volcano. His bite isn't remotely gentle, just like mine wasn't. No doubt there will be a bite mark on my skin for days to come. No one has ever bitten me back. Who the fuck is this guy? I struggle against his grip, but he doesn't let go, he just glides his lips along my shoulder, to the crook of my neck, then up my cheek so he can press his mouth against my ear.

"What's the ruling?" Benji asks, his breath hot against the shell of my ear.

I struggle against his grip again, but only half-heartedly this time. His weight presses me into the bed, his cock hard against mine. I'm not going to answer him with words. I roll my hips up until our cocks slide together through his boxers and my pants.

"Thought so," Benji whispers against my skin with a sinful chuckle. He lifts his head up to press the tip of his nose against mine, making my eyes blur as I try to keep my gaze on him. "I've been told what you like, but I clocked you the minute you walked through that door." Benji untangles his hand from my hair to pat my cheek in an infuriatingly mocking manner. "How about I run the show tonight? Turn off that brain of yours?"

I swallow loudly, fear sluicing through me. "You won't tell anyone?"

Benji cocks his head in confusion. "Tell anyone what?"

"That you... that I let you..."

Benji stops me with a bone-melting kiss. When he pulls away, my body is liquid gold, my brain quiet as he swirls his fingers against my still overheated skin.

"I signed an NDA, but even if I didn't, tonight would be just ours, hmmm?"

Okay, yeah, that makes sense. What's the difference between giving pain and receiving anyway? It's all the same receptors in the brain. At least that's what I try to convince myself as Benji kisses down my chest, lips leaving fire in their wake. Pain is all I know, pleasure is a less common experience. Benji carefully undresses me, fingers touching any spare skin he can find, lips lingering on the skin of my thighs, even the scarred pieces that are hidden by tattoos.

His fingers dip to the back of my knees, carefully pressing up until my feet are flat against the bed, knees bent. Everything is too slow, too sweet. The anxiety is welling up inside me, I can't take it. Just when I'm about to kick him, shove him the fuck away, his teeth press into my inner thigh. A low moan escapes me at the sweet pleasure of the pain. His teeth stay there long enough for me to feel my heartbeat pounding under my skin, the decadent promise of a bruise tomorrow.

Benji proceeds to bite the hell out of my thighs. The feeling is so indescribable, so perfect. I stare up at the unlit chandelier hanging above us. The glass is dull in the dark, no sparkle left in it. Sometimes that's how I feel when I perform. The only time I mean anything is when I'm on stage, when I'm performing for my fans, for the fucking label. Like a damn chandelier that's only worth anything when lit up.

I toss my arm over my eyes to stop the thoughts wanting to invade this moment I've paid a lot of money for. Benji stops biting and smacks my thigh hard, the slap ringing through the silence of the room. Removing my arm from my face, I turn my gaze back towards him.

"Did you take a shower at the arena?" Benji asks, voice firm, but low.

I swallow hard. "Yes."

"On your hands and knees."

"No."

Benji rises up to his knees on the bed and places his hands on either side of my head. His gaze is dark, fathomless, even in the dim of the hotel room. God, his eyes are so light blue. Like a fucking husky. Who even has eyes like that?

Lifting one hand, Benji pinches my chin between his fingers. "Get on your hands and knees, Nolan. I won't ask twice. Don't you want my cock?"

My entire body goes liquid. "Yes."

Benji sits back on his haunches, watching me like a hawk with those damn impossible eyes. I let my gaze linger over his taut abs, his hard cock hanging heavy between his thighs in a small patch of light brown hair. I roll over onto my hands and knees with a quiet exhale. Benji runs his hands over my back, tips of his fingers skipping up the curve of my spine.

Folding my arms, I bury my face in the silky soft comforter. My breath puffs against the material, rebounding back up against my face with each heavy exhale. Benji is quiet behind me until I hear the telltale sound of a lube bottle. This part I know, this part is easy. Giving myself over to someone until my body is no longer my own, belonging only to them. After all, I always belong to someone else, never myself.

Instead of feeling lube-slick fingers pressing inside me, the soft touch of Benji's tongue jerks me out of my thoughts.

"What are you doing?" I exclaim, voice high-pitched as fear rolls through me.

Benji presses down on my lower back until I curve back towards the bed. His skin is so hot against my own chilled body.

"Who's in charge tonight?" Benji whispers against the skin at the small of my back.

I kick at him hard, my heel connecting with his thigh. "I'll let you think you're in charge, but we all know it's me. Get on with it, motherfucker."

Benji rewards my attitude with a stinging slap to my ass. I dig my fingers into the thick comforter as Benji returns his attention to my ass. His fingers bite into my thighs as he holds me still, holds me so that I can't squirm away from his seeking mouth. When he presses his tongue into my hole, I clench my thighs hard to keep from crying out. My vision goes black for one solid second as he moans softly. He turns his head away, resting his face against one ass cheek. I have no idea why that's so fucking endearing like he has to keep touching me even as he catches his breath.

"It's a trip having a tattooed rockstar at my mercy," Benji admits quietly, words uttered so softly I don't think he intended me to hear them.

"Stop saying cute shit and just fuck me."

Benji's sigh is long and loud, but he listens. He stops trying to fuck me with his tongue and crawls back up my body.

"Put your hands on the headboard, Nolan," Benji orders, breath fanning across my back with each word.

Against my better judgment, I do as Benji says. I stare listlessly at my tattooed knuckles wrapped around the wrought iron headboard. The metal is freezing under my palms. I use the cold to anchor me to the now, in the moment, so I don't float away on a spiral of overthinking.

Benji's lube-covered fingers reach underneath me to touch my cock, and I slap his hand away. "No."

Benji is scarily still behind me. "What are you saying no to?"

"Don't touch my dick, dude. Just fuck me."

Fingers bite into my hips as Benji breathes heavily behind me. For one taut second, he drops his forehead over my shoulder blades, breath puffing hot against my chilled skin. Benji's warmth disappears, making my skin prickle with the cool air around us.

One, two, three, four.

Benji returns before I can reach five. His large palm presses against the small of my back, steadying himself as he pushes his condom-covered cock into me. The burn is familiar and I grit my teeth through it. Something about being fucked centers all the emotions inside me going a million different ways.

Once Benji bottoms out inside me, he curves his upper body against my back, his fingers wrapping around my wrists. He presses his face against mine, the heat of him bringing me back to life after weeks of feeling detached from my own body.

"Next time, we fuck with you on your back so I can watch you," Benji whispers against the shell of my ear.

I shake my head to make him go away. "Come on."

Benji chuckles darkly and rises up, his hands finding a home on my hips. "Fine, Nolan. Have it your way."

He pulls out all the way, only the tip of his cock still inside me. When he slams back into me, he knocks all the wind out of my lungs. Seconds go by before I can gulp in a breath of air, just in time for him to do it all over again. Benji is relentless, pummeling into me until all the air inside me has evaporated. My vision darkens, just in time for him to bend over, pace not faltering for a second. His fingers curl over my throat, squeezing so tightly that any ounce of air making its slow way down my throat is frozen in its tracks.

"Lift up," Benji orders. His breath comes in low pants against the side of my neck.

I lift up slightly and gasp at the change in angle. Benji presses his pleased grin into the sweaty crook of my neck. He dips his fingers between mine on the headboard, anchoring me in the exact position he wants to take my body for himself. My eyes roll back in my head as he seeks his own pleasure inside of me, as the heat of him seeps into me, giving me life after so many months on the edge of destruction.

"Are you going to come?" Benji pants against my shoulder, teeth biting down so hard I lose my breath all over again.

"No."

Benji squeezes my neck again, harder, tighter, perfect. "Come."

My brain is a traitor of epic proportions. Teeth buried in my skin, fingers curled over mine on the headboard, my brain turns right off, and the pleasure dials up to one thousand. Lightning zips down my spine, curling my toes into the soft, plush comforter. With a quiet scream, I come untouched as Benji relentlessly fucks me. The moan that rattles around us as he stills inside me almost has me ready to go again.

This is when I usually kick Trevor away, make him go order room service, anything but touch me when I'm most vulnerable. But Benji doesn't even give me a chance. He pulls out of me slowly, either ignoring my hiss or noting it to remember for the next time. Instead of plopping on the bed, Benji lifts me from it, standing me on my shaky feet at its edge.

He cups my face in his palms, lifting my chin, imploring me to meet his gaze head-on. His smile is shaky, his eyes warm as he curls his fingers behind my ears.

"Good? Tell me, Nolan."

"Good," I say woodenly, not sure if I really mean it.

Benji nods quickly as if he takes my words at face value. "Okay, okay. Come on."

Benji's fingers tangle with mine as he leads me towards the en suite bathroom. He carefully positions me against the vanity, my back against the cool granite so I don't have to look at myself in the mirror. Does he know? There's no way. Not even Trevor knows I hate the sight of myself in the mirror. Even a glimpse of my reflection disgusts me.

I warily watch Benji move around the bathroom. Sweat glistens over his muscles. His hair is mussed from fucking, and there's an angry bite mark on his neck that'll be there for days. Some weird satisfaction rolls through me that I'll leave a mark on him. I always liked it with Trevor too. As if these men might leave me behind but I leave them with an indelible impression, one that can only be removed with time.

Benji finishes preparing a bath, then climbs into the tub, all long limbs and a gentle smile. Curling his fingers in invitation, he wordlessly waits for me to join him in the warm, amber-scented water. Every instinct in me says to run, says to flee, says to cut my losses before the weekend can progress any further.

But I don't.

I let him tug me into the water, and position me between his warm thighs. His hands trail over my arms, my chest, and any inch of skin he can find as he gently washes me of its sins.

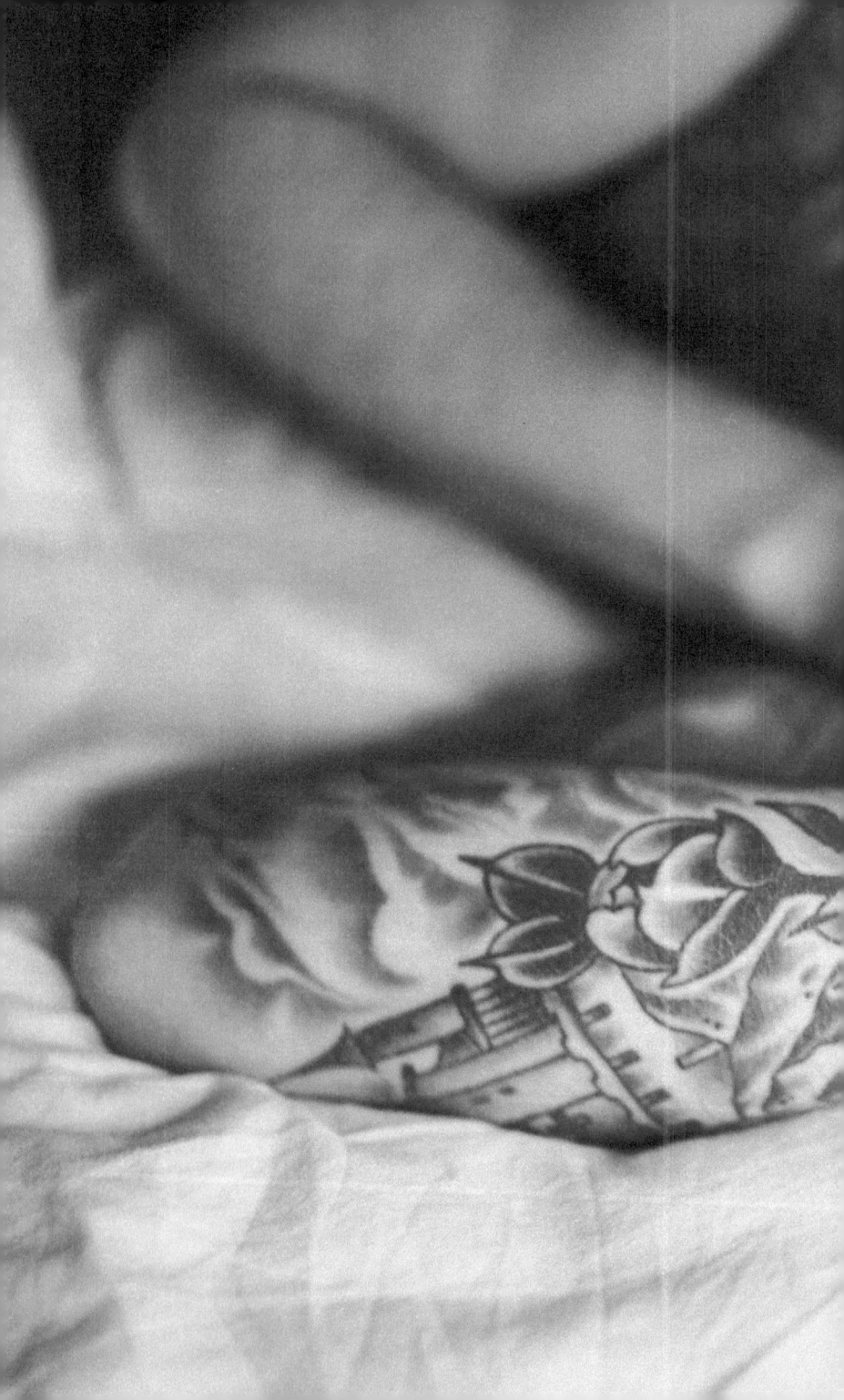

3

BENJI

OCTOBER 2026

Pain shoots through my entire body when I roll over on the heavenly hotel bed. I feel like I ran a marathon, then promptly got into a fight with a werewolf right after crossing the finish line. My body is beat to shit after just one and a half days with Nolan Hastings. Turning my head slowly to the side, my gaze lands on the sleeping man beside me. After fucking into the early morning, it must be afternoon now if the light streaming through the windows is anything to go by.

We'd slept until noon yesterday, fucked all throughout the afternoon, then Nolan had disappeared down the hall into another bedroom in a fit of irritation, before returning to me in the evening to fuck some more. He'd smelled like cigarettes and felt like rage personified. Three orgasms later, he was pliant under my hands, and willing to take another bath together. Maybe that's the trick to Nolan Hastings, fuck him until he gives me what I *need*. And what I need is to not be so at him because fucking nonstop isn't really my scene.

I slowly lift my arm to press at the cro

where the bite from the first night still tingles. After that initial bite, Nolan had spent less time biting, and more time seemingly accepting what we were doing for the weekend. The man is covered in tattoos from tip to toe, but I already knew that from all the magazine covers I've seen him grace over the years. I don't remember him being so thin though. His ribs stick out as he breathes softly, the sheet just barely covering his bare ass.

A Grim Reaper tattoo covers the entire expanse of his back. Beautiful brightly colored flowers cover his ribs, looking like they're wrapped around his bones, blooming to life as he breathes.

I'd expected a lot of things this weekend, but all expectations fell short of the actual Nolan. He's terrifyingly quiet and watches me like a hawk inside and outside of the bedroom. Yesterday afternoon I'd shaved and he'd watched me from the bed, eyebrows furrowed, fingers slowly tightening and releasing the messy sheets underneath him. Once I'd returned to the bed, he'd goaded me into fucking him again, on our knees as usual. We've fucked ten times by now, and still, he doesn't let me touch his cock. But each time he comes untouched with a small, pained gasp as if the action hurts him.

Nolan rolls onto his side, facing me on the bed. Lips parted in his sleep, he murmurs something that I can't understand. His words sound slurred in his sleep, making it hard for me to parse the words. After a few quiet seconds, a clear, pained, and terrified *no* floats from his lips. His arm comes up to protect his face from his dream just in time for another clear *no* to escape him.

"Nolan," I whisper softly, gently touching his bicep.

Nolan gasps and sits up in the bed, eyes wild and terrified.

His chest heaves with gasps as he tries to gulp in air. When he notices I'm watching, he squeezes his eyes shut tight against whatever look I must have on my face.

"Make yourself useful and order food," Nolan orders quietly, no bite in his voice. His fingers come up to rub at his temples.

"Okay," I say softly.

Nolan flops back against the bed with a giant huff, fingers still working at his temples as if he can massage out whatever dream woke him so abruptly. I take my time ordering us a late breakfast considering it's earlier than I'd initially thought. We'd only gotten five hours of sleep. I'm exhausted from the weird hours, but Nolan seems to be used to them. Rockstars, I guess.

The shower turns on just as I finish placing our breakfast order. Steam fills the air of the bathroom as I gently push the door open. Nolan's just about to step into the shower, but he casts an odd look at me over his shoulder.

"Up for one more round?" Nolan asks, a dangerous smirk lifting up the corner of his mouth.

"Aren't you tired?" I ask because honestly, I'm exhausted.

Nolan rolls his eyes and steps into the large shower. The overhead waterfall showerhead pours down over him. Tipping his head back, he runs his hands through his drenched hair, causing a cascade of water to sluice down his body in gushing rivers. Once he's fully soaked, he takes a step back to lean against the cold tile. Crooking one finger, he beckons me closer, eyes void of any emotion.

"I've got to get my money's worth. Get in here, stud."

My nose wrinkles in distaste at the nickname. Gross. But my cock hardens and I join him in the shower regardless. His dark chuckle reverberates around us. His hair is somehow even more inky when wet, eyes so black that they look perpetually rimmed with eyeliner. The skeleton hand tattoos around his neck also oddly do it for me, as if the bones are a guide for where I should place my own hands. Unable to resist, I do it now, laying my fingers over the inked skeleton's hands teasingly choking him.

His eyes flash at my touch. "Wanna choke me?"

I swallow loudly. "Never seriously done that before."

Nolan hooks his leg around my hip, tugging me closer until our cocks are lined up. A hiss escapes me and Nolan grins so widely that I can almost see his molars.

"I can teach you, stud," Nolan murmurs before wrapping his thin fingers around my wrists. He pulls my hands harder against his body until the pressure feels like too much against my freckled skin. "Tighten your fingers."

I do as he says, but hold back just a little, slightly terrified at the idea of accidentally killing one of the world's biggest rockstars because I downplayed my own strength. His pulse beats harder against my palms as his mouth parts on a silent gasp. Looking down between us, I notice his cock hardening even further at my touch, the angry red tip leaking pre-cum in the humidity of the shower. I wish he'd let me touch his cock. I want to swallow him whole, bring him pleasure just with my mouth.

"Pretty, isn't it?" Nolan asks, voice strained from the pressure I'm applying to his throat.

My eyes flit back to his heated gaze, mouth dry with want. "Let me suck you."

Nolan's eyes flash again. "Make me."

I squeeze his throat tighter, until the air whistles when he breathes in through his nose. Pressing him harder against the wall, time goes syrupy-slow. "I'm going to suck you off, and you're going to come down my throat. And you're going to like it."

Letting one of my hands drop from his neck, I move the other around to the front to splay my fingers around the center of that damned tattoo that's slowly driving me insane. The tiles are cold against my knees, but the quick drop is worth it when I look up at Nolan to find him staring down at me with wide, worried eyes. I squeeze my fingers tightly around his throat, arm stretched as far as it can go to keep my grip on him. Without further hesitation, I suck his cock to the back of my throat, swallowing around the perfect taste of him exploding on my tongue.

His fingers tangle roughly in my hair, keeping my face buried in his groin. When I lift my gaze back to him, his head is tilted back against the tiles, eyes squeezed shut to blot out the sight of me on my knees for him. Slowly lifting off his cock, I use my other hand to steady him at his base so that I can lick around the sensitive head. His knees tremble, so I suck him back down before he can collapse to the floor. Three good sucks and a hard throat squeeze later, he comes quietly down my throat. I swallow every single drop, then slither back up to stand toe to toe with him.

Nolan's eyes slowly blink open as if just realizing this wasn't all a dream. I dip down to kiss him softly, carefully coaxing him to open up for me so that I can share the taste of him on my tongue. He moans softly before pulling away with an annoyed grunt.

"Happy now?" Nolan asks with a snarl. He pushes me away so that he can grab at the body wash in the corner of the shower. I can't help but notice that his hands tremble as he squeezes soap onto a loofah, then angrily spreads it over his body to wash himself clean. The man makes no sense, running more hot and cold than the bad water heater at my mom's house.

"I'd be happier if you sucked my dick too."

Nolan's annoyed gaze dips to my neglected cock. "It'll be my parting gift."

"Blue balls?" I ask incredulously with a laugh.

"Sure," Nolan replies with a lazy shrug.

I try to keep my gaze off Nolan as he finishes up his shower, stepping out before I've finished washing my hair. The steam distorts the shape of his body through the foggy glass door, but it's easy to watch the shape of him. He dries off carefully, then hangs the towel on the bar with a gentle tug to ensure it lies correctly. He leaves the bathroom without a single glance in the mirror and for some reason that makes me feel something I can't explain.

Once I'm finished, dried, and dressed in sweatpants, I find Nolan in the living room of the penthouse with the breakfast I'd ordered spread across the table. He's slowly munching at a strawberry when his eyes flick over to me.

"You ordered enough food for an army," Nolan points out, sounding slightly annoyed.

I shrug as I toss myself in the chair opposite him. "Didn't know what you liked."

Nolan smirks as he licks bright crimson strawberry juice off his palm. "You'll learn."

I dive into the fancy-as-hell omelet on my plate with gusto because I'm fucking starved. In just a few inhales I'm done, so I move on to the fluffy French toast. Nolan leans back in his chair, appraising me as I gobble down my food like I haven't eaten in weeks.

"I'll have Chris reach out to you in a few more months for another weekend. It'll probably be in Los Angeles by then since I'll be recording the next album before going on the world tour at the end of next year."

"You like it?" I ask with a mouthful of French toast.

Nolan skewers me with a confused look. "Like what?"

"Performing? Making music?"

"No, and yes," Nolan answers as he bites into another strawberry.

"See you in a few months, I guess."

Nolan slowly licks his fingers clean of all evidence of the strawberry before speaking. "Give my love to Trevor. I'll contract with you going forward. And remember you signed an NDA."

I roll my eyes. "Kind of hard to forget. I don't have much, but I don't want to lose what I do have from breaching a contract I'm required to sign to fuck a rockstar."

Nolan pushes away from the table with a bitter laugh. He surprises me by coming around the table to kiss me hard and deep, tongue dipping into my mouth.

When he pulls away, he roughly slaps my cheek with a cruel smile. "You taste like breakfast. Now fuck off."

He disappears towards the large suite we've spent almost two days desecrating. A second later my packed duffel bag is thrown out of the bedroom. The door slam echoes through the quiet penthouse, setting my teeth on edge. What a fucking brat.

———

ONE ANNOYING FLIGHT and a long rideshare later, I arrive back at headquarters. It's early Sunday evening, so I don't expect many people to be hanging around. I probably should've gone straight to my own apartment, but I oddly felt like trying my hand at seeing who I could bother.

Lucky me, Eli is lying on the couch, reading some thick book that's probably required for one of his classes.

"Sup, bestie?" I ask, tossing myself on the other end of the couch.

Eli drops the book to his chest with a sweet smile. "So?"

I shrug helplessly. "He said he's canceling the ongoing contract with Trevor and wants to see me again in a few months."

Eli arches one eyebrow in surprise. "Oh?"

"He's a piece of work, for sure. I think I can handle him though."

"That's a different tune than you were singing a few days ago," Eli deftly points out. He's irritatingly right.

Before meeting Nolan I'd assumed it would be one huge failure of a weekend. But now I'm intrigued by the bitter man. He sets me off-kilter, makes me feel like my body isn't my own, in a way that doesn't terrify me.

"He's the weirdest fuck I've ever had."

Eli hums thoughtfully. "You sound like Trevor. Although, I'm not sure Trevor actually *liked* being with Nolan. You know how Trevor is."

I grunt in agreement. "Well, he's my client now. Pays a shit ton. I might take a few weeks off and travel somewhere. If Claire will let me."

"Somewhere sunny, I presume?"

I grin widely at him. "Of course, maybe Costa Rica. We'll see. What are you up to today?"

Eli sighs loudly. "Schoolwork. Jackson is gone for a week with a client. Trevor disappeared somewhere but Claire is keeping her mouth shut about it."

"It's odd," I point out, slightly concerned for Trevor. He's the most reliable of all of us.

"I'm not too worried. If it was bad, Claire would tell us. Send me pictures wherever you end up. And buy me a—"

"Magnet," I interrupt him with a grin.

Eli grins back with a small laugh and a flush staining his cheeks. I stand from the sofa, and lean over to tenderly kiss his warm cheek. Grabbing my duffel bag, I head towards Claire's office, pleased to find Davis gone for the day and Claire sitting quietly at her desk.

She perks up at the sight of me. "I just got an email asking for an *exclusive* contract between you and Nolan."

"What's that mean?"

Claire all out grins. "It means, he doesn't want any other boyfriend but you for the foreseeable future. He never even did that with Trevor. Look at you, nailing down Nolan Hastings with your wily ways."

"Say that ten times fast," I dare her.

Claire rolls her eyes. "Are you good with an exclusive contract?"

"Yeah, sure. By the way, I want to take a vacation. Disappear somewhere for a few weeks. All good?"

Claire clicks through the computer with deep concentration. "Yeah, it's fine. Chris estimated Nolan will want you again early next year."

"He told me."

Claire blinks slowly as she swings her gaze back to me. "Told you what?"

"Nolan told me before I left."

"Nolan told you?"

I tap the side of my head with a smirk. "Are you alright, boss lady? You're just repeating what I say."

"I'm fine," Claire says slowly, her gaze sweeping over me. "Are you fine?"

I pause slightly. "Yes?"

Claire makes a disbelieving sound, then returns to her computer. "Alright, I'll email you the contract for you to sign digitally. It's double your normal rate, by the way."

Double my normal rate? Jesus Christ. This means I can be choosier about the clients I do take since I'll be making so much with Nolan. More vacations. More surfing, more sand, more absolute quiet instead of the grind of the city. Perfect.

"I'll sign it. Now I'm going to go home and sleep off my sex hangover. Nolan is insatiable."

Claire's tinkling laughter follows me out of HQ. Once I'm showered and dressed in pajamas, I curl up into a tight ball in my bed with my phone cupped in my palms to sign the Nolan contract. Sleep claims me moments after signing on the dotted line.

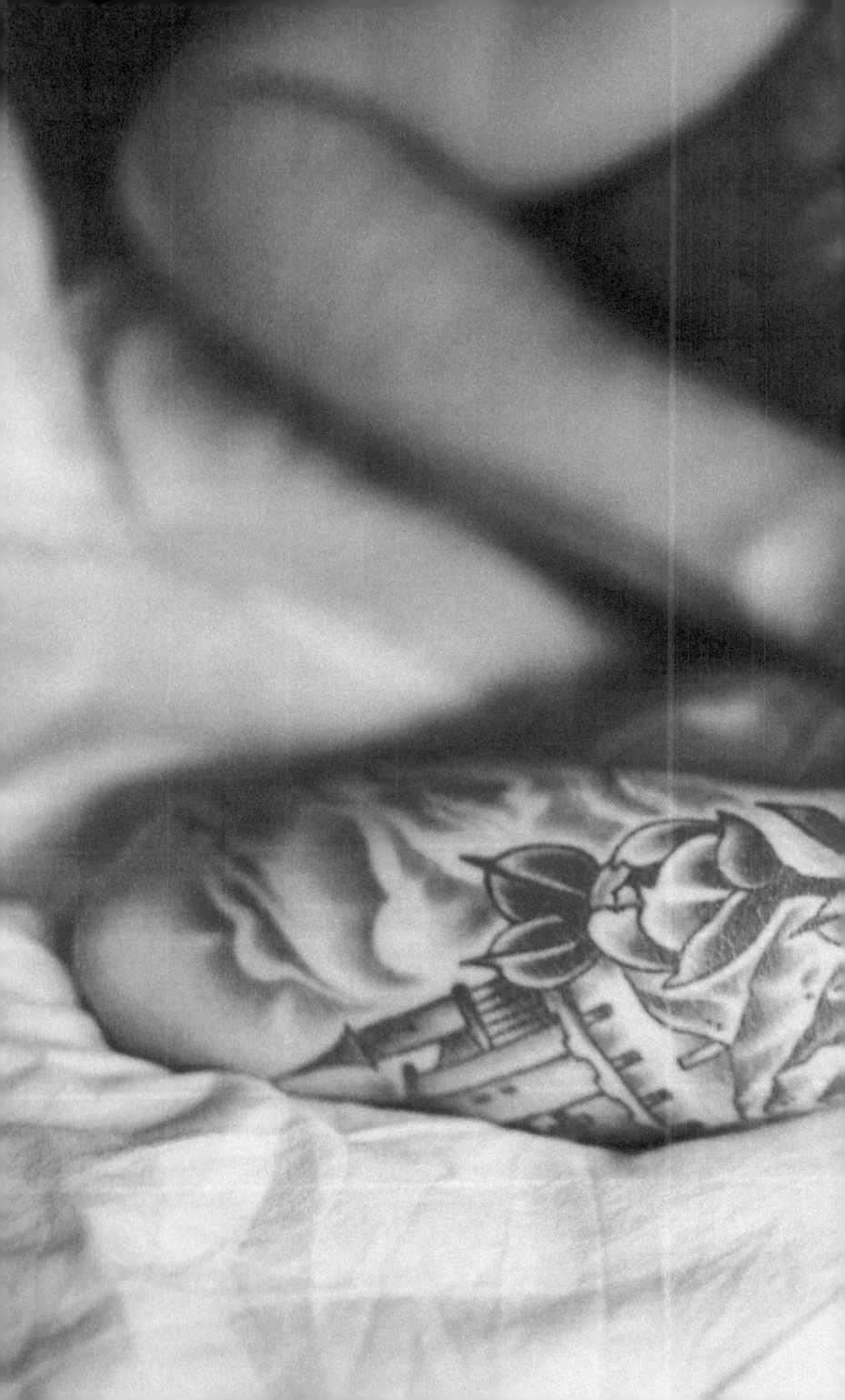

4

NOLAN

FEBRUARY 2027

M aking new music is the only good part of this hell called fame. All the tours, every meet and greet, and every magazine cover all take a small piece of my soul until one day, there will be nothing left at all. But every new record recaptures a part of me that I always worry will be lost forever.

I wrap up, laying down one of the final album tracks, and leave the recording room behind with a deep breath. Chris sits on one of the couches, a pleased-as-punch grin on his usually tight lips. Of all the managers in the world, I was lucky to land one that isn't a piece of shit, but I still only trust him as far as I can throw him.

"It sounded good!" Chris says gleefully, his eyes sparkling.

"I'll love it until I have to sing it a million times in front of crowds that make me want to chop my own ears off," I complain as I toss myself onto the sofa beside him.

"It was good," Mike, my producer, points out with a gentle smile under his long beard. "You beat yourself up too much kiddo." He skips around and plays the chorus of "No Longer Here" with a small divot between his brows. "This part could use some heavier guitar though. Are you good with me bringing Clive back in to lay it down?"

I wave him off. "Whatever you think it needs."

Mike bends back over the board, messing around with the track that I love but I know I'll hate in only a few months. That's the way it goes. I write a song, love it, record it down, and then hate it for the rest of my life.

Chris taps my leg with his phone to get my attention. "Benji's back at your house."

My face goes hot at just the thought of another weekend with Benji. "How long is he here for?"

"Open-ended," Chris answers as he types away at his phone.

"What?" That can't be right.

Chris shrugs. "Let me know when to send him packing. You're out here for a few more weeks and you're making good headway on the album. You deserve a break. Maybe it'll help you get your brain back in the game too."

"Maybe."

Sometimes I think the only way to get my head back in the game is to take my head off, empty it out, and screw it back on. But I don't say that to Chris because I don't want him to worry more than he already does. The label has already thrown around *mental health retreats* a few times after I got sober a few years ago. Back when I was drinking, everything was so much easier. Using liquor to kill all the worst parts of myself off so that I couldn't even remember most days. They're lucky I can still write now that I'm sober.

Nerves roll through me as I drive back to my house

tucked away in the Hills. The sky darkens the further up the hills the car goes, as the lights from the city bleed away. When I pull through the open gate, I notice a few lights are already on inside, indicating that Chris was telling the truth, and that Benji is waiting for me inside.

I sit silently in the car for a few moments, gathering myself. Steadfastly avoiding the mirror, I run my fingers through my hair, hoping that it's not a rat's nest after today's recording session. Alright, time to go inside and get fucked mindless.

The alarm system beeps as I step quietly through the front door. For the first time, my house smells like something besides whatever supplies the cleaning crew uses. My stomach growls at the savory smell. God, I can't remember the last time I ate a full meal. The sizzling sounds of food on the stovetop drags me towards the kitchen. The sight that greets me sends my heart thundering in my chest, my rib cage suddenly ten times too small.

Benji turns his head to take in the sight of me, a small smile tilting up his plush lips. His eyes are just as light blue as I remember, the color of the sky in the early dawn. A few more freckles than I seem to recall him having last year are smattered across his nose. He's infuriatingly cute, it makes me want to bite him, maybe even kick. Is this cute aggression or just my normal fury?

"Sorry, got hungry waiting," Benji apologizes sheepishly.

"Help yourself. Mi casa es su casa," I tease with a sweeping gesture of my arm.

Benji snorts as he returns his attention to the bubbling food on the stovetop. "I've made enough for us both. Figured we could eat so we have energy to go all night."

I wander deeper into the kitchen, only coming to a stop

once I'm beside him. He smells the same, like fresh clean sheets, with a hint of something flowery, maybe lavender. A sleepy kind of smell.

"What are you cooking?" I ask, voice small in the large, usually empty kitchen.

Benji grins and dips his head to hide his face from my gaze. "You didn't have much, so I just threw something together. It's just garlic, zucchini, chicken, spices, and some noodles I found in your pantry."

"Smells good," I tell him, because it does.

Benji shyly meets my gaze. "Yeah?"

"Yeah, make me a bowl. I'm going to go shower the recording studio off of me."

I can feel Benji's gaze prickling at the back of my neck as I quickly flee the kitchen. That entire interaction was too much. We should definitely stick to just fucking. The hot water rolls over my skin as I bathe the day away, burning everything about Nolan Hastings from my brain, until I'm just any other man. I spend a few extra minutes prepping for our fuck fest, because I'm a good little bottom. I'm bad at a lot of things, but never that.

By the time I return to the kitchen dressed in just low-slung sweatpants, Benji is plating our dinner. His gaze lifts to slide over me, from my toes, all the way to my messy, still slightly damp hair.

"Dinner's ready," Benji says quietly, voice small. He reminds me of a baby bird, terrified of its impending first flight. Good thing I can shove him off the edge without a care in the world.

I take a seat at the dining table with a perfectly respectable grin. Benji falters slightly as he sets the bowl down in front of me, but then he moves to sit opposite me with his own dish of food.

"Thanks, honey," I say before digging in.

Benji's lips twitch, but he doesn't reply to my dig. We eat mostly in silence for a while. The food is good, savory and covered with a layer of cheese that I didn't even know I had in the fridge. Usually the housekeeping service stocks it on Sundays, tosses everything I didn't eat the week before, then stocks it again. A repeating cycle of waste. But this is good, and I eat almost half the bowl before falling back in my chair with a groan.

"Who taught you to cook? It's good."

Benji licks sauce away from his lip and my stomach clenches with need. Asshole. "My moms."

"Moms? Plural?" I ask.

Benji nods as he pushes his own plate away. "My moms are lesbians. Mom is Piper and Mama is Juniper."

I blink slowly at this piece of Benji knowledge that I've been gifted. "The lesbians part is cool as hell but those names sure are something."

Benji chuckles, although the smile doesn't reach his eyes. "They're old-school hippies. They had me when they were already in their forties."

"Where'd you grow up?"

Asking Benji about himself is easier than letting him know anything about me. Although, all the details about me are scattered all over the internet. All he has to do is google Nolan Hastings and there's a feast of information for the entire world to know. Nothing about my life is secret. Except maybe my proclivity to get fucked rough by escorts, but that's not because the label says I can't be gay. It's because maybe, sometimes it's nice to have something just for myself that not everyone else knows.

"I grew up on a commune in Georgia," Benji answers easily.

"Come again?"

Benji stands from the table with both of our plates, and heads towards the kitchen to do the dishes. "I said they were hippies."

"A commune? Like a cult?"

Benji shakes his head with a shocked laugh. "No, not a cult. Just a group of likeminded people that wanted to live the same kind of life. I was homeschooled until I was a teenager and begged to go to the local public school."

"Huh."

Benji's biceps bunch as he scrubs at the plates and suddenly I've had enough chitchat. Enough of us playing like we don't know exactly what's going to happen this weekend. Pushing back from the table, I stalk over to him with a single-minded mission. I carefully reach around him to slowly turn the faucet off. A smile twitches at the corner of my lips at his light, eager sigh. Bingo.

"Benji," I say softly.

"Hmm?"

"Can you fuck me now, please?"

Benji turns around between my arms, pressing the small of his back against the counter. He sneaks his hands to my waist, his thumbs pressing hard against my hip bones. Without a single word, he dips down to take my mouth in a gentle, but thorough kiss. The night shifts around us, going from mellow, to knowing, to flat-out needy as I wrap my arms around his neck to tug him closer to me. Benji moans into my mouth and nips hard at my lip, pulling a moan from me.

"What's on the list this time, huh?"

My brain barely boots back online to understand his question. "What?"

"Well," Benji says, thumbs sweeping at the skin just under the waist of my sweatpants, "what do you need? Want me to fuck you so hard you can't remember your own name? Want me to bite you all over until you're covered in bruises? Want me to fuck you on your hands in knees in front of the fireplace in your bedroom? What does Nolan Hastings want from his escort?"

Rage rolls through me at the use of my full name. Fuck. Some emotion must flicker on my face because Benji's hand comes up to curl in the hair at the nape of my neck, tugging my head back so I have to fight to keep my gaze on him.

"Maybe you want me to decide?"

"I want you to shut the fuck up," I tell him, teeth gritted in annoyance.

Benji smiles softly. "No can do. Gotta do a lot of talking to keep fucking for money safe and sane."

"Who the fuck are you?" I ask as the rage lowers to a simmer.

"The man who's going to leave you walking funny." Benji abruptly lets go of me and gives me a gentle shove. I stumble back in confusion, but he only nods towards the stairs. "Go to your room. Hands and knees on the rug in front of the fireplace. I'll be there in a second."

"No."

Benji grins, wide, and just a little mean. "Don't test me."

"No," I repeat, this time unwilling to move.

Benji crosses his arms over his broad chest. "Fine. Then we're going to talk through our limits. I've got your brief, but I want to hear it from you. No hard limits? Bullshit."

My chest heaves in anger. "Excuse me?"

"Your hard limit is giving up control. You didn't like me ordering you around just then, did you? What else didn't you like? If you don't tell me, then I might repeat it. I'm not much in the mood for unnecessary mistakes."

Yeah, fuck this guy. I pick up the glass of water on the island, and throw it at the ground so that it shatters into tiny pieces. Water sprinkles the floor, a river flowing through the jagged, broken edges. The rage inside me disappears into a cloud of embarrassed smoke. Turning around in a fury, I flee downstairs to the bedroom. Huffing and puffing, I look for more things I can break. But my bedroom has been carefully curated to be absent of anything breakable.

The soft padding of Benji's footsteps echoes down the stairs behind me. For some reason, the idea of him not cowering in the face of my tantrum calms me. Most people would flinch and run the other way at my bad behavior. It's a learned assumption after so many years. Act out, people leave me alone. They don't look close after I've behaved like a toddler with their favorite toy taken away.

Benji pauses just inside the room, hands carefully hidden in the pockets of his sweatpants as if afraid to reach out for me. Good. He should be.

"Don't speak to me like that in my own home," I tell him loudly, just barely avoiding a shout.

Benji nods in understanding. "Okay. But you've got to tell me what you like, what you don't. I'll never know how to give you what you want if you just act out instead of communicating like an adult."

"Fuck you."

Benji shakes his head with a tired sigh. "Alright, Nolan."

I cross the distance between us in a flurry of limbs and my

mouth is on his before I can even blink. He tastes like sweet tea. I didn't even realize I had any in the fridge. Benji backs us up towards the rug and shoves me down until my back hits the ground hard enough to make me gasp, my mouth breaking from Benji's. His normally light blue eyes are a shade darker, frighteningly intense as he stares down at me in the shimmery orange glow of the warm fire.

He slowly dips down to nuzzle at my throat. Pleasure rolls through me when his lips feather over my pulse. I dig my blunt nails into the bare skin of his back when his teeth bite into my skin hard enough to send my eyes rolling back into my head. Oh yeah, that's the stuff. He rolls his hips against mine so that our cocks slide together through our clothes. Fuck, he feels so good against me, his heavy weight pushing me down. I've missed this so much.

"We need a safe word," Benji mumbles into the tense air between us.

"No."

Benji's eyes flash and his movements freeze. "Yes. Pick one or this stops now. And I have to know you'll use it. I'm serious."

Why is this guy always fucking pushing me? His stare is hard, his thighs even harder against the sweaty skin of my own as I wonder if this is really worth a fight. Pick a safe word and get fucked or don't and lose whatever this is with Benji. Fuck.

"Azure," I bite out. It's the color of Benji's fucking perfect annoying eyes. The last thing I ever want to say.

Benji's teeth flash white in the dark room just before dipping down to bite at my neck. Fuck. Sharp pain shoots down my arm, sending a dizzying rush of euphoria through me. Benji breaks away from my neck to take my lips in another burning kiss. His tongue slides into my mouth, tangling with my own as his fingers tug at my hair. He rolls his hips again and I have to bite back a whimper that so badly wants to break loose.

"Fuck me, you motherfucker," I whisper against Benji's mouth, just before biting down hard on his lip.

Benji's fingers disappear from my hair to trail over the burning skin of my back. His hands come to rest on my ribs, a seemingly favorite place to rest them. Rising up on his knees, he stares hungrily down at me.

"Lift up," Benji orders, and for some stupid reason, I obey like a total lemming. He rips off my sweatpants, leaving me nude under his heated gaze. His eyes rake over me as his throat bobs, seemingly overcome while looking at me. Blue gaze locking with mine, the world tilts dangerously sideways.

Benji rolls to standing, muscles flexing with the fluid motion. Stepping out of his own pants, he falls back to his knees between my splayed legs. His large palms slide up my inner thighs in quiet reverence, causing goose bumps to appear in their heavy wake. Benji's eyes lift back up to meet my questioning gaze.

"Tell me what the tattoos mean?" Benji asks softly as his stare is fixed on the blooming flowers across my ribs.

I swallow roughly against the emotion threatening to choke me. "Life can come from something decaying if you only let it."

Benji tenderly sweeps his thumbs over the flowers tangled with my ribs. "What's decaying?"

"Me," I reply quietly, then tug him down to kiss him once more.

His weight blots out the terror threatening to break free.

What I can't say with words, I say with the silent press of my lips to his mouth. Benji devours my mouth with a single-minded focus as he rolls his hips against mine. My thighs tremble against his from the force of the pleasure rippling through me. His cock is hot and heavy against my own. The memory of him inside me all those months ago comes rushing right back. I need it so bad that I can barely see straight.

I bite his lip hard again until he pulls away from me with a startled hiss. "Fuck me, Benji. Come on. This is your chance. Fuck the rockstar everyone wants. I could have anyone in the world but I've got you. Do it."

Benji growls before kissing me again just to shut me up. A gasp breaks free when he presses two lubed fingers into me, immediately seeking out my prostate like he's on a mission from God. When I open my eyes to stare at him, I find his hot gaze trained solely on me.

"Don't look at me." I shove his face away until I can't see his stupid puppy dog eyes anymore. Benji bites between my forefinger and thumb, right into the fattiest part of my hand. The pain shocks me into stillness, despite his exploring fingers inside me.

Benji lifts onto his knees again with a pained groan. His left hand presses hard against my stomach to steady himself as he wraps a condom over his cock. Without a single word, he hooks my legs over his shoulders, and pushes into me in one fluid movement. I breathe through the pain, wanting it, needing it to feel like I'm not still stuck on this miserable fucking planet.

Rocking slowly into me, Benji spares me only a few moments to adjust. The pace he sets is so brutal that my teeth crack together from his unforgiving thrusts. I dig my fingers into the skin of his back, raking down so hard that I know he'll have marks for days. Perfect.

Time ebbs and flows as Benji fucks me in front of the fire, our sweat mingling between us. He rotates between kissing me breathless and biting whatever skin he can reach. Bruises will mar my skin for days, only hidden by the colorful sheen of my tattoos. They hide more sins than I ever thought they would. So many. The years of scars are hidden by beautifully expensive tattoos.

"Can I touch your cock this time?" Benji asks against my mouth. He swipes his tongue along my lower lip until I'm trembling with need beneath him.

"I don't know, can you?" I retort.

Benji growls again before taking my mouth in a painfully hard kiss. Our teeth knock together as he fights to dominate me, to show me who I belong to. But I belong to no one but myself. Not even this beautiful man fucking me within an inch of my life can own me. Benji abruptly pulls out of me with a loud groan.

"Hey!" I shout as I lift up onto my elbows.

Benji falls between my legs and swallows my cock down as he roughly shoves two fingers inside me. Oh fuck. My brain shuts down at the feeling. Benji uses his other hand to pinch my inner thigh. The weird mix of pleasure and pain skyrockets my orgasm through me. My vision goes black for a solid three seconds until the glow of the fireplace filters back in.

I'm coming slowly back to myself in pieces when Benji straddles my hips with a soft whine. He bites his bottom lip as I stare up at him in stricken awe. His hand flies over his cock, the condom now gone. Pressing one hand beside my head, he looms over me with a pleasure-filled groan. The muscles in his neck are so tense they look like they could snap. He needs to come. I want him to come.

"Do it," I goad him, knowing he needs to hear me say the words.

Benji squeezes his eyes shut just in time to paint my stomach with his release. The heat of his cum boils my blood, almost making my dick rally with the force of it. Benji presses his sweaty forehead to my chest as he loudly gulps in air.

Benji chuckles darkly. "Fuck."

"We did, yeah."

Benji snorts as he slowly rises to his knees. He smears his cum all over my chest, then dips his hands to my ribs to rub the mess all over the flowers he's weirdly obsessed with. He's goddamn glorious. I've been fucked by a lot of men in my life, but something about Benji is different. Borderline special. And that's how I know that after this fuck fest, we need a long break before we fuck again. Only time can stop me from developing useless emotions for a man who's paid to use his body to bring mine pleasure.

Seemingly shocked at his claiming gesture, Benji awkwardly clears his throat and stares listlessly into the fire. Seconds tick by before Benji rises to his feet, holding his hand out for mine.

"Bath time," Benji urges quietly.

Just like the first time we fucked, Benji guides me to my bathroom, carefully situating me so that I don't have to look at my reflection. He roots around the jars of bath salts and soaps in the shelf beside my clawfoot tub, coming away pleased with a scent that is hidden from my nosy view. Bright red scratch marks grace the broad expanse of his freckled back. As the warm water fills the tub, so does the soft scent of lavender. The scent is calming and my already tensing muscles slowly relax.

Benji crawls into the tub, crooking his fingers once again to invite me to join him. The biggest deja vu of my life. The fuck might've been different, but the caretaking after is so familiar to me even now. I melt against him in the tub, bone-less and wrung out after one single good lay.

Maybe a weekend of this on repeat will cure me.

Maybe it won't.

Who the fuck knows anymore.

5

BENJI

FEBRUARY 2027

The Nolan effect. Something about him makes me crazy, makes me behave in a way that's so absolutely opposite of myself. I'm Sunshine. I'm jokes and teasing and the one friend that no one ever has to worry about because I say what I mean and mean what I say. But holy fuck, Nolan makes me see red.

Maybe something inside Nolan echoes inside of me.

I don't know how long they've got me out here for, but it's not going to be long enough to wear Nolan down.

Nolan mumbles in his sleep like he did the last time we shared a bed. I listen for words, but they're still all nonsensical at this point. The fire is still on in the bedroom that faces the Hollywood Hills. Lights glitter in the distance since the sun still has a while before rising. It had been surprisingly easy to get Nolan to fall asleep late last night. All it took to be a warm lavender bath, a heavy make-out session, then wrapping him in my arms like a beasty, tattooed blanket.

Not long after falling asleep, he pulled himself out of my embrace to flop on his stomach on the other side of the bed.

53

Even in his sleep, he hates being touched without his permission. I can't fault him because I've seen all the videos of fans grabbing him. Between fans, photoshoots, and tattoos... I'm starting to think that maybe Nolan doesn't feel like his body belongs to him.

I carefully roll over onto my side to grab my phone. Dimming the brightness, I swipe through my notifications to land on my text chain with Eli.

Me: Are you up?

Eli: Sadly

Me: I think I'm already in too deep with Nolan

Eli: Uhmmm... Explain

Me: I don't know! He makes me feel like someone else

Eli: ....

Eli: Explain further

Me: I'm a total top with him

Eli: Okay

Me: I'm not usually THIS toppy

Eli: Sounds like you've got a fun dynamic going on idk bud

Eli: Is he still biting

Me: Yes

Me: Hard

Eli: Yikes

Eli: Bite back

Me: I DO

Eli: You should tell Jackson

Me: No, not yet. Just me and you for a while. Then I'll tell Trevor.

Eli: IDK why you're afraid of Jackson

Me: DADDY!

Eli: Gross

Eli: More like Papa

Me: Yeah true

Eli: gotta go sunshine

Me: ELI

Eli: love you

I LOVE my friends so much, but I always feel disconnected from them, even when in the same room. Maybe it's the years growing up on the commune, but I never quite feel like I belong. Plus, I'm always just the comedic relief, so it doesn't feel natural for me to share feelings or emotions. But sometimes I wish I could, especially now that I'm getting more and more tangled up with Nolan. I wish it was easier for me to share how I feel with Eli, Trevor, or even Jackson.

Blowing a wheezy breath through my nose, I roughly toss my phone onto the bed beside me. Nolan moves around restlessly, so I carefully roll onto my side, gently resting my hand at the small of his still sleep-warm back. He settles under my touch and tucks his head into the crook of his arm with a soft huff.

Well, now's the time for me to be sneaky. I use the peaceful quiet of morning to quietly catalog his body, noting all the varying colorful tattoos that cover his skin. The ones over his ribs are rapidly becoming my favorites. The flowers are so intricate, beautifully tattooed as if watercolors on his skin. Those damn skeleton hands are probably runner-ups. Along the expanse of his back is a Grim Reaper with a scythe, his arm reaching out as if trying to take the person looking at Nolan's back to the depths of hell.

"Stop staring at my tats," Nolan says gruffly.

"They're pretty."

"They're expensive," Nolan argues. "Part of the rockstar aesthetic."

"Don't you like them?" I ask, running my finger over the broad lines of the reaper.

Nolan shrugs hard as he turns his head in my direction. "They're fine."

"What's your viewpoint on morning kisses?" I want to kiss him so badly.

Nolan's nose wrinkles even further. "Too intimate."

"Bummer," I say sadly.

Nolan's eyebrows furrow as he carefully appraises me. With a large, put-upon sigh, he heaves himself up onto his elbows and leans over me. His dark messy hair beautifully frames his face. I can't help but tangle one of my hands in the wavy strands, softly rubbing my thumb at the underside of his defined jaw. There's an old scar overlapping his left eyebrow that's faded with age, but it looks like he's cut a line clear through his eyebrow because of it. Aesthetics, he'd probably say.

Nolan leans down to softly brush his lips over mine, a gentle, barely there kind of kiss. My toes tingle as his lips glide over mine. I fight back every instinct to pull him closer, to delve into his mouth to taste him. Maybe he is right; maybe early morning kisses are too intimate for us, at least at this moment.

He pulls away with a weary sigh to flop back on the bed. His gaze cuts to me as he tangles his fingers in the silky soft sheets.

"What do you normally do on days off?" I ask curiously.

Nolan snorts with a roll of his eyes. "Days off? Far and few between. You're just here because I'm almost at the end of recording and they want to keep me happy."

"Who is 'they'?"

"The gods that be." Nolan turns his head towards me with a calculating, slightly manic sort of look. "There's a dive bar an hour from here that has great local talent. Wanna go?"

"Hell yeah!" I say around a delighted grin.

Nolan's eyes get that confused look again before he rubs it away with the heels of his hands. The urge to feed him again is almost unbearable. He looks so fucking tired, despite the vivid color of the tattoos. His skin has this slightly sick pallor to it and there are huge dark bags under his eyes. Sometimes when he moves he seems exhausted just by breathing, just by having to walk a few feet.

"Can I cook breakfast?"

Nolan rolls his eyes. "Can you?"

I grit my teeth against a sarcastic reply. "May I cook you breakfast?"

Nolan points towards the door. "Have at it. I'm going to go back to sleep, so you can bring it to me."

Nolan burrows back under the blankets with a huff as he tugs the sheets over his head. I leave him to "go back to sleep." After slipping on my sweatpants, I pad down the hallway to get started on breakfast. The easiest option is scrambled eggs and toast, which is probably more nutrients than Nolan normally gets on a daily basis. I end up adding some cream cheese to the eggs to make them fluffier and a little fattier. A few ripe avocados sit at the bottom of the crisper drawer, so I add them to the toast like the spoiled yuppie I've become. At least that's what Mama says.

Nolan is still curled into a ball under the sheets when I return to the bedroom.

"Breakfast," I call out.

Nolan peeks his head out from under the blanket to judge the food options. He sniffs once, twice, then shrugs as if in awful acceptance of the meal. I sit down crisscross applesauce beside him and dig into my own plate of eggs. Nolan accepts the fork I offer him with a weary, cornered-animal sort of look. But after the first bite of eggs, his shoulders lose their tension and he shovels the food down as if I might take it away before he can finish his share.

He even eats the avocado toast. It takes everything inside me to not beam with pride.

"That was good," Nolan says with great reluctance.

"Eggs are good for you."

Nolan snorts. "Are you a nutritionist?"

"I just believe in getting a well-rounded diet to fuel my body. Eat the rainbow and all that."

"I bet that's shit your moms say."

I smile at the mention of my moms. He's right. That is shit they say.

"My mom does believe in eating the rainbow."

"Awful euphemism in certain contexts." Nolan wiggles his eyebrows obnoxiously.

"We're up with the sun. What should we do?"

Nolan tiredly points towards the backyard. "Go swim some of your golden retriever out. I'll watch."

I do love to swim *and* he has a nice pool. The sun just starts to break over the horizon, splashing the sky with pinks and purples as I walk naked out to the pool. I can practically feel Nolan's eyes on me the entire walk. Dipping my toes into the warm water, I turn my head over my shoulder to meet Nolan's heavy gaze. When I toss him a grin, he scowls and shoos me along with a wave of his hand.

Diving into the water, I break through the surface with a pleased sigh. It's the perfect temperature, almost like bath water. I swim a few laps to warm up, then do exactly as Nolan said. My muscles burn as I swim back and forth without pausing, thinking over the past twelve hours at this hidden mansion in the hills. Thoughts of Nolan and the way he was with me last night run on repeat in my head. Figuring him out is going to be impossible.

I only stop swimming when Nolan's figure shimmers through the turquoise water. Coming to a stop at the edge, I rest my arms against the pool deck while gasping in much-needed air. Nolan stares down at me in serious contemplation. He's still only wearing those loose sweatpants that always look one breath away from falling to the floor.

"You've been swimming nonstop for thirty minutes," Nolan points out, sounding just shy of petulant.

I grin up at him as I wipe water from my face. "You told me to swim my golden retriever out."

"I was joking."

I frown. "Oh."

Nolan casts his gaze out to the hills spread out behind his house. Something in his eyes hurts me; his gaze is beyond tortured. He always looks one moment away from spilling some dangerous secret that might tear him apart to speak aloud. I reach out to curl my fingers around his warm ankle, and smile when his skin is warm beneath my touch.

"Join me," I whisper softly.

Nolan angrily kicks my fingers away with a snarl. But he shoves his sweatpants down to the ground, kicking them off towards the sunning chairs. He doesn't jump into the pool like I did, instead he slowly walks in on the stairs. The sun hits the water at just the right angle so that he looks like some sort of miserable god returning to their ocean kingdom. He's stunningly beautiful, despite the pain that radiates from his very core.

"What?" Nolan asks roughly as he pauses in front of me.

"You're beautiful," I say and immediately regret it.

But Nolan doesn't hiss or spit at me, instead he flushes slightly and looks away. I curl my palms around his slim hips and tug him closer, until he's close enough that I can smell the rich amber scent of him. His fingers dig into the meat of my back as I kiss along his neck. Pulse pounding beneath my lips, I grin against the skeleton fingers tattoo. When I take his ear between my lips and suck, his breath stutters out of him, his fingers digging even more painfully into my back where the deep scratch marks from last night are still fresh.

I bite down hard on his lobe and Nolan presses closer until I can feel his cock growing warm and heavy against my leg in the chlorinated water.

"Don't call me by my full name," Nolan whispers into my hair. I tug away from him, but he lifts a hand to the back of my head to hold me to him. "Don't look at me right now."

"Why?" I whisper back.

"That's the name people use when they think I belong to them. Don't call me that."

"Is that why you reacted the way you did last night?"

Nolan shrugs enough for me to feel the uneasy movement. "I don't know."

But I can tell he's lying. He does know. He just doesn't want to spill more truth than he already has this morning. I tug against his grip on my head and press my mouth to his in a warm, drowsy kind of kiss. Nolan whimpers into my mouth as I back him up against the edge of the pool. I curl a protective arm around the back of his neck so his head doesn't hit the edge. Another whimper escapes Nolan when I change the kiss from drowsy to demanding, plunging my tongue into him to lick every crevice, to own his mouth with mine.

I pull away from him panting, finally meeting his half-lidded gaze. "When I'm here, you belong to me."

Nolan slowly closes his eyes to blot me out. "I don't belong to anyone."

I squeeze my arm tighter around his neck. "To me," I growl.

"Fine, Benji," Nolan relents, sounding tired beyond belief.

I kiss him again because I can, because at this moment he's hurting and I want to fix it. That's what I do. I fix everything for everyone, keep them smiling, keep them happy. It's all I've ever known. Sunshine personified. We kiss long enough for Nolan to lose patience with it. He finally shoves me away with a tired, frustrated sort of look.

I watch him flee the pool, his fingers flexing at his side as he strides naked and uncaring back into his bedroom. God, he makes no sense. And he makes me act in a way that I've never acted before. Makes me feel territorial, possessive. I don't know how to contain it to keep him from being angry with me. I'm just here to fuck him when he needs the release, when he's gone too long without human touch.

Giving him what he needs, while simultaneously getting what I want, is going to be the hardest game I've ever played.

———

"MY BEST FRIEND HAS A G-WAGON TOO," I tell Nolan as I climb into his Mercedes.

"Oh yeah?" Nolan asks, totally disinterested.

I nod quickly while buckling myself in. "Yeah, Jackson. He's got a matte black one. It's his baby."

A hint of a smile tugs up the corners of Nolan's mouth. "The matte ones are nice."

"Right?"

Nolan hums as he pulls out of the gate surrounding his home. I tried to cook dinner for us but Nolan had waved me off, saying something about eating snacks at the dive bar. I'd not quite believed him that it would be enough, so I ate one of the protein bars I found in his pantry. Next time I'm here I need to bring my protein shakes with me or maybe his grocery crew could grab me some.

Nolan had tossed an outfit to me, perfectly my size and ordered I'd wear it. Black skinny jeans and a black T-shirt that hugs all the muscles on my torso. When I'd walked out of the bathroom, Nolan had almost smiled at the sight of me. Nolan wears something similar, but he has a silver chain around his neck with a crucifix. Artful rips dot his jeans showing peeks of his myriad of tattoos. He's hot as sin and I want to fuck him again.

"Why are you an escort?" Nolan asks, apropos of nothing.

I turn slightly in the passenger seat so I can let the full weight of my gaze fall on him. Nolan squirms slightly in his seat, but otherwise remains unaffected.

"I like to fuck and I'm good at it, might as well be paid to do it."

Nolan laughs and my heart triples in size. Oh, he has a nice laugh. Just as deep as his voice. It rolls through me and lights me up inside. He bites the corner of his lip and flicks his gaze quickly to me, before returning it to the road.

"Guess that's a good enough answer as any."

"What would you be if you weren't a rockstar?"

Nolan taps the steering wheel thoughtfully. "One of those guys who run the rental chair business at the beach."

The answer is so shocking that a laugh startles out of me. "What?"

Nolan nods slowly. "You know, those guys who charge like twenty bucks for a chair at the beach? I'd do that. Just have a nice little business so that I could spend all day by the ocean."

"I think that's the most original answer to that question ever."

Nolan turns the music dial up to signal he's finished with the conversation. Heavy rock music fills the inside of the car, but I can tell it's not his music. I've spent the past few months listening to Nolan on repeat. While his music is definitely heavy rock, he sings lighter ballads sometimes. Those are my favorites. The songs that showcase his low, sultry but sad voice. But the songs where he screams and yells are also good, probably better for the people that like that sort of thing.

The remainder of the way to the dive bar is silent. Nolan parks in one of the remaining empty spots without any fanfare. For a Sunday night, the place is packed. It's a small joint, painted black, with a neon sign that flashes *The Anti-Social*. Nolan hops out of the car without a backward glance toward me, all but forcing me to hustle out of the car to sprint after him. He aims the key fob over his shoulder to lock the car, then pauses in the middle of the packed parking lot to stare blankly at me.

In the darkness, surrounded by cars, with the pulse thumping around us from the dive bar, Nolan tugs me to him to press a rough kiss against my mouth. His kiss steals the breath from me like he's sucking the air out for his own parched lungs. When he pulls away from me, his eyes are dark and that miserable look he often wears is back on his too-beautiful face. Angrily swiping his hand across his mouth, he shoves me back a step with two fingers against my chest.

"Don't touch me in there. No matter what. Okay?"

With that lone demand, Nolan stalks off towards the bar before I can even summon an answer. I follow him inside, walking as close to him as I dare. As long as I can still smell him, I figure I'm close enough. Bright red and blue neon signs flash over the walls. The bar smells familiar, like sweat and beer.

Heavy rock music drifts from the stage that's surrounded by people milling around. The words from the band are muffled, barely understandable to my untrained, untalented ears. Nolan avoids the bar to instead stand among the crowd.

He pushes through the sweaty bodies, and I follow after him like a planet in his dizzying orbit. Nolan comes to a stop halfway to the front, hands tucked into his jeans as he stares listlessly up at the stage.

No one around us seems to notice that Nolan Hastings is standing in their presence. The boy who rose to fame from YouTube, handpicked by a television show host, to become one of the most famous rock musicians of our generation. In the darkness of the bar, he's hidden away so that he can only be himself. And for a wild second, I get it. At this moment he's not Nolan Hastings, he's just Nolan, standing in a crowd listening to mostly shitty music.

Nolan bobs his head to the music with an assessing look in his eyes. It takes every ounce of restraint inside me to stop myself from reaching out to him. I want to feel the music quaking through his bones, through the flesh of his body. I want to kiss him in the dark bar and fuck his mouth with my tongue until he melts against me with burning need.

Nolan makes me want, after so many years of just going through the motions. But he also pisses me off like nothing else. Nolan's an enigma of epic proportions that I think I could spend my entire goddamn life trying to solve. Only to end up empty-handed. Like a bird fleeing the nest once big enough to fly.

The music comes to an end after what feels like forever. The stage goes dark and Nolan presses his body against mine for one thrilling moment.

"Stay here," Nolan whispers for only me to hear.

"Okay."

I watch him disappear towards the edge of the throng, my eyebrows scrunched in confusion. The crowd murmurs among themselves for an endless age, until someone from the bar climbs onto the stage with a frenzied grin. Oh no.

"We've got a special treat tonight, folks! Give a big hand to Nolan Hastings!"

The entire crowd is silent for a brief second before breaking into raucous applause. My stomach roils at the sight of Nolan walking to the front of the stage. He curls his fingers around the microphone, his eyes dark, hiding a depth of something that I wish I understood. He carefully situates himself on the stool and grabs the acoustic guitar to his left.

"Hi," Nolan says into the microphone with a breathy laugh. Someone in the crowd whistles and Nolan squints their way. "Thanks, love. I felt like doing something acoustic tonight. Anyway, if you know the song, sing along. If you don't know it, then shut the fuck up so everyone can hear me."

The crowd laughs and a few more whistles fill the air again. Nolan places the mic back in the stand, then turns his attention to the guitar. He plucks a few strings slowly, setting the mood for whatever song he's about to sing. When he opens his mouth, I suddenly know what people are talking about when they say someone has the voice of an angel. Nolan's voice is melodic, deep, and it feels like a punch to the chest when I finally understand the words. Despite listening to his songs on repeat for months, something about hearing him in person is different. His tone is deeper, striking through the tender core of me.

His fingers glide over the neck of the guitar, easily bringing the melody to life. But his voice is haunting as he sings lyrics about being ruined at a young age. Toward the end of the song, his gaze lifts from the guitar to flit over the audience. I'm not sure he can see me with the lights, but his gaze somehow lands on me anyway, and the corner of his mouth tips up in a poor imitation of a smile.

When he finishes the song, the entire crowd claps like they've just seen God return to the earth. Maybe they have. Nolan has that effect on people. He carefully places the guitar back in its stand and gives a wave to the crowd, before climbing offstage. I push through the bodies to beeline it straight for him. My blood is rushing in my ears, fingers itching with the need to grab him, do anything. Just touch him.

By the time I reach the stage, Nolan is surrounded by fans. He happily takes selfies as if his fame doesn't haunt him at every fucking step. The perfect celebrity. It takes fifteen minutes before everyone is satisfied with pictures or hastily drawn autographs on arms. Nolan tips his head in the direction of the back of the bar once the fans are gone. I follow along behind him, and join him at a two-seater table top.

"You want something to drink?" Nolan asks, voice low and going straight to my cock. Fuck.

"Can I?"

Nolan rolls his eyes. "Can you?"

I can feel my eye twitch in irritation. "I'll get something to drink. You want something?"

Nolan shakes his head. I disappear toward the bar without a backward glance. I return to Nolan with a cheap bottle of beer in my grip. He tilts his head to the side when I rejoin him.

"I took you for a liquor boy."

I shrug and take a slow sip of my beer. "Not much of an alcohol drinker at all."

"Shame," Nolan says sourly. "Drink for me."

"Why?"

Nolan digs around in his pocket for his wallet, pulling out a thick coin. He moves it around between his fingers a few times, the perfect picture of a gambler before placing a bet. His smile is wry and teasing as he finally shows it off to me.

"Five years sober."

I'd forgotten the headlines. He'd been drunk on stage, puked everywhere, then carted off to rehab for a few months. He'd just barely been twenty-one at the time. Uneasiness rolls through me as he pockets the medallion back into his wallet.

"Is it safe for you to be at a bar?" I ask like an idiot.

Nolan rolls his eyes again. "I'm a rockstar. There's alcohol and drugs everywhere I go."

"Ever scared of relapsing?"

Nolan stares at me for a few seconds as if in disbelief I'd deign to ask him such a question. He presses his elbows against the table, leaning closer so that he doesn't have to speak so loud.

"There's a higher chance of me ending up dead than me ever drinking again."

I carefully set my beer down on the dirty table and lean over so that our faces are only inches apart. Nolan's lips twitch at the corner again, as if working hard to hold back laughter.

"Isn't being in a bar tempting though? One sip and it all goes away?"

Nolan narrows his dark brown eyes at me. "Fuck you."

"Nah," I say with a cruel laugh. Leaning back into my seat, I grab my beer and take a slow sip. "I think it works for us the other way. I've got plans for you later tonight."

Nolan makes a pitying look at me, lower lip popping out in a pout. "Aw, cute little puppy. What are you going to do?

Finish your beer so that we can get the fuck out of here. I'm tired of them all looking at me."

"If you don't like them looking at you, why'd you perform on the stage?"

Nolan flicks his hand in a dismissive wave. "Keep your friends close, but your enemies closer."

"Your fans are your enemies?"

"Bloodsuckers," Nolan murmurs darkly.

I gulp down the rest of my beer with a barely restrained grimace. "Let's go. I'm going to fuck you by the pool until you're crying."

"Whatever," Nolan says blandly, but I can clearly see the shape of his hardening cock in his jeans.

But I'd forgotten that Nolan always has the upper hand in every situation. The moment we're alone in the car, he lunges across the console to attack my mouth with his own. It's more of a biting, angry kind of kiss than anything close to sweet or slow. Again it feels like he's trying to suck me dry through a kiss alone.

Nolan pulls away from me with a gasp and glances down at my lap while biting his plush bottom lip. My cock is painfully hard in the tight jeans he dressed me in, pressing against the zipper in a way that makes my brain hurt.

Nolan glances back up at me in the dark of the car, face closed off. "I'm going to suck your cock. You're going to choke me with it until I can't breathe, until tears are leaking from my eyes. And you won't stop unless I tap out. Do you understand?"

"That sounds dangerous," I argue, voice cracking on the words.

Nolan's answering smirk is beyond wicked. "You'll learn, stud. There's pleasure in the pain."

Nolan unbuttons my jeans and dips his warm hand into my pants to wrap around my cock. He squeezes me once, before pressing his warm mouth against my ear.

"Fuck my mouth, then when we get home, I'll let you suck me off while you press a hand to my throat." Nolan slowly licks my ear, then blows his warm breath over my skin, sending a violent chill down my spine. "You're so much fun, Benji."

I have just enough presence of mind to remember where we are. Grabbing the back of Nolan's neck, I tug him away and watch his eyes blow wide at my rough touch. There are too many people that could see us, and while I love the idea of the entire world knowing Nolan is mine, this man protects his privacy like it's a precious secret in the palm of his hands. Fucking his mouth outside of the bar isn't going to work for me.

"Not here," I say roughly.

Nolan squeezes my cock hard, making me buck up into his grip. "Are you saying no to me?"

"Yeah, I'm saying no, Nolan. If you can wait until we get home, I'll give you everything you want and more. But I'm not fucking you outside this bar."

I'd expected a tantrum, maybe even a punishment, but Nolan just stares at me with his hand still down my pants. Movement outside the bar catches my attention, but it's just someone smoking, too far away to see us in our current precarious position.

"I can't believe you said no to me," Nolan whispers in disbelief.

"Well, I did. So. Can you stop squeezing my dick?"

Nolan carefully removes his hand from my pants, then just as carefully zips my jeans back up. His fingers press against the warm skin of my stomach for a moment before pulling away as if he was burned.

Nolan stares blankly out the windshield as he peels out of the dark parking lot to point us back to his house. Streetlights blur behind the window faster than my eyes can hone in on them. When I'm with Nolan, I feel swept away by an uncontrollable tide. He gets under my skin, making me do things I'd never once in my life considered doing. Some would call it danger, but the more I get to know him, the more I think maybe he's just waking me up inside, after a long time asleep.

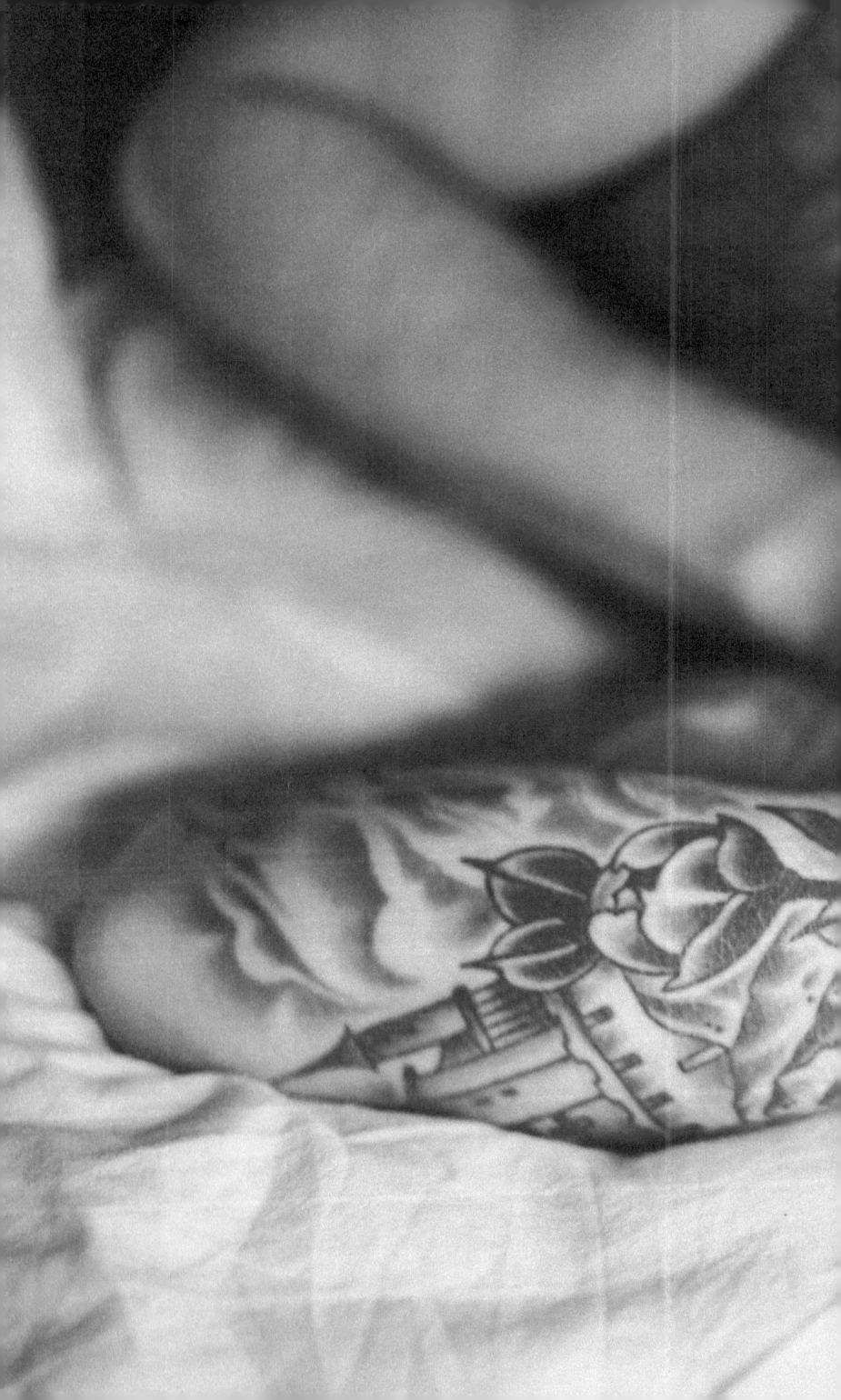

6

NOLAN

AUGUST 2027

The only part of fame that I like is making music. Tours? Hell. Photoshoots? Awful. Fans thinking that they own some part of me? Degrading. But I've made a deal with the devil, so there's no out for me. Six months in Los Angeles was all I got to record the next album. In four days, I leave for the world tour.

And I am rapidly deteriorating under the pressure.

At this point, there's an entire team to make decisions for me. All I've got to do is show up for a sound check, perform, do the meet and greets with fans, and collect a check for the record label and promoters. All of this was so much easier when I was lit all the fuck up.

"Are you ready?" Chris asks as he walks into my house as if he owns it.

"Do I have a choice?"

Gently closing the front door behind himself, Chris checks me out from head to toe. I try not to squirm under his gaze, but it's difficult. Chris is probably one of the rare people in my life who cares about me. Like actually cares.

not the rockstar the label has so carefully curated. When I was drunk off my ass constantly, it was Chris who was there to clean me up, give me coffee to sober me up even when I didn't want to be sober. Yeah, the label forced me into rehab when I'd been fucking my life up for years, but it was Chris who held my hand through the entire process. It's always been Chris.

"Do we need to cancel the tour?" Chris asks, voice carefully neutral.

"Nope," I say, popping the *P* like the asshole I am. "Oh my God, can you imagine? The label would have a conniption."

"Not if you relapsed," Chris points out shrewdly.

I freeze with my hand halfway up to my hair. "I haven't relapsed."

Chris shrugs, uncaring. "They don't have to know that."

"We're not faking a relapse."

"I'm just saying if we have to, the option is there."

"Noted."

Chris follows along behind me as we make our way through the house, heading toward the kitchen. I hop up onto the island to perch in wait for Chris to share whatever news he has for me. As if he lives in my home, Chris picks through the contents of my fridge, only pulling away satisfied once he finds a soda which I only keep in stock for him.

Taking a large gulp of the soda, he makes an annoying smacking sound before leaning heavily against the counter opposite of me. The vibes in my kitchen could kill a small Victorian child with how rank they are.

"Spill it," I tell him.

Chris spins the soda carefully in his hands with a twitch in his eye. "I'm worried about the tour."

"Who isn't?"

74

"Nolan," Chris says gravely. "We cannot have a repeat of the last tour."

"What happened on the last tour?" I ask innocently.

"Don't be a little shit."

We stare at each other for a moment, daring each other to speak. Unable to take the attention, I look away towards the backyard. The pool sparkles under the midday sun. I can almost picture Benji leaning against the edge with that crooked grin on his lips if I try hard enough.

"I have the stupidest idea," I say slowly.

"Oh boy."

I've actually been thinking about it a lot lately. What it would be like if Benji joined us on the tour, if Benji was there as the crutch I will need to survive. Sometimes my brain is so terrifying, the thoughts so loud, that having someone like Benji there to keep those thoughts at bay is probably exactly what I need.

"What if we bring Benji with us?" I ask quietly, dancing my fingers along the cold granite of the island.

Chris stares blankly at me for a moment before taking a small, pained-looking sip of his soda. "Are you fucking serious?"

"Yes."

Chris sets the now half-empty can down behind him. "That raises the risk of you being outed."

I snort, as if I care about that. "The entire world can know I'm gay. I don't give a shit. It's just... if he goes on tour, I want him to be only mine. Just mine."

"He's not a toy, Nolan."

Chris isn't getting it. I jump off the island to pace around the kitchen. To his credit, Chris stays cool as a cucumber, leaning casually against the counter beside the fridge. His eyes follow me as I pace, but he doesn't look worried, probably because I'm radiating anxious cat energy instead of *I'm about to do something that'll get us on the front of a tabloid* energy.

"We both know the tour could kill me," I say simply, hands buried at my scalp.

"Nolan—"

"Don't!" I yank at my hair in a brief show of vulnerability before straightening back up. "I want Benji on the tour with me. The entire tour. You'll do what you can to protect us from being found out. The band already has an NDA, so they won't say shit, so does the stage crew. Just... fucking make it happen, Chris."

"Alright," Chris whispers quickly before I can say anything else.

Relief like I've never felt before in my life sweeps through me. Breathing slowly, I stand straighter, and stare out the back windows toward the hills illuminated by the sun. Maybe this will solve all my problems. Maybe this will cure me. Maybe, maybe, *maybe*.

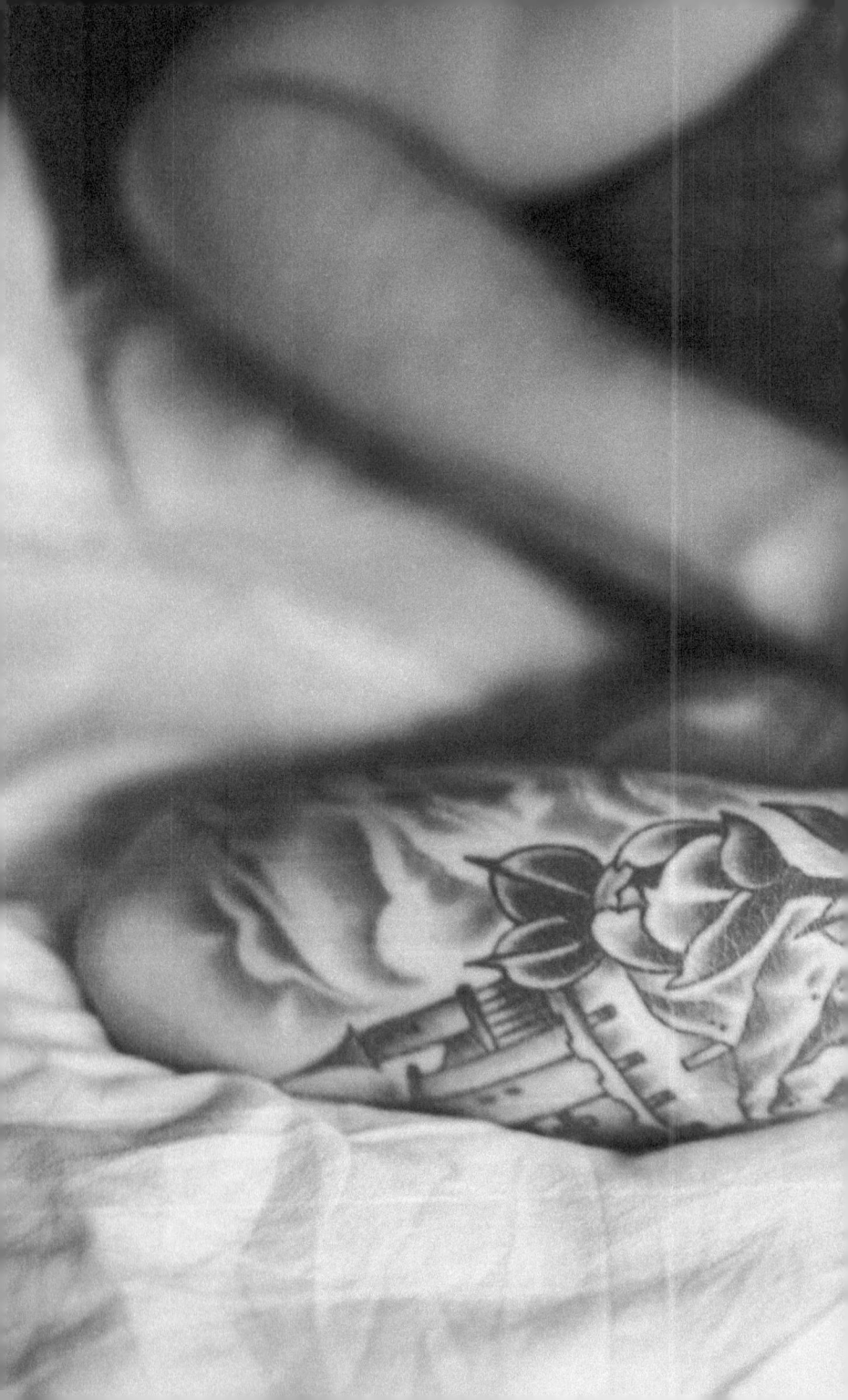

7

BENJI

SEPTEMBER 2027

All of my friends are falling in love. Eli is all shacked up with Colby, and no one can fault him because Colby is a *serious* snack. Then there's Trevor with the giant Beau. Seriously, these guys are drinking something different from the rest of us. Now Jackson is all goo-goo for the snarky redhead.

Meanwhile, I'm hopelessly pining for the rockstar I can't get out of my head no matter how hard I try. I haven't even seen him since February. But those five days in Los Angeles are burned into my mind.

After a fun day at the autumn festival, we all gather at Trevor and Beau's house. We shoot the shit for a while, and I fill Trevor in on the contract Chris and Claire want me to sign. A world tour with Nolan. Once Jackson heads back to the mother-in-law suite over the garage at Colby and Eli's place, I corner Trevor in the backyard of Beau's house.

"You've got to tell me if I'm making a mistake with Nolan."

Trevor stares at me hard, gaze unblinking in that intense way of his. I do my best not to squirm under his stare, but it's difficult because the man has a serious intensity.

"I can't answer that for you, Benji," Trevor finally says with a resigned sigh.

"Trevor," I whine.

"Sunshine," Trevor mocks.

I'm going to punch him. Reaching out to take a swipe at him, Trevor ducks with a dark chuckle.

"You've just gotta do what you think is best, you know? You've already been with him a couple of times, so you just have to figure out if you could do it for months on end. A world tour is a serious commitment," Trevor says with all the gravity of a parent explaining something to a child. Which he kind of is, despite him being younger than me. Most of the time Trevor *feels* like the eldest of all of us. "And you've got to think about the cost that twenty-four seven with Nolan is going to do to you. Is it worth that? I can't tell you."

"I just want you to decide for meeeeeeee."

"Can't, sorry. But Nolan isn't a bad guy, we both know that. He's just fucked up."

"A little," I hesitantly agree.

Trevor leans against the back porch railing to stare blankly out at the forest of trees swaying in the gentle breeze behind Beau's home. I scoot over beside him to also lean against the railing, pretending like I can see in the forest whatever he's able to see. But after a few minutes it gets boring, so I straighten back up with a sigh. Leaning my back against the railing, I stare at the side of Trevor's face until he turns to look at me.

"What was he like with you?" I ask softly, a little afraid of the answer.

Trevor's mouth pinches, and he steals a look behind him to ensure Beau is safely inside the house. "Aggressive and mean. He always topped from the bottom, bit and scratched and egged me on until I got aggressive too. I never liked it much. I always left feeling worse, which wasn't something I hated back then. But with Nolan it was always a little more difficult. Especially dealing with his emotions."

"It seems he has a particular dynamic that he likes," I comment, not wanting to confirm or deny to Trevor that Nolan's the same way with me. Because while I think there's similarities, I don't think Nolan opened himself up to Trevor the way he has with me. Similar dynamics, but different approach.

Trevor nods tiredly. "Just be careful." He stands up slowly and pats my cheek fondly. "And if it goes south, you can always come running home with your tail between your legs."

I stick my tongue out at him, earning me a real Trevor laugh. "I'm going to do it."

"Well, good luck. You'll need it."

Trevor offers to drive me back to Colby and Eli's place but I wave him off. Walking through the woods at night isn't new to me after growing up on the commune. Plus, usually a walk helps me get my mind right, helps me figure shit out. The stars flicker in the sky over me as I walk along the gravel road. Hands tucked into my pockets to ward off the slight chill in the air, I think about the contract that Chris emailed me earlier this week.

Eight months on a world tour with Nolan and three million dollars. That amount of money will change *everything* for me. If I let Jackson invest some of the money, I could probably retire off of it. But I also don't know if I'm strong enough to handle eight whole months with just Nolan. His emotions are volatile and hard to withstand at times. He's a barreling hurricane and I'm a dandelion caught in his raging storm.

When Colby's farmhouse comes into view, I pause beside one of the large oak trees a little down the way. A breeze blows over the grass, settling whatever wary feeling that's been slowly growing in my chest. Chris lists his number at the bottom of his email, so my impulsiveness wins when he makes it so easy.

"Hello?" Chris says after the third ring.

"It's Benji... I want to talk to Nolan before I sign the contract."

"You want to talk to Nolan," Chris repeats in obvious confusion.

"Yeah, I want to speak to him. Can you give me his number?"

There's a mild scramble for the phone, hushed noises, and then a very serious smacking sound. That's weird.

"What?" Nolan asks into the phone, his tone clipped like always.

"Hi," I say with a small smile.

"Hi?" Nolan repeats, sounding just as confused as Chris.

"I'm going to sign the contract for the tour, but I wanted to talk to you first. Can you step away from Chris?"

The sound of Nolan moving around echoes through the phone, shuffling his feet and a quickening in his breath. A few moments later, a door closes.

"Alright, you've got me alone. What can I do for you, Benji?"

"I'm going to have some rules."

"You're going to have rules?" Nolan repeats with a skeptical laugh. "Who do you think is running this show?"

"Me."

"You?"

I spin around in the gravel, kicking my right foot in the

rocks. When I look up at the moon, it stares unblinking back at me like it also knows I'm a big fucking idiot. And maybe I am an idiot. But if I'm going to do this, then I want to do it my way, not Nolan's.

"Yes, me. I'll come on the tour, fuck you when you need the release, but you're going to do what I say when I say it. Because I think you like that idea, don't you, Nolan? You hate giving up control, but at the same time, you kind of like it."

"Benji," Nolan growls.

"So I'll go, but I'm in charge. Okay?"

"Fine," Nolan finally relents after a few charged moments. "But you need to remember that for eight months, you're mine; I'm not yours. No matter what you think. I'll see you in New York next week."

Nolan hangs up without another word, leaving me standing alone in the dark. The moon is still as bright as ever, mocking me and my idiocy. For the first time I notice the ring circling the moon. I rub at my chest, trying to ward off the ominous feeling of danger looming on the horizon. *A ring around the moon means hold steady, things are about to get bumpy,* my mama's voice murmurs in my head. Maybe for once she'll be wrong.

THE WORLD TOUR starts in London, but instead of flying separately, I'm meeting Nolan in New York to fly on his private jet. It takes far too long for me to find my way toward the section of JFK with the private planes. The security guard looks at me dubiously when I give my name, and he even looks mildly pissed off when my name is on the list. I frown as I step inside and look down at my faded, ripped jeans and an old T-shirt. It's travel attire. I want to be comfortable.

After a few minutes of wandering, I locate Nolan sitting in a leather chair, both legs tossed over the winged back and head hanging close to the ground. He doesn't hear me approach him because of the large headphones over his ears. Fingers tapping a beat against his thighs, he's the picture of a musician. My heart does this dizzy sort of leap in my chest at the memory of what his mouth tastes like. I wonder if he still tastes the same, like spice and bite and rage.

"Don't bother him," Chris murmurs from behind me.

I jump a little. "Jesus, you scared me."

Chris smiles sheepishly, then nods toward Nolan. "He's picturing himself on stage. Helps his anxiety."

I turn back to Nolan and swallow thickly. A little furrow of concentration rests between his brows. His shirt slowly slides down to reveal his concave stomach, the tattoos a storybook across his skin.

"I'm going to bother him," I inform Chris, moving away before he can have the option to stop me.

Crouching down in front of Nolan, I lightly boop him on the nose. His dark brown eyes take me in, that furrow in his brows slowly disappearing, only to be replaced by a wicked smirk at the corner of his lips.

"Hey, stud," Nolan teases.

The terminal is empty minus for us, so I dip down to kiss him. Nolan startles just a little but gets with the program quickly, opening up for me so that I can lick into his mouth. He tastes just like I remember but with a coffee bite. His tongue tangles with mine, but he doesn't fight for dominance. Gripping his neck in my palm, I squeeze and steal his breath from him. When I pull away, his eyes are glassy, and he stares up at me.

We look at each other for a few long moments, before I stand, never breaking eye contact.

"Ever been blown on an airplane?" Nolan asks as I toss myself into the seat beside him.

"Can't say that I have."

Nolan closes his eyes again. "First time for everything."

He ignores my presence, seemingly getting lost in the music again. We don't sit long before Chris stands, taps Nolan on the shoulder, then disappears toward the gate. Nolan stretches out like a cat, legs pulled taut, arms stretched so the tips of his fingers touch the dark gray carpet.

Nolan heaves himself out of the chair and holds his hand out for me. I slip my hand into his, enjoying the touch of his calloused fingers against my wrist. His headphones slip down to his neck as he tugs me toward the gate, his fingers gently squeezing my own.

The private plane isn't as small as I was expecting. Sleek tan leather seats dot the cabin, and there are two doors in the back. Chris settles quietly in a seat up front and starts amiably chatting with the older stewardess. Nolan drops my hand and makes a beeline for the seat at the back of the plane. I'm not sure where to go. Do I follow Nolan? Do I sit with Chris?

My internal struggle is put to rest when Nolan stands back up with a roll of his eyes. "Hello? Come sit back here."

Sassy fucker. Plopping my trusty backpack on the ground, I slide into the seat beside Nolan. He keeps his headphones around his neck and angles his head against the seat so that he can fix me with his weird, hard gaze. My eyes dip down to the skeleton hands around his neck, then back up to his suddenly grinning mouth.

"Oh, Nolan, if I come, I'm going to be in charge," Nolan mocks, lips curled up in a mean sort of smirk. I have the odd urge to take him over my knee and spank him. Instead, I curl my fingers against my jeans to keep myself from reaching out for him.

"I am in charge," I point out, voice thready.

Nolan rolls his eyes. He fumbles around in his jeans pockets, making a victorious sound in the back of his throat when he pulls out a stick of gum.

"Juicy Fruit, it's the best." He carefully unfurls the gum from the silver jacket, then pops the yellow stick of gum into his mouth. A small, pleased smile tilts his lips up as if he's forgotten to be a shit if only for a moment. "Aptly named gum since I am also a juicy fruit."

"You're sassy today," I point out.

Nolan shrugs indifferently. "Either that or be wrecked out of my mind worrying about this fucking goddamn world tour."

"You don't like tours?"

Nolan turns his hard gaze on me. "We've talked about this, Benjamin, I don't like *singing* for crowds at all. Keep up."

"We didn't talk in-depth about it," I point out.

Nolan looks sarcastically thoughtful, if that's a thing at all. "Pretty sure we did. Hey, wanna fuck me in the bedroom when we're over the Atlantic? You can put a sock in my mouth to keep me quiet."

Jesus Christ. I squeeze my eyes tightly shut to stop myself from getting a boner. I'm not going to fuck him on the plane. It's what he wants, but not what I want.

"I'm not fucking you on the plane," I say, doing my best to keep my voice level.

"Boring." Nolan tosses himself back in the seat, tugs his headphones over his head, and proceeds to do his best to ignore my very presence.

The plane takes off without a hitch. Once we're in the air, the stewardess comes back to offer me drinks. After ordering a ginger ale, I lean against the seat and look out at the sky. The city disappears beneath us as we climb higher and higher, the cloud cover hiding the city from sight. An hour into the seven-hour flight, Nolan falls asleep beside me. His head dangles precariously for a few moments, before falling onto my shoulder with a gentle thump.

Slowly, I raise my hand to sift my fingers through his messy hair. He stays asleep through it, but mumbles a few words I can't make out. I turn my head to press my nose into his hair, trying to inhale the familiar scent of him without seeming like a damn creep. Of course, that's the moment that Chris wanders back to observe us.

"You have a way with him," Chris points out, eyes stuck on where my fingers gently curl around his arm.

"He's sleeping."

Chris rolls his eyes and releases a small laugh. "The man never fucking sleeps."

Chris disappears back toward the front of the plane with an odd sort of smile. I don't know what he's talking about. Nolan hasn't ever struggled to sleep when I'm around. Although, usually it is because I've fucked him into a giant heap of exhaustion. I lose track of time just watching Nolan sleep. His lips stay slightly parted, gentle breaths puffing against my face as he sleeps. Rock music filters from the ears of the headphones, but not loud enough to disturb his quiet slumber.

My arm and shoulder ache from staying still to be a good pillow. I use the time to once again catalog his tattoos. As fond as I am of the flowers on his ribs, I also like the odd mishmash of tattoos that line his arms. The one on his right arm is a sleeve depicting a glowing forest with small, wood-land creatures throughout. The closer I look, the more I notice that the creatures look slightly rabid, almost evil. Cool. He has an evil forest on his arm.

A ding goes on overhead and the captain tells us all to buckle in for landing. Not wanting to unsettle Nolan, I care-fully reach across him to grab the seat belt. Nolan comes awake with a startle, his fingers reaching out to grab at my forearm.

"Hey, it's me. I'm just buckling you in." I carefully pull the seat belt across his lithe waist. His eyes remain on me the entire time, his gaze sharp despite just returning to wakeful-ness. "Okay?"

"Fine," Nolan mumbles before clearing his throat. "What time is it?"

"Well, you slept the entire way, angel. We're landing."

Nolan either ignores the nickname, or doesn't hear it, because he presses his pointer finger and thumb against his eyes. He seems annoyed that he slept the entire way. The shake of his leg accompanies us all through landing, even as we come to a stop on the tarmac. Chris stands once the door opens and waits for us to join him. I hold a finger up in the universal sign for him to give us a moment. The man must trust me a shit ton because he leaves the plane without a single argument.

I slip my hand around the nape of Nolan's neck and

squeeze hard. Using my firm grip, I tug him toward me and kiss his still sleep-soft mouth. He fights me for a moment, fingers pushing against my chest, before they curl into the fabric and tug me closer as he moans quietly into my mouth. The shake of his leg stills and his body slumps against me as I swipe my tongue into his mouth, making him pliant and *mine* under the onslaught of our kiss.

"Better?" I ask against Nolan's slack mouth.

"Fuck you," Nolan whispers back, but the absence of tension in his body belies his statement. I relaxed him and he's pissed about it.

I grin broadly when he clamors out of the seat, and my grin grows even wider when he waits for me before stepping out of the plane. Nolan strides straight for the car waiting to no doubt take us to the hotel close to the arena. Chris sits in the front while the both of us climb into the back.

"How's Trevor?" Nolan asks as he stares out the window at the passing London scenery.

"Fine. He found love, quit escorting."

Nolan's head turns to me, a small frown on his lips. "Really?"

"Mmm, yeah. Nice guy. Tall, southern, quiet."

"Hope it lasts. Trevor was nice."

Nice seems like a big compliment coming from Nolan. I want to ask him a million questions. I want to ask him why he seems so set on me after having a turn at almost every other guy on the boyfriend roster. What makes me different? But I don't ask because I'm not quite sure I want the answer.

The car pulls up to a fancy-ass-looking hotel that I'm definitely not dressed well enough for, but Nolan isn't either in his skinny jeans and tight black T-shirt. Doesn't seem to matter though when we walk into the lobby and a hush falls over the people milling around. I have this odd urge to pull Nolan into my arms, shield him from the view of everyone around us. But I also know Nolan would hate that with the burning passion of a thousand suns, so I stay a few feet behind him as he heads straight for the elevators.

He stands anxiously by the elevator doors, fingers tapping against his thigh. I slowly reach up to slip the headphones back over his ears, thinking maybe the loud music will calm his restless tapping. His anxious movements stop and his dark eyes stare at me in some weird mix of confusion and gratefulness. A moment later, Chris reappears while brandishing a hotel key card.

"Your room key for the next three nights," Chris says as he slaps the card against my chest.

I grab the slim key with a frown. He didn't hand one to Nolan, just me. But Nolan doesn't seem confused or surprised by it, instead pushing his way into the elevator to lean against the furthest wall as he waits for me to hit the penthouse button.

"I'll see you at the arena in two hours for warm-up." Chris exits the elevator with a wave. "Make sure he eats something," Chris calls without a look back.

"I'm not eating," Nolan mumbles under his breath as the elevator continues to climb to the penthouse level.

"Something small?"

"No."

"For me?"

"Definitely not."

"What if I say please?" I tease with a flutter of my eyes.

"I would hope you know me well enough by now to know that saying please won't endear me to you further, but will probably make me even more of a little shit. Unless saying

90

please leads to you fucking me, then maybe I could get on board." Nolan strides out of the elevator, head turned to look back at me. "You could feed me your cock."

"Nolan."

"Benjamin."

"That's not my name," I growl as I fumble the key into the lock.

Nolan chuckles beside me, his breath fanning over my face. "Frustrated, stud?"

Nolan reaches around me to grab the card, fingers trailing over my overheated skin. With one gentle swipe, he pushes the door open, then proceeds to toss the card at my face. I take a slow, steady breath to stop myself from grabbing him and fucking... I don't know... eating him whole. He'd probably like that too much though. He needs better punishments.

Nolan heads straight for the bedroom to the right but pauses just outside the door.

"Are you going to do that thing where you pretend like you don't want to give me what I want, argue with me, let me get you riled up, then fuck me and be nice afterward? The bathroom here is nice for all those post-fucking soaks you like to take."

"Is that what you're doing now? Trying to rile me up?"

Nolan shrugs as he slips off his headphones. His shirt slowly disappears over his head, his thumbs slowly working at the button of his jeans. Messy hair and a stare that makes heat pool in my stomach. Backing slowly toward the bathroom, Nolan holds my gaze. I follow him like there's a string connecting us, tugging me toward him as sweat prickles at the nape of my neck.

"Benjamin, why are you playing this game with me?"

Nolan pushes his pants down, revealing his semi-hard cock. Fuck. He was commando this entire goddamn time. "You're here for one thing. And you know what would relax me before this fucking concert in ten hours? A good hard fuck. The kind where you shove your fingers in my mouth until I choke."

"Stop it," I say firmly.

Nolan freezes. "Excuse me?"

"I said stop. We're playing by my rules now. My rules are that we don't fuck before a show, only after."

"You can't be serious," Nolan says around a shocked laugh.

"Deadly serious. I'll fuck you after a show, when you're pliant and tired, when you need the release to go to sleep. Before a show, we can kiss, but that's it."

"You can't—"

"I can and I will," I interrupt him.

Nolan visibly fumes, nostrils flaring, gaze going hard. He steps closer to me and shoves me, but I don't move. We might be the same height but I've got enough weight on him that his shove is fruitless. He seemingly realizes this and scrunches his adorable nose up in annoyance.

"Give me all the rules," Nolan mumbles, eyes refusing to meet mine.

I carefully wrap my palms around his neck, letting my fingers tangle in the curly hairs there. "No fucking until after a show. Then I'll give you whatever you want, however you want it. Before shows, I'll kiss you as much as you want, feed you, make sure you're relaxed. And on days off, we have dates."

Nolan winces. "Dates are for suckers."

I chuckle as I gently brush my fingers against the warm

skin of his neck. "Then I'm a sucker. Give me what I want, be good for me, hmm?"

Nolan's eyes meet mine as I dip down closer, our lips a breath apart. "Someone who looks like you shouldn't talk the way you do."

"Look like what?"

"Sweet and soft."

"I'll show you sweet and soft," I murmur just before closing the gap between us. I kiss Nolan until he's supple under my hands, boneless, putty for me to make into what he needs to be for the show.

And later, when I watch from the stands as he sings in front of a crowd of more people than I can count, I know the lack of tension in his body is because of me. I count that as a win.

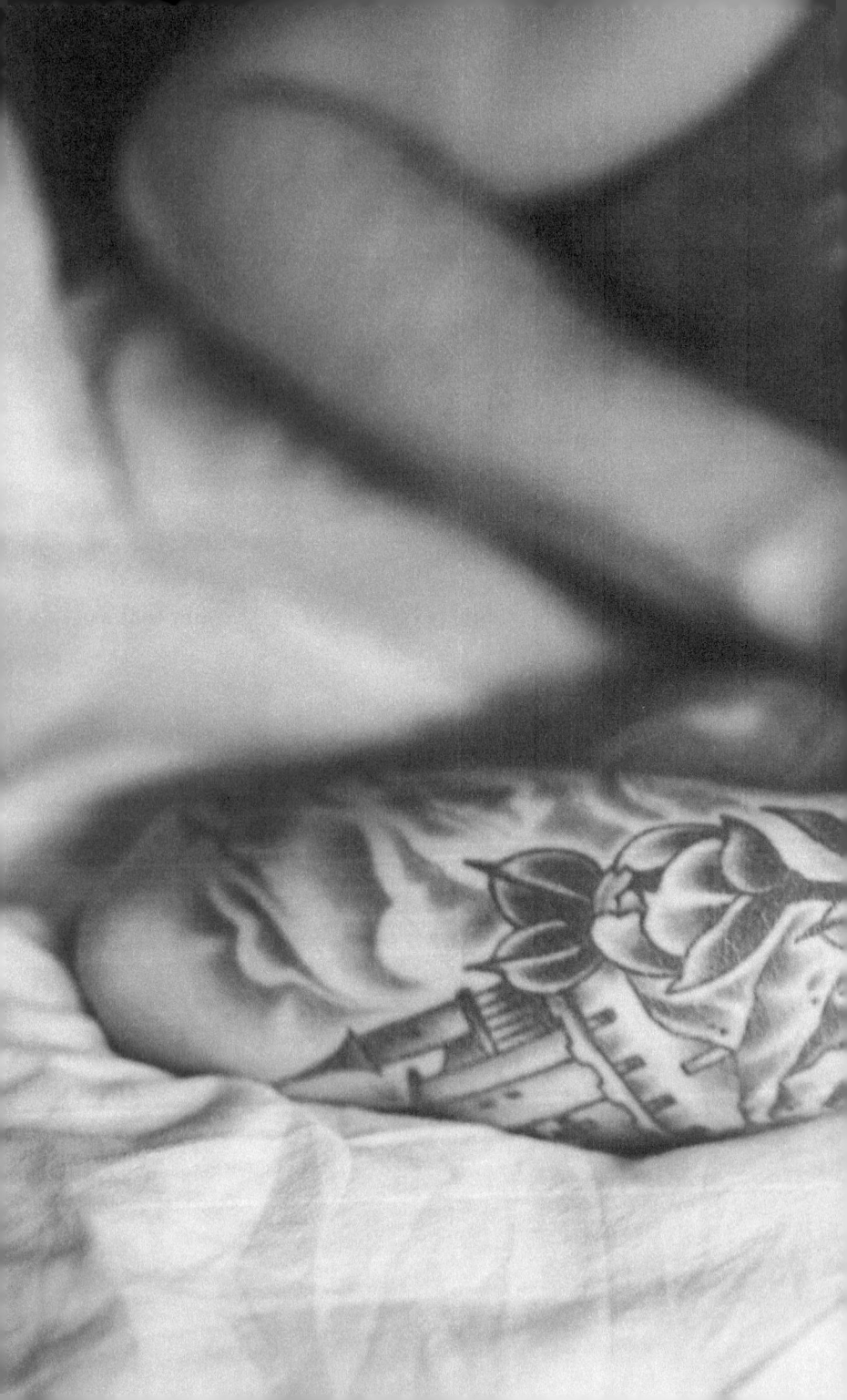

8

NOLAN

OCTOBER 2027

Six shows down and Benji keeps to his word because he's supremely annoying. Golden retriever piece of shit. Before every show he kisses me senseless until all the tension bleeds from my body like a balloon slowly losing air. After shows, he fucks me however I want, which usually means a quickie in the bathroom of the VIP room in the arena. When we're finished, he always rests his forehead against my shoulder, panting like he's run a marathon.

A small part of me is pleased that I can break him down.

But he's not a cure-all.

The stage is still one of the worst places in the world. Standing in front of the crowd, hearing them sing my own words back to me, feels like a thousand fire ants crawling over my skin, biting me until their venom finally stops my heart. One of these days, I'm going to drop dead on stage, a cautionary tale that sometimes the thing you want most in the world is the thing that kills you in the end.

"It's date night," Benji announces as he brushes his teeth. "I have to do an interview with the local..."

Benji rolls his eyes. "Tomorrow after the show," he mumbles around his toothbrush, foam creeping out of the corner of his mouth.

"Yes... I need to prepare for it, you see," I say blandly. "Do my due diligence."

I watch as he spits the toothpaste into the sink, wiping his mouth with the back of his hand like a fucking caveman. Why the hell does that turn me on? Everything about this man is so annoying. Benji hurriedly grabs his ratty shirt from the counter and slips it over his head, looking way too good for only wearing dark jeans and a navy V-neck. His eyes are so startlingly light blue that sometimes I get caught up in staring at them. It's like staring at the sky after a storm, with no cloud in sight. That's Benji, no clouds at all.

"Don't try to wiggle your way out of it. You know the rules." Benji crawls back onto the bed to lie over me. His warmth seeps into my slightly chilly skin. "Nolan, be good."

And then he kisses me despite my morning breath. I try to turn the kiss from slow and gentle into filthy; maybe he'll fuck me if I'm nasty enough. But Benji pulls away to smirk down at me.

"Stop."

"I'm not doing anything!"

"You think if you distract me with your nasty mouth, I'll change my mind about the date."

Well, he's got me there. I shove him off, but instead of getting mad, the fucker just laughs as he falls back onto the bed. His messy hair and easy grin stir some odd feeling in my chest that I can't explain. I don't want to try to explain it either. Benji is dangerous. Not in the sort of way I'm used to with the guys who fight back, but in the way that I think if I let him, he could do serious damage to my already tenuously hanging-on heart.

"I've never been to Ireland, so I want to see the countryside," Benji says as he tangles his fingers together over his chest. He's the picture of absolute serenity.

"We're in Dublin."

Benji turns his head to aim those annoyingly beautiful eyes at me. I have to suppress a shudder as I tug on a pair of ripped jeans. Black is my go-to color because it attracts the least amount of attention. So, black jeans, black T-shirt, and a black hoodie are my standard outfit. Plus, a good hoodie covers up all my tattoos which are my most recognizable feature.

Benji rolls off the bed with an annoyed sigh, at least I assume it's annoyed. After tugging on a grandpa cardigan, he comes to an abrupt stop in front of me. Using his knuckles, Benji tilts my head up slightly so that he can press a soft kiss to the hollow of my throat. He nuzzles against my skin, taking a deep breath.

"You always smell so good in the mornings," Benji whispers against my skin.

What the hell. I back away from him and roughly smack his hand. "Cut it out."

I leave him standing forlornly in the middle of the bedroom. After brushing my own teeth, I stride toward the entrance of the penthouse, knowing that Benji will follow me without a word. Benji orchestrated the driver to take us somewhere that I have no clue about.

Surprises suck. I always want to know what's happening. The driver is thankfully quiet as we climb into the car. I hate chatty drivers. Downtown Dublin rolls past outside the window in flashes of dark green. Everything is sort of dreary, the air crisp. Ireland reminds me of Northern California.

Benji makes a small sound, tugging my attention back to him. He's wearing this dopey sort of smile that makes my stomach do that weird fluttery thing again. I push my sunglasses up over my eyes and turn back to the window so I don't have to look at him. We ride along for almost an hour until we come to a stop in a small town hidden among grassy hills.

"You'll wait?" Benji asks the driver.

The guy looks at him like he's crazy but nods anyway. Poor Benji doesn't realize this guy has been paid to take us wherever we want without question. Like the goddamn puppy he is, Benji grins at me as he comes around the car to grab my hand.

"There is a castle," Benji says excitedly.

I want to reply something sarcastic, something caustic, something *biting* but I can't in the face of his genuine excitement. His hand is warm in my own. He leads me along the cobbled streets, fingers squeezing mine as he navigates us toward a castle in the distance.

"Isn't that fucking cool," Benji says breathlessly.

Sure, the castle is pretty cool. Kind of looks familiar. I tilt my head to the side thinking about it for a moment, going through the rolodex of images in my brain.

"It was in *Braveheart*."

Benji turns freaked-out eyes toward me. "What?"

I point toward the castle. "It was in the movie *Braveheart*. They'll never take our freedom!" I do a really poor Irish accent that has Benji somehow looking even more startled.

"You knew that just by looking at the castle? That was a

neat fact I was going to share with you as we walked around..."

Benji looks so put out that I yet again feel kind of bad. With a sigh, I start walking toward the castle and tug him along with me. "We can pretend I don't know, stud. Okay?"

"It's not the same..."

"Oh my God." I stop in the middle of the path leading to the castle. With wide, dramatic eyes, I turn toward Benji. "Isn't that castle so big! Look at it! I wonder if they've ever used it in a Hollywood movie. Wouldn't that be cool?"

Benji's puppy dog eyes turn grateful and he grins at me. "It was in *Braveheart*."

I gasp in feigned shock. "Seriously?"

He stands up straighter. "Yes, they shot parts of the movie here."

"So cool," I say very seriously.

Benji tugs his hand out of mine and slings his arm over my shoulder. "Come on."

Despite my perpetual want to stomp my feet in the ground, the day ends up being pretty nice. Benji plays the perfect tour guide, giving me facts about the castle as we walk around. Once we venture out of the castle, he even gives snippets of facts about the town.

"Did you google this place before bringing me here?" I ask curiously.

Benji smiles shyly. "A little. One should always be prepared. Oh, do you want to go into this pub? I know you can't drink but maybe we can get some real Irish food?"

I'm oddly helpless against denying him when it's not in the bedroom. He leads me to the pub that's half full considering it's a weekday and early evening. Air thick with the smell of beer and fried food smacks me in the face when we push through the door. But the plus side is no one here seems to recognize me. Maybe there are still some parts of the world where I'm just Nolan Hastings.

A small table in the corner calls to us. When we sit down, Benji sits at the chair beside me instead of the one across from me. I realize it's to block the view of me from the outside of the bar. Jesus. Why is that also hot?

"Hello." A woman stops by our table with a sweet smile. Messy blond hair, kind eyes, she grins down at us totally unknowing that a worldwide rockstar is seated at her table. "What'll ya have?"

Benji grimaces as he looks down at the menu.

I grin up at her and wink. "Bring us your favorite dishes. We want to experience the real Ireland."

"Ya sure?"

I nod. "And bring a beer for him. Guinness, right? Just water for me."

She happily stuffs her notepad back into her small apron. "Easy enough."

Benji blinks over at me, sheepish. "I was going to impress you by ordering like I knew what the fuck I was doing."

"You don't have to impress me," I reply.

That weird look flits across his face again. The look that I have trouble parsing. Like maybe I've hurt his feelings somehow. I'm not good at this sort of thing, talking to people, being pleasant. When I meet fans, I have to fake it until I make it but Benji and I are living in each other's pockets.

"It's boring sitting here staring at each other. Tell me a story."

"What kind of story?" Benji asks.

I wave a dismissive hand at him. "Anything."

Benji's lips purse thoughtfully as he thinks about it. A few moments pass by before he grins again, obviously having thought of something.

"I almost drowned when I was six years old."

"What?"

"So there's this pond on the commune and apparently I just assumed that I could swim. I'd seen the older kids swimming. My moms had me in the shallows sometimes. So, I was out wandering alone, which was pretty typical for the commune. But, anyway, I was wandering around and just decided to swim. I got undressed, waded out, and when my toes couldn't reach, I just kept going... but then I got scared. The water was so dark and the bottom of the lake disappeared..." Benji trails off with a frown, lost in the memory. He shakes himself loose from it. "One of the older boys was passing by and saw my hands waving. He came in to save me. After that, he spent the summer teaching me to swim. My first crush. Cody Carrol."

"That's a serious name," I say but really I want to ask him why he was wandering alone around this commune he speaks about.

A crimson blush dots Benji's cheeks and suddenly I've never wanted to murder someone I don't even know so badly before. Fuck Cody.

"He was sweet. He left for college and never looked back. I think he's a doctor now, the last my cousin told me. Well, she's not really my cousin. But all the kids that grew up with me are basically my cousins."

I lean forward on the table. "This isn't some polygamy thing, is it?"

"No!" Benji shouts frantically, waving his arms around. "No, it was very normal. My moms are just fucking hippies."

"If you say so."

"What about you? What about your childhood?"

I scowl just as the waitress returns with her arms laden with food. Thank God. The food smells delicious and my traitorous stomach growls just at the sight of it. What was I thinking? Ordering all this damn food. Hopefully Benji won't notice when I eat just a few bites.

"This is a lot of food," Benji mumbles right before digging into his plate of steaming food.

I pick at my own plate, carefully moving food around so it looks like I've eaten a lot. I've been a professional at appearing to have eaten a lot over the years. It's not that I don't want to eat. Not even that I don't like food. My anxiety just constantly makes me *not* hungry. When hunger does finally hit me, I feel like a garbage disposal that can't stop consuming until I'm sick with it.

The bread is good at least. That's a safe choice. I dip the bread into the stew, watching as the thick brown gravy drips from it. Flavor bursts on my tongue, rich and hearty. It's not too bad.

"Good?" Benji asks around a mouthful of food.

"Good," I reply, because it is good.

We eat quietly, the conversation ebbing as Benji gorges himself on the spread before us. Every time we share a meal together I'm always surprised just how much he can put away. But I don't know *why* I'm surprised considering how often he works out. If we aren't fucking, going on these stupid dates, then he's at whatever hotel's gym working out. Not that I'm going to complain because he has the body of a Greek god.

Benji pays the bill with another shy grin. I stay quiet on the ride back to the hotel, some odd feeling creeps up inside me that's threatening to break loose. Most days are a blur. Every day takes so much effort just to keep on going. Sometimes, I think about stopping it all together. That deep, dark seed of something inside me that whispers terrifying thoughts into my ear. Thoughts about going to sleep and just never waking up because the world would be a better place without me in it. What a fucking thought.

I didn't know there was a word for what happens to me before a show until I googled it a few years ago. My brain disconnects from my body until I'm just going through the motions, just barely hanging on. On stage, I become someone else. I become Nolan the rock god that they all clamor to tear apart. Every single person seated in the crowd wants Nolan Hastings. They either want my voice, my body, or my money. Something about me belongs to them. And the entire time I'm singing, it's for them, not one single moment of it is for me.

I miss when singing was mine. When it belonged to me. Nothing belongs to me anymore. Nothing has for a long time, except for Benji.

The arena blurs in front of me until all I know is the microphone in my hands, the sound of my drummer behind me. If Chris didn't carefully curate the people backstage, I know there would be no way for me to remain sober. Despite years of sobriety, the temptation would be too much with how my brain feels off-kilter by the time I stumble off the stage after a three-hour set.

"Nolan," Benji says loudly, hands gripping my shoulders.

I blink everything back into focus. "Hi."

Benji's smile barely meets his eyes and I hate that. I can't explain why but his smile being dimmed when he looks at me is like a cloud passing over the sun. Miserable. Covered in sweat, feeling like I'm dead inside, I reach up to push the corner of his mouth up with my thumb.

"Smile like this," I instruct him.

Benji's lips quiver as he fights a smile. "That was a good set."

I look back out to the emptying arena, feeling some weird, too-big emotion that I can't put to words. Pieces of myself remain out on the stage, pieces I'll never get back. Everyone out there is leaving with a part of me.

"You know what would make it even better?" I ask as I walk forward, forcing Benji to walk backward.

Benji arches a curious eyebrow. "What?"

I lean forward to whisper in his ear, smiling when a shiver rolls through him at the touch of my lips to his overheated skin. "Fuck me in the bathroom, hand over my mouth so no one can hear me scream."

"Whatever you want," Benji agrees quietly.

I return to myself bit by bit as Benji shoves me against the wall, covers my mouth with his hand, and takes me so hard my toes lift off the floor with each torturous thrust. In these charged moments, I belong to myself, and Benji belongs to me. My pleasure and his pleasure blend together until the world spins only for us, only for the soft gasps, the bites that almost break skin.

Afterward Benji leans against the wall, eyes closed as he pants through his release. I carefully tug up my pants, grateful for the twinge in my ass when I lean against the sink to slap at my cheek. As I take a rare glance at myself in the mirror, I see my eyes are dull and lifeless, hair flat, and I don't recognize myself at all anymore. There's solace in knowing everyone thinks they know me, but no one really does. Not even myself.

9

BENJI

NOVEMBER 2027

Nolan sleeps like the dead. It's almost terrifying. His back barely moves, eyelashes perfectly still, mouth closed tightly as he sleeps away the cobwebs of the show from last night. One month on tour has taught me that being a rockstar is definitely not as fun as they make it look in the movies. If Nolan isn't sleeping, practicing, or playing for crowded arenas, then he's begging me to fuck him until he falls into a deep, deadly sort of sleep.

I'm still learning how to strike the perfect balance with him. It seems the longer the tour goes on, the more sullen he appears. He's also getting more difficult to handle, his emotions volatile, his want for borderline violent sex increasing at a rate that kind of terrifies me. I mean, sex is sex, but with Nolan it has this edge to it that makes me wonder if he really wants it, or if he's just going through the motions. Sometimes it feels like I'm just a tool to increase whatever pain he's simmering in.

Only our dates make me feel like maybe this isn't the worst idea known to mankind. When I take Nolan tourist trap in whatever city we're in, when I make him laugh despite the exhaustion radiating off of him, when he's quiet and pliant in my arms at night after a fuck that steals my breath, I wonder what it would be like to keep him. While the tour is grueling and mostly miserable, I like spending time with Nolan. I like the way his brain works and his derisive commentary on just about everything.

But after a month, I still can't get a read on how he feels about me. Every emotion Nolan has is carefully hidden behind steel walls that are impossible to permeate. Impossible to climb. I only see what he wants me to see and nothing more.

An incoming call from my mom lights up my phone, shaking me from my reverie. Not wanting to wake Nolan, I roll out of bed and pad toward the balcony that overlooks Milan, Italy. Afternoon has the streets bustling below, the scent of food from nearby restaurants wafting up to the balcony.

"Hey, Mom."

"Where's my world traveler today?" Mom asks.

"Milan."

Mom sighs wistfully. "We spent a few weeks in Italy before you were born. Loved it there. I prefer the Amalfi coast." Mom's voice dips down into a whisper. "The nightlife there was bonkers."

"Why are you whispering?" Mama's shout echoes through the line. I can't help but grin. They're kooky and weird but they're my moms. I miss them so much it hurts.

"Well, I didn't particularly want you to hear."

"Why?" Mama says with an accusing lilt to her voice.

"Oh, here we go," Mom mutters.

"No fighting! It's afternoon here, so it must be early there. Everything alright?"

"Oh, yes," Mama says, having obviously commandeered the phone from Mom. "Are you coming home for Thanksgiving?"

"Probably not. My travel plans won't bring me home until next year."

"What?" Mom asks in confusion. "You won't be home for Christmas?"

Oh, here comes the guilt. "Probably not until your birthday, Mama."

"Oh."

The phone goes deadly silent. "Sorry, guys."

"It's okay!" Mom says because she's always the one to save face, the one to fix any sort of problem. "You'll just have to meet the new additions to the family when you come back home. Everyone misses you."

"I miss them too." No matter how I feel about growing up in the commune, growing up so sheltered, I do miss the people. I keep in touch with a few of the kids my age via social media, especially the ones who left like I did.

"Are you okay, honey?" Mom asks in her sweet-as-honey, Georgia-peach accent. The familiar sound of it rolls over me, soothing some of the bumps and bruises I've gathered over the past month.

"I'm fine. I promise. I miss you guys soooooo much."

"Now you sound more like yourself. Well, it's early. We'll let you go. But we love you, Sunshine. You're the light of our lives."

"I know. I love you, too."

The sound of a small skirmish filters through the phone and I can clearly hear the sound of Mama stepping out onto the porch, the small creek behind the house bubbling through the phone speaker.

"Mi corazon, mijo. Are you sure you're alright?"

"Yes, I promise. Don't worry!"

Mama sighs heavily. I can practically see her leaning against the porch railing, black hair shot through with gray. "If you say so. Your mom is driving me up the wall, you know. She's doing that whole mural thing again. We've painted and repainted the bedroom three times."

Crap. Mom only does that when she's anxious because of me. "I'll text more. Promise. Also, I hope it's flowers and not insects again. The beetles were super freaky."

"It's galaxies now," Mama says with an air of resignation.

I try really hard to not laugh. But I can practically envision the black wall with weird splotches of color splattered across it. "Oh, space. Nice. The best of a lot of bad options."

I can practically hear Mama's shoulders lowering from her ears. "Alright, mijo. We love you. Call soon."

"Love you," I murmur just before the line quiets.

I glance back over my shoulder and sigh in relief when Nolan is still sound asleep in the messy bed. Rubbing at my face, I shake off the phone call. It's fine. They'd just worry if they knew the mess that I was in. And it definitely is a certified mess. The room is chilly and breaks goose pimples over my skin as I tread back into the bedroom. Nolan makes a small disgruntled sound when I lie quietly back down beside him.

His dark brown eyes blink open slowly, as if there is an insurmountable amount of something weighing them down. As the tour goes on, he looks closer to death than life. I want to feed him, make him sleep, pull him into my body to keep him safe. I have this odd sense of feeling that he's slowly slipping through my grip, like sand at the beach.

"Morning," I whisper into the soft beige sheets.

Nolan grunts and leans forward to bury his face in my neck. A few seconds go by where he just simply breathes me in, his fingers dancing across the expanse of my back before settling at my shoulder blades. His skin is so cold against my own overheated body. The shape of his hand feels like a brand, one that I'm not sure I'll ever be able to forget.

"Are you making me go out on a date today?" Nolan murmurs against my skin, his teeth lightly nipping at my throat with each word.

"Making is such an odd choice of words, Nolan."

He snorts and snuggles closer against me. I close my eyes tight against the small, rare show of want from him. Usually by now he's fled the bed, pushed me away until I feel tormented with some odd sense of loss. He's still naked after last night, so I curl my hand over the hard curve of his hip, the bone biting into the softness of my palm.

"Are you *taking* me out today?"

"Yes."

Nolan hums quietly. When he pulls away, his eyes are full of more life than they have been for weeks. "Do you need to go home for Thanksgiving?"

"Were you eavesdropping?"

Nolan rolls over onto his back, bringing me with him. His leg curls around my hip, his slowly hardening cock nudging against mine. Fuck.

"You talk very loudly."

That's definitely not true. "I was whispering."

I shiver when Nolan scratches at my scalp. He blinks slowly up at me. "Your whisper is very loud."

I can't take one more second of his fingers working their magic in my hair. I grab his wrists and press them down into the pillows above his head. The pulse in his wrist pounds against my palm, proof of life. Nolan stays quiet, only arching one eyebrow as he waits for my next move.

"Nolan, what do *you* want to do today?"

Nolan's eyebrows furrow, his fingers curling to bite into my knuckles. "What?" he asks, sounding slightly affronted.

I dip down to brush a kiss over his cheek. He gasps slightly, just barely audible, but it's a sound that settles low in my gut.

"Do you want to go out? Stay here with me? Dates don't have to be us gallivanting around whatever city we're in. We can do something in this hotel room until it's time for you to get ready for your show."

"Can we fuck?" Nolan asks, voice pitched low. The sound settles low and warm in my chest, sending a zip of lightning shooting through my body.

"After the show."

Nolan tilts his head back in frustration. "Whatever. Fine. I don't know why you're so set on spending time with me anyway. Just collect your paycheck and fuck me after the shows."

Something about his tone rings an alarm in my brain. He's not even being sarcastic or irritable. I can tell now what his tones mean, and that one means everything he said was a statement of fact to him. Even without the fucking, I'm so curious about Nolan that I'd happily spend days getting to know his irritable, sour self. If only he'd let me.

"Bath first." I roll out of bed and bite back a laugh when Nolan stares up at me, annoyance painted across his face. I wiggle my fingers in invitation. "Come on, angel. It's my date day. I'll give you what you want even if you don't know how to ask for it."

An emotion that I'm not privy to crosses Nolan's face. His eyes crinkle and his mouth turns down into a new frown that I catalog in my memory bank. I think I've shocked Nolan so greatly that he has no other choice but to go along with me. His fingers tangle with mine, making it easy to tug him out of the bed.

The bathroom has a large clawfoot tub that'll probably, maybe, *hopefully,* fit us both. If not, Nolan can sit comfortably on my lap, and I won't complain. Turning the water on high and to the type of hot, scalding temperature I've learned Nolan likes, I toss in some of the bath salts and oils the hotel provided. The air fills with the scent of lavender and vanilla. When I glance over my shoulder, Nolan is leaning against the sink, carefully keeping his gaze pointed away from the mirror.

"Come on, angel." I climb into the tub and wiggle my fingers again in demand for him to join me. He never fails to smile when I do this. It's a small Nolan smile, the one that tips just one corner of his mouth up, but I always count it as a win.

"We're too big for this," Nolan mutters as he climbs in, easily settling between my legs.

I wrap my arm around his cold chest, pulling him tightly against my front until he's snugly pressed into the curve of my body. His heart pounds a rapid beat against my palm, so I gently swipe my thumb across his damp skin, hoping to calm it.

"Tell me something I can't learn from Google," I whisper into the skin of Nolan's neck.

His hands rub up and down my thighs, as he sighs deeply. "My entire life is on Google. You know everything."

"I haven't looked you up, so I don't know anything already."

Nolan's hands still their questing journey on my thighs. "You haven't looked me up?"

I shake my head and nuzzle deeper into his neck. Pressing a kiss against his pulse point, I slowly raise my hand to cup his throat. "No. I want to know what you *want* me to know. Nothing the internet says means shit."

"You're so fucking weird, Benjamin."

"That's not my name," I whine, because it's actually starting to have a ring to it when he says it.

"I know," Nolan quietly admits, almost quiet enough for me to miss it.

"What's my name?"

"Sunshine," Nolan whispers, fingers dancing across the skin of my thigh.

"How do you..."

Nolan chuckles lightly. "Chris does background checks on all my men. Just like I knew everything about Trevor's past. I know your name is Sunshine and that you dropped out of college after two semesters."

This fact should probably piss me off but it doesn't. "Doesn't seem fair that you know that about me but I've never googled you."

"Well..." Nolan trails off with a soft, barely audible sigh. "I don't call you by your name, do I? It's pretty obvious you don't like it."

"I go by my middle name," I admit quietly.

"I'll offer you a trade," Nolan says just as quietly. Goose pimples pop up in their wake as I trail my fingers over his forearms. "The first time I performed on stage for a crowd of around one hundred people... I ran off as soon as I finished singing and vomited all over the stairs behind the venue."

The biggest rockstar in the world has stage fright. "Then what'd you do?"

Nolan turns his head to aim an annoyed look at me. "I taught myself to not vomit after being on stage. What else is there to do?"

"What do you mean you taught yourself?"

Nolan huffs and turns back around. His hand splashes in the water a few times, sending ripples through the warm, soapy water. Back to chest, I can almost imagine we're one person like this, like when we get out of the tub, we'll still be stuck together, just one solitary human. I wonder if it's possible to share my breath with him, when he so desperately needs the air.

"I taught myself to not feel nausea. What else is there to do?"

"How did you do that?"

Nolan lets out a deep groan. "Benji, seriously, it's not that fucking deep. I go on stage, zone out, then come back off stage and you fuck me. That's it. What other tidbits about Nolan Hastings do you want, hmm? Want to know how many men I've fucked? Want to know about how my druggie parents dropped me off at my great-grandma's house when I was a kid because the drugs meant more to them than I did? Want to know about the group home I was in after my grandma died and how the other boys relentlessly bullied me, going as far as to kick me in my sleep? I can cry if you want, if that'll get you going."

I squeeze his throat until he turns his head enough to gaze at me. "Stop."

"Don't ask for something if you don't really want it, Benji."

"I want to know *you*. Not whatever factoids you think the press would eat up. Not the bits of information in the message boards that fans froth at the mouth over."

Nolan turns his head to press his forehead against my cheek, his breaths stilted, rib cage moving rapidly under my palm. "You're going to make this so hard, Benji."

"Make what hard?"

Nolan swallows loudly. "I hate being me. Sometimes I don't want to exist anymore."

Fuck. What the hell do I say to that? I squeeze Nolan tighter against me, desperately fighting back the urge to cry. My throat feels tight and my heart cracks in half as I slowly lift my hand to curl my fingers into his damp hair.

"Nolan," I whisper, a secret between us.

Nolah shakes his head hard, his hair tickling my chin. "Don't, Benji. Pretend I never said it. Forget everything about this, just remember me wanting to be fucked, wanting to be used. Remember that, okay?"

"Nolan," I say again, throat thick with unshed tears.

"Forget it, Benji."

And then Nolan turns around in the tub, causing water to slosh over the edges onto the marble tile of the bathroom. His soapy palms grip my cheeks and his eyes bore into mine.

"Remember me that way when this is over. Remember me wanting you so badly it hurt me, okay?"

I don't like hearing him say the word over. I hate how flat his eyes look, all the emotion gone. I despise the way his hands tremble slightly against my cheeks. I've got to speak in the way Nolan understands though, because words will never be enough to get through to him. Curling my hand against the nape of his neck, I tug him down until our lips are pressed painfully together, teeth gnashing as Nolan sneers against my mouth.

"I can't need you," Nolan growls into my mouth.

The words taste raw and painful, dipped in the very need that I know Nolan doesn't want to feel. I tangle my fingers in his hair and tug his head back to bite his throat hard enough to steal a gasp from him. The air from my lungs won't be enough, I think I need to give him my heart.

"I won't leave until you tell me to leave, Nolan. If you want me at the end of the contract, I'll still be here."

Nolan melts against me as his body loses every ounce of fight. One month in and I've lost the ability to steer this ship. We're so far off course that I know I'm beyond fucked.

"You know what I've always wanted?" Nolan whispers, the words caught between us like sneakers on a telephone wire.

"What?"

Nolan presses his cheek against mine, his breaths panting and hard in my ear. "I want to say no and I want you to fuck me anyway. I want to fight and scream and claw at you, but you don't stop until you're fucking me into the ground, getting off on me saying no. That's what I've always wanted."

"Have you done that with anyone else?" I ask, almost regretting the words the moment they're out.

Nolan chuckles darkly. "No, stud."

"I'll do it," I say quickly, despite being fucking terrified at the idea. I want to give Nolan everything he wants. If he asked for the moon, I'd fling a lasso around it and pull it down to earth just for him, just for one single ounce of joy to flit across his face.

"Not now. But one day soon, before this is all over. You'll do it raw too, because I was tested a long time ago in case I ever wanted that with you." Nolan's fingers curl over my biceps, nails digging into my skin, hard enough to make me grit my teeth. "You'll remember me like that, okay? That's how we'll remember each other. I'm just a sick fuck."

"Shut up," I growl before tugging his mouth to mine. I don't want to hear him talk that way about himself. This entire conversation is turning my brain to mush, so I've got to end it. The idea he was tested for me though, sends a rush of longing so deep through me that I'm afraid I'll keel over.

"I haven't fucked anyone else since Los Angeles. I got tested before we came on this trip." I lean forward to kiss the corner of his mouth, knowing he'll push me away soon if I'm too mushy. "You're safe with me."

Nolan's gasp sounds painful, just before he presses his mouth to mine. We kiss until the water turns cold, until our fingers are pruned. I've got to get him fed since he has to be at the arena in just a handful of hours. Ignoring the conversation we just had is going to be basically impossible, but I've got to at least pretend with Nolan. He's surly and shut down even as I tenderly dry the cascading water droplets from his body.

"What do you want to eat?" I ask him as I tug a shirt over my head.

Nolan shrugs one tattooed shoulder. "Whatever."

"Is there something that sounds good that you'd happily eat?"

A flicker of emotion crosses his face, then disappears like a wisp of smoke. "Not really."

"Tell me the thought you just had," I demand, walking up to him to cup his cheeks.

His eyes flit up to mine and his eye twitches. "Burger King."

Okay, that's a little off-beat. But whatever he wants, I'll give it to him. "What do you want? A burger?"

"Yeah with their special sauce... and some extra sauce on the side for the fries."

"You got it."

I drag Nolan by the hand into the small living room of our hotel suite. I've barely used Chris since we arrived, mainly giving the man a break from managing Nolan twenty-four seven since I've taken on that task myself. But this is definitely a mission for him since I don't speak any Italian, and I don't want to leave Nolan alone in the hotel room, not after that weird little confession in the bathtub.

Nolan looks so small on the sofa, legs tucked under himself, eyes distant even as he stares blankly out of the balcony at bustling Milan.

Me: Nolan wants Burger King

Me: A Whopper with extra sauce and fries

Chris: I'm sorry

Chris: Who wants what

Me: Please, it's what he asked for.

Chris: Twenty minutes

I sit beside Nolan on the sofa, close enough that he can feel the heat of my body, but far enough away that he doesn't feel overwhelmed by touch. His fingers twitch on his thigh before reaching out to tangle with mine. Eyes still firmly looking out the balcony, Nolan easily misses the way my lips twitch at the corners as I do my best to contain the smile that so badly wants to break free. Slowly, but surely, Nolan is starting to trust me. Maybe by the end of this godforsaken tour, he'll trust me with his heart, not just his desires.

A knock at the door is followed quickly by Chris pushing through. His eyes flit from me to Nolan and my heart does this weird sort of loopy thing in my chest when Nolan keeps his fingers tangled with mine despite Chris entering the room.

Chris drops two bags on the table with a serious, hard look at Nolan. "Do you need me to cancel tonight's show?"

"No," Nolan says firmly.

Nolan disentangles his fingers from mine and reaches for the bag with a trembling hand. He basically buries his head into the paper bag. When he lifts his head, his eyes are crinkled, and there's a barely there grin tugging at his lips.

"Thank you, Christopher."

Chris rolls his eyes and waves his hand dismissively, turning to look intently at me next. "I got you something too." He looks down at his watch with a sigh. "We need to be at the arena in two hours."

"We'll be there," I tell Chris with narrowed eyes, hoping he gets the vibe and scoots the hell out of the hotel room.

Chris obviously picks up what I put down because he leaves with a wave over his shoulder. When I turn to Nolan, he's already got the burger half unwrapped and is delightfully stuffing his face.

"What?" Nolan asks around a mouthful of food.

I shake my head to stop myself from saying something disgustingly sweet like *you're cute* or *I think I really like you* or *you terrify me when you abruptly pull away*.

Grabbing my own bag, I open it to find a burger, chicken nuggets, and fries. Bless your heart, Chris. We eat quietly despite Nolan reaching over to take one of my nuggets. Normally I hate sharing food with people, but I don't mind so much when Nolan steals my food. He needs it more than me.

"Hey, what's your favorite flavor of Jolly Rancher?"

"Cherry," Nolan mumbles while stuffing a fistful of fries into his mouth.

"Best flavor," I murmur in agreement.

Nolan lifts one eyebrow. "Your favorite too?"

"Yeah, all the others taste like—"

"Cough syrup," Nolan interrupts me.

I huff out a laugh. "Well, yeah."

Nolan tosses himself back on the sofa with a pleased sigh. He pats his stomach a few times, eyes closed, head tipped back against the plush pillows. Nolan pops one eye halfway open to look at me.

"Are you an exclusive top or..."

I shrug. He doesn't need to know I've only *ever* topped. "Mostly."

"So you're vers?"

"Eh... I prefer to top."

Nolan sighs softly. "Good, I prefer to bottom. Lie back and let someone else do all the work."

"Obviously," I say under my breath.

Nolan stands from the sofa with a huff. He shakes out his limbs, twists his neck a few times, then looks down his nose at me. "I think I'll get to the arena early tonight. I want to perform a song that's not on the setlist. I'll need the time to practice."

"Okay," I say in confusion.

Nolan trudges off to the bedroom to put on his practice clothes. I busy myself by cleaning up the mess from our impromptu lunch. When I wander back to the bedroom, Nolan is standing with the heels of his palms pressed to his eyes.

"Nolan?"

Nolan removes his hands and spins to look at me. "It's fine."

But he's clearly not fine. The tension in his shoulders is back and the happy, full-of-food guy from a moment before is gone. I cross the distance between us and tug him into my arms, kissing him softly until he melts against me. His breaths are soft and slow when I pull away, his eyes only open enough to show a peek of the dark brown irises.

"It's fine," Nolan repeats, that weird edge to his voice now gone.

I squeeze his shoulders and rub my thumbs over the tense line of his neck. He leans heavier against me for one single moment, before pulling away to finish getting dressed. The ride to the arena is silent, but Nolan's fingers tangle with mine, so I don't take it personally. Sometimes he needs silence more than me.

The arena is bustling as the crew gets the stage ready for the concert in a handful of hours. Nolan bypasses the VIP room downstairs to head straight for the stage. His band stands with wide eyes, probably wondering why the fuck Nolan is a few hours early.

"I want to add a song tonight," Nolan declares, chin lifted defiantly in the air.

"What?" Chris asks from beside me, voice frantic.

I shrug helplessly. "He just told me back at the hotel."

"We can't just add songs... we don't do this. There isn't a spot for this in the lineup." Chris rubs at his temples making some aggrieved noise back in his throat. "Fucking hell shit fuck damnit."

"Oh wow, never heard that combo before."

"Fuck," Chris says once more with emphasis.

Nolan pulls his crew in tighter, hands moving fast as he explains whatever is going through his mind. The drummer, Drew, looks excited, while the guitarist, Hanson, looks a little peeved. But they all exchange some weird handshake before Nolan toddles back off to the front of the stage to stand in front of the mic.

"Sometimes I don't know about him..."

"Let him have an ounce of joy about something he usually hates, okay?"

Chris startles a little and looks over at me. "Really?"

I wave my hand in Nolan's direction, eyebrows furrowed as I watch on. "Let him be."

Nolan closes his eyes as he strums the guitar, his fingers flitting up and down the neck in a way that makes my gut clench with want and need and some other word that hurts to even consider. The song is immediately recognizable: "House of the Rising Sun." It's the song he sang back in the dive bar in Los Angeles.

Nolan's voice is so deep, so raw, that it makes the song sound even more painful somehow. I stand frozen at the edge of the stage, eyes caught on him. When he gets to the chorus, he turns his head to look at me, throat working as he belts the lyrics.

And when he finishes, he winks and blows me a kiss.

He does the same thing in front of a crowded arena.

I can't help but feel like it's some weird, tortured version of a love song. A song with a warning to avoid the fate of someone lost to destruction. *Too late*, I want to tell Nolan. I'm already lost.

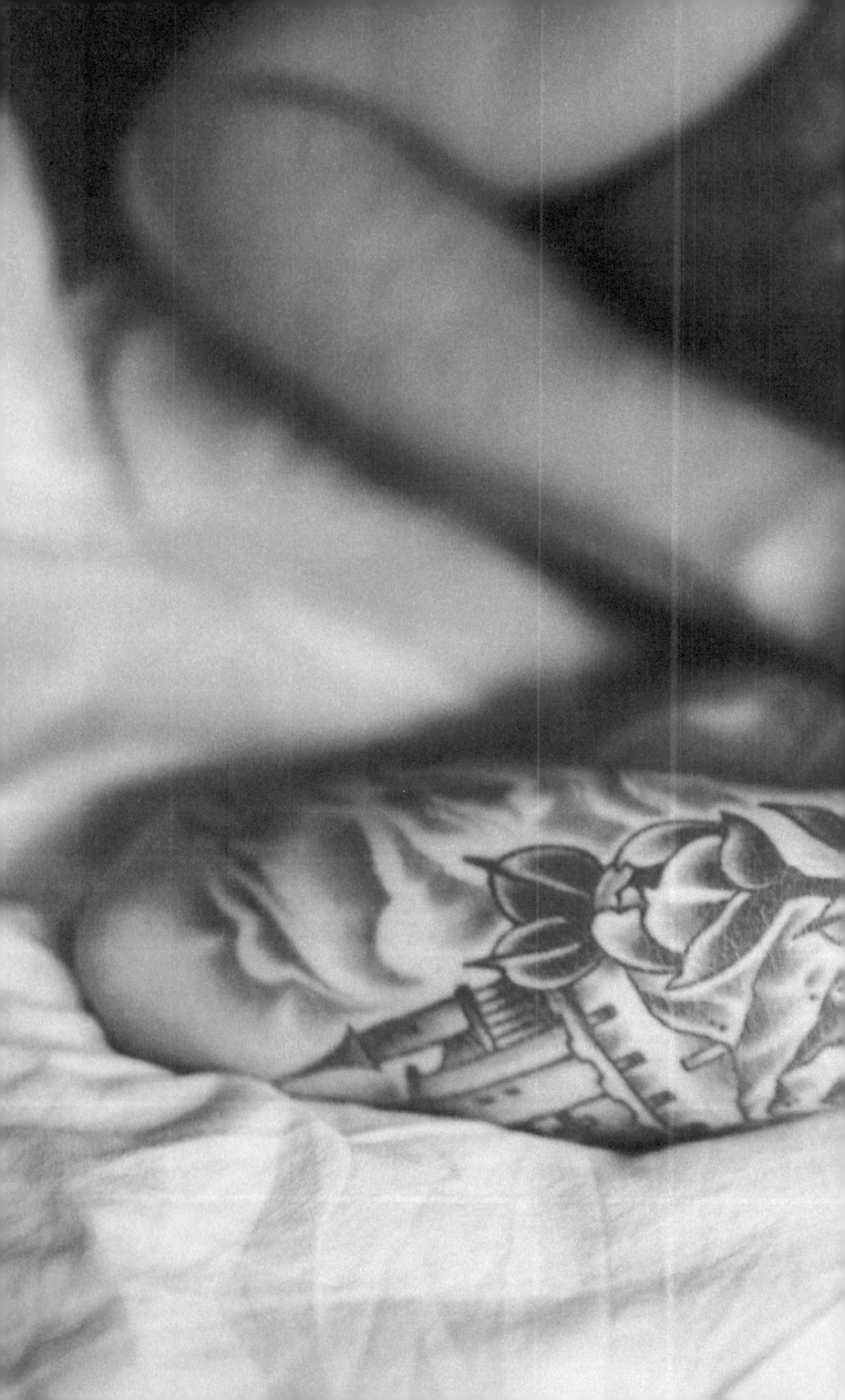

10

NOLAN

DECEMBER 2027

Everything is blurry. The people in the crowd, my thoughts, the tenuous string that connects me to my body, all of it is blurry. The only thing I see in startling clarity is Benji. It feels like there are blinders on my eyes. I can only see pinpricks of light, everything else is so fucking dark. Benji's the sunshine, the light at the end of the dark, damp tunnel, he's the promise of land on the endless horizon.

So I have to push him away.

He's getting too close.

He's going to figure me out.

Five days in France is a nice break, but at the same time it unsettles me to the core. I need to keep moving. As long as I'm moving, my brain doesn't have a chance to think the thoughts that send a chill down my spine. The kind of thoughts that say it would be so easy to end all of it, not just the tour, but *everything*. Down some pills. Step in front of a bus. Jump off a ledge.

The thoughts scare me because even though I want to die, I don't know how. Before Benji it was easy. Every me want to die. Every night on stage makes death the easiest option to escape. But when I fall asleep at night, he's there now. What am I going to do in May at the end of the tour? He'll leave me like everyone else. Everyone always leaves, including me.

"So the cover back in Milan was a hit," Chris announces as he strides into the hotel suite.

"It's been all over my social media feed," Benji agrees. His fingers run through my hair repeatedly, nails softly scratching at my scalp.

I keep my eyes closed and tilt my head harder against his thigh, silently asking for more scratches. Benji chuckles softly and acquiesces, because he's the best boy. Always doing what I ask even when I ask without words.

"I'm not doing it again," I say firmly.

Chris sighs so loudly it sounds like he's hurt himself. "I told the label as much already. But, Nolan, you really should consider it."

"No," I mumble sleepily. "It was for Benji."

Benji's fingers stutter in my hair for a moment before restarting. Everyone is quiet for a few long moments and sleep starts to claim me until the sound of Chris shuffling closer prompts me to open my eyes. His shadow looms over us on the blue velvet couch and his eyes radiate concern. Gross.

"Nolan, you're okay, right?"

I wave him off. "I'm fine. I'm always fine. Sober as can be."

Chris squeezes his eyes shut tight and pinches his nose. "I'm not worried about your sobriety. I'm worried about *you*. You'd tell me..." He trails off, his gaze quickly flicking to Benji before bouncing back to me. "You'd tell me if you needed anything, right?"

I snort. "Definitely not."

"The label isn't my client. You are. Remember that?"

With a large amount of regret, I sit up to stare blankly back at Chris. "Is this some come-to-Jesus moment or something? What the fuck is going on?"

Chris holds his hands up like I'm a velociraptor on the prowl. "No, I just wanted you to hear the words." He pulls out his phone and scrolls through something. "So, we've got these five days in France, three days in Sweden, a small break for Christmas, after we fly to South America for New Year's and start the second leg of the tour."

"I don't need a break for Christmas," I tell him pointedly.

Chris rolls his eyes. "Yes, but your crew does, and so do I. I need to go home and see my wife and grown children."

I always forget he's married with kids. Mostly because half the time it feels like he's some weird type of father figure to me. Although, I'll never admit that out loud. Ever.

"Fine."

"Thank you," Chris says sarcastically.

He shares one final look with Benji before disappearing back out of the hotel room. The sun is setting beyond the building, an orange glow casting over the hotel room. I'm exhausted from traveling to France. I just want to curl up on the couch and let Benji pretend I'm something worth his time. But our time is also coming to a close and there's something very particular I want on our rare night free from practice, from the stage, from Nolan Hastings. Tonight, I'll just be Nolan.

"I want to say no tonight," I say bluntly.

Benji's startled blue eyes flick to me. "Seriously?"

I crawl across the velvet couch to straddle his lap. His

palms settle on my hips, a familiar, reassuring weight. "I'll say no and you'll fuck me anyway. Be rough with me."

Benji's eyebrows furrow in deep thought. His thumbs sweep over my hip bones in this maddening swiping motion that already has me half out of my mind.

"One day you'll let me be soft with you," Benji says quietly, like a secret.

My heart cracks in half. "No, that's a dream, stud."

Benji looks away from me, throat bobbing on a hard swallow. "It's a good dream."

I curl my fingers over his jaw, turning his head so that he has to look at me once more. Our eyes meet and it feels like a flash of lightning. Want and need and another word that I can't put a name to flash through me all at once. I dip down to kiss him, gliding my lips softly over his always sweet mouth.

Benji pulls away from me to roughly grasp my jaw. "Tell me exactly how you want it to go. I need a plan."

"I'll be in the bedroom, undressing by the bed, and you'll rush into the room riled up and angry. You'll shove me onto the bed, push my face into the pillows, and fuck me face down on the bed, ignoring every single one of my cries and stops and noes. That's what I want. That's *my* dream."

"And your safe word?" Benji asks, voice carefully neutral.

I grin with all my teeth. "Azure."

Benji's cock is hard underneath me when I shift over him. Perpetual sunshine has a kinky side, that much I know. After a few quiet moments, Benji shoves me off his lap. He runs a shaky hand over his face, then nods toward the bedroom.

"Go on. You've got fifteen minutes to get ready." His eyes narrow slightly. "And I'm fucking you without a condom so I can see my cum drip from your ass afterward."

"You're learning," I comment, hoping to sound like an

asshole but knowing I sound more besotted than anything. I hate myself for it.

Benji gestures toward the bedroom. "Go."

For once in my life, I listen. The walk from the living room to the bedroom is twenty-three steps. Each step feels like it takes hours. Asking an escort to do this with me was never in the cards. Something about doing this with Benji is so vulnerable, like I'm showing him my hand of cards that I keep so tight to my chest.

My hands tremble as I get myself ready for Benji in the bathroom. I won't meet my gaze in the mirror, I can't, not now. I wonder what Benji sees when he looks at me. Does he see someone whole? Does he see someone perilously close to the edge? Or maybe he just sees me for what I am; a broken and lost man.

Time slows to a crawl. I'm just about to go back out to the living room, demanding something stupid from Benji, when he barrels into the bedroom. I have a split second to gather that he's shirtless, ratty jeans unbuttoned but hanging on to his hips. My teeth gnash with the force of his shove as I fall onto the bed. His fingers dig into my shoulders as he shoves me down.

"Stop!" I yell, feeling some weird joy at this role play.

"No," Benji growls into my ear. His skin is molten lava against my own. A shiver rolls through me when his hand rips at my shorts, tugging them down until the cool air of the hotel room slaps the bare skin of my ass.

I try to elbow him, get him to stop, but he just presses me down onto the bed harder. His hand comes around to roughly grab my throat. He squeezes so hard that I'm not sure I'll ever be able to swallow again.

My head spins when he wraps his other arm around my

middle, tugging me up until I'm on my knees. I fight him, trying to get leverage to kick him off of me, but he's got enough weight on me that it's impossible to move him. He's a rock, immovable. His hand squeezes my throat again just as his cock notches against my hole. Benji doesn't even wait, he just pushes in, ignoring the resistance as my body fights me to relax. It hurts, but exactly the kind of pain I want.

"No, please," I whimper, but I'm not asking him to stop fucking me. I'm asking him to stop invading all my senses, stop making things seem *easy* when really they're fucking hard. Everything is so fucking hard. Everything is so exhausting. My body feels like it weighs ten thousand pounds as he pushes me harder into the bed.

Benji is abnormally quiet as he fucks me, even when he bites hard at the sliver of skin between my neck and shoulder blade, his favorite place to bite. By the time he leaves, there'll be permanent imprints of his teeth on me. Not as permanent as the tattoo of him on my heart. I'm ruined. I know that now.

His cock throbs inside me with each torturous thrust. My hips ache from the angle and my mouth is dry, tongue thick in my mouth.

"No," I say one more time, tears gathering in my eyes.

Benji slows his pace, his arm coming around to tug me up until we're both kneeling on the bed. His hot palm comes up to cup the side of my face, turning my head until he can stare unflinchingly into my eyes. He's the bravest man on earth.

"Can I do it my way now?" Benji asks quietly, tears in his eyes.

I nod slowly, unable to form words.

I'm lightning and Benji is the thunder, the protective boom that follows my bright flash of light. If only I could hold on to him, maybe the storm wouldn't be so terrifying when I get lost to the darkness. But it's not fair to Benji to use his thunder. Not fair at all.

Benji takes my mouth in a gentle kiss as he switches from aggressor, from brutal taker, to life giver. He tastes so familiar, so startlingly real when everything else around me is unrepentantly fake. He lets go of my face to squeeze his fingers around my wrist, pressing his thumb where my pulse pounds. Benji presses my hand to my abdomen and I gasp at the feel of him moving inside me.

"That's me, inside you, feel it?"

"Benji."

"Do you feel it?" Benji repeats, each word enunciated with a hard thrust.

"Yes," I admit. But the word is double-edged. I feel his cock in me, moving deep inside me, owning me in ways no one else ever has, but I also feel him in my chest when my ribs move with each breath. I feel him inside me in every single way that matters.

"Nolan," Benji whispers against my neck just as he rolls his hips.

"I feel you everywhere," I mumble as he takes me apart.

His lips glide over my neck, like butterflies on my skin. Benji sighs in relief and then tips us over to lie on our sides. Grabbing my thigh, he tugs my leg up so that he can get a deeper angle. I gasp and grab his forearm when he slides so deep I can feel him in my throat.

"Jesus, Benji, I..."

"Just feel it, angel."

And then he takes me apart and puts me back together. Every time he pulls out, he drags his cock along my stretched rim, only to slowly slide back in so deep that stars explode in my vision. All I feel is Benji. All I hear is the sound of his breaths against the shell of my ear. He tangles our fingers together and brings them to my chest, just over my heart.

He fucks me for what feels like hours. I'm delirious and begging for something that I can't put words into. Only *please* and *now* and *need you* fall from my lips. But Benji doesn't go anywhere, doesn't leave me alone in my want. He meets me right in the middle, beat for fucking beat.

"I've never fucked someone raw before," Benji whispers, cheek pressed against my own. "It feels like you were plucked from heaven and brought down here for me. A perfect fit. When I come inside you, a part of me will stay there forever. I'm giving a piece of myself to you."

I want to bite him, I want to slap him, I want to fight against the overwhelming tide of emotions, but instead I pull his arm tighter around me and squeeze my eyes shut to blot out everything else but *him*. Only him. Only ever Benji. My thunder.

He licks his other palm and takes my cock in a tight grip. I hadn't even realized I was hard, my orgasm a distant thing in the back of my terrified brain. He curls his hand around the base, squeezes tight, then slowly brings his palm up to cup the head of my cock. Every thrust inside perfectly hits my prostate, so much so that my toes tingle, and the air gets caught in my rib cage.

"I need you to come first so I can watch you fall apart on my cock. Can you do that, angel? Can you come for me?"

The words trigger some hidden part of me that I've never known. My orgasm flows through me like the waves of a violent black ocean. Distantly, I'm aware that Benji orgasms too, his release hot, and so very real inside of me. For this solitary moment in time, I'm alive. Benji pulls out and I feel so fucking alone without him inside me. But because Benji can read me line by fucking line, he rolls me over and slips two fingers inside me.

His eyes are freshwater blue as he stares down at me. "Did I give you what you need?"

I lift my hand and curl it around his jaw, dancing my fingers behind his ear. I'm ruining him. His eyes are so troubled. The sunshine is bleeding out from him and it's because of me. I'm not good for him. I'm not good for anyone. I'll take and take and *take* from them until they have nothing left to give. I'm not better than anyone in the crowd. Time is slowing, the end getting closer to us.

"You gave me what we both needed, hmm?"

Benji sighs and leans his forehead against my stomach. He lies there for so long, fingers still inside me, that I worry I've fucked up somehow. I wouldn't be surprised if I did. With a shaky inhale, Benji crawls up my body to kiss me soft and slow, the kind of kiss you have while slow dancing under the stars. A kiss that says *you're mine* and *wait for me* and *don't go*. But I can't say it back. Not yet. If ever.

11

BENJI

DECEMBER 2027

France changed something between us. Maybe it was the way I handled Nolan when I realized it wasn't the fight he wanted, it was the tender care that no one has ever shown him in his life. I'm losing track of time as we roll on. France to Sweden and now to South America.

Christmas was me and Nolan alone in a beautifully expensive hotel room in Brazil to wait out the next part of the tour. Nolan didn't even care that it was Christmas Day. He was unusually quiet minus the strumming of his guitar as I called my moms to wish them a merry Christmas. As time goes on, Nolan becomes more sullen, not meeting my gaze even when I beg to take him out on dates. I can't shake the feeling that something is wrong. I don't know how to fix it, fix whatever the divide is between us.

Three months in each other's pockets and I can suddenly say this isn't transactional anymore. Nolan means something to me. I can see right through his need to act to kick me away. Every slash of his claws reveals himself little more to me. He has a soft underbelly that he's terrified people might see. When he gently cups my face, eyes staring up at me in wonder, I know that's the real Nolan behind whatever careful shield he puts up.

It's New Year's Eve now, the first show was yesterday, and there's another tomorrow. But today we are free just to be with each other. I've come to look forward most to these days. They're usually the days Nolan lets me be kind, even sweet, and handle him in a way that works for *both* of us.

The hotel room is too quiet, it's wrong. Dressed in just sweatpants, I pad through the rooms until I come to the balcony that lines the large living room. A rumple of clothing on the ground outside sends my heart skyrocketing through my chest, until I inch closer and find that Nolan's just lying on the ground. His head is tilted to the sky, lips pursed deeply in thought.

He doesn't hear me coming because of the headphones covering his ears. But my shadow forces his head to turn my way, his eyes still hauntingly distant. I lower myself to join him on the hard concrete. I inch closer until we're almost touching, but not. I let my pinkie softly graze the palm of his hand where it rests on the ground. Nolan's eyes close softly at my touch.

"What are you doing out here?" I ask quietly, knowing he'll hear me despite the music in his headphones.

He turns his head back to the sky. "Staring at the sky. They have good birds here."

I turn my head to look up at the bright blue sky. Only a few clouds dot the expanse above, but a handful of birds float along on the wind. Carefree and beautiful.

"They look happy."

"I've always wanted to be a bird," Nolan murmurs, sounding utterly defeated.

"Why a bird?"

Nolan clears his throat awkwardly. "So I could fly away, high up into the sky and never be found."

It's a perfectly Nolan answer that still somehow has the ability to shoot me straight through the heart. I roll over on the hard ground to lean over him. His dark brown eyes flick from the sky to my face, a small moment of relief passing over him. I cup his cheek in one hand, gently sweeping my thumb under his tired eye.

"We could be birds together, fly away from here. Sound good?"

Nolan's eyes close slowly, his exhausted breath puffing against my palm. "Okay, Benji."

Unable to stand the sight of him so pained, I swoop down to kiss him softly. I smile against his mouth when his fingers tangle in my shirt, tugging me down to rest my weight against him.

"What do you normally do on New Year's Eve?" Nolan asks when I pull away. He's been asking these sorts of questions lately, clearly wanting to know what my life is like outside of him, when I'm away from tour.

"Usually I go to a party with my best friends."

Nolan hums quietly as he squeezes my wrist. "Tell me."

"Well..." I scrunch my face in thought, trying to remember last New Year's. "Jackson usually gets us into the good parties. The four of us go and have a good time. We dance and drink and scope out guys. Usually only Eli would go home with someone, he's the prize. But now Eli is happily almost basically married to a former client. Trevor is settled down with this huge farmer. Like seriously, he's a giant.

Jackson is, well... I don't keep in touch with him as much as I should. We fight like cats and dogs."

Nolan looks thoughtful for a moment. "Why do you fight?"

"Oil and vinegar. We just think so differently."

"I used to fuck Trevor," Nolan says as if I don't already know that.

"I know."

Nolan's eyes turn sad, but he darts his gaze away. "I was rough with him. I don't think he liked it much."

"It was a job."

"And Eli? I never met him."

I smile despite myself. "Eli is everything good in this world."

"I believe it, the way you look when you talk about him."

I swallow thickly, suddenly missing them all so much. "I miss them a lot. They're... my family in a way."

Nolan reaches out to pat my cheek. "You should call them. Say happy New Year."

Nolan rolls up to sitting. He gives one final lingering look at the sky, before heaving himself to his feet with a withering sigh. I watch as he disappears into the hotel room, leaving the glass door wide open without a care in the world.

I pull out my phone because the urge to speak to one of my best friends is so strong, I could cry at the idea. Trevor wins the lottery today.

The phone rings before Trevor picks up. "Benji! How's it going? I've been thinking about you constantly."

"I... Trevor, I'm not doing so great."

"Hold on," Trevor murmurs quietly. The sound of him moving around filters through the phone. Distantly, I think I hear waves. "Benji, tell me."

"Are you at the beach?"

Trevor breathes hard through his nose. "We're all at Colby's beach house."

Oh. I wish I was there. I miss them all so much, even Jackson. "Nolan isn't what I thought. He... Trevor, I don't know what to do. I think I'm in like with him."

"In like," Trevor repeats carefully.

"Feelings are involved now. I want to keep him."

"Oh, Sunshine."

The sound of my real name doesn't even piss me off, it just makes my heart miss a beat in my chest, painful and raw. "Did he ever seem... off to you? Like, not okay?"

"Every time," Trevor admits, voice pitched low. "But I was an escort. What was I supposed to do? He paid me to fuck him and bite him and leave bruises on him. And he left those bruises on me too. That's all it was with us. Nothing more."

"He lets me see him."

Trevor goes eerily silent. "What do you mean?"

"I think... Jesus, Trevor. I've got to save him."

"I hear you, Benji. But I also don't think you're capable of handling this by yourself. I really think you need to talk to Claire."

"No, no. I can't tell Claire. She'll... she'll pull me. I can't leave Nolan. I can't leave him." The idea of leaving Nolan is terrifying.

"Jackson's here. He wants to talk to you," Trevor rushes out.

I close my eyes tightly and press the heel of my hand to my forehead. My heart is beating rapidly in my chest. I feel sick like I could puke up all my internal organs. The sound of guitar filters out of the hotel room, prickling at my overwhelmed senses. God, I don't know what the fuck to do. But I have to be strong. I can't... Nolan reminds me of my mom so badly. When she was at her worst when I was a kid, I can't see Nolan going through that, too.

"Are you safe? Did he hurt you?" Jackson asks, voice gruff and worried.

"No, no, Jackson," I whisper, voice barely audible. "I'm fine."

"You've got Trevor pretty worried. Tell me what's going on," Jackson demands, leaving no room for argument.

I blow out a shaky breath. "I'm fine. I promise. Tell Trevor to chill. I just needed... I needed someone to know."

"Know what?"

"That I'm in way over my head," I admit before hanging up.

I turn back to the living room to find Nolan sitting on the couch, carefully strumming the cords of the guitar. The tune is oddly familiar, reminding me of the records that my moms used to play late at night after they thought I'd gone to sleep. When I step into the hotel room, Nolan's gaze stays on the guitar, but his lips start to move with the haunting lyrics. Words about time and loss and his voice is so haunting that my stomach curdles as I stand barefoot before him.

He finishes and slowly lifts his head to look at me. "'Time in a Bottle.'"

"Nolan," I say, carefully stepping closer.

"That's my favorite song," Nolan whispers.

The moment is so fraught, the rope holding us together pulled so tight I'm afraid it might snap. I want to call Trevor back and ask him to hold my hand. I want Eli to come and stand beside me, just quiet and full of life. I want Jackson to come and tell me I'm not fucking up. I want my friends so badly that my heart cracks into small little splinters. I don't know what to do anymore. Nolan's slipping out of my grasp and I feel so alone.

"Benji," Nolan says quietly. "Go take a shower, put on a nice outfit and a smile, then join me on the balcony, okay?"

"Nolan."

His smile could shatter a million hearts. "Please?"

My feet carry me to the shower. I do as he said, using Nolan's preferred shower gel so that I smell like him when I'm done. With wet hair, and pain in the pit of my stomach, I dress quickly and hurry to rejoin Nolan on the balcony.

This time, my stomach plummets to the ground. Nolan sits on the railing of the balcony, legs dangling over the edge. He doesn't turn to look at me when my steps echo out onto the cold concrete. Heart pounding in my chest, I do the only thing I can think of to do. I climb up on the railing beside him, fighting desperately against the dizzy vertigo that over-takes me.

Nolan turns his head slowly. "What are you doing?"

"Being with you," I answer softly.

Nolan stares at me. "I can't do this anymore, Benji. Do you understand? I have to..." He trails off and gestures at the ten stories below us. Cars honk and pass by, no doubt getting ready for a night of celebration. Nobody knows Nolan Hastings is about to jump and end it all. And nobody knows I'm going to follow him down.

"If you jump, I jump too. I can't let you die alone. You've spent so much of your life alone. I..." A cry gets caught in my throat. "I can't let you be alone in those last moments too."

A tear slides down Nolan's cheek. "What?"

"I... I'll go with you."

"No."

"Yes," I say as I shakily nod. "It's us, okay?"

"Us." Nolan repeats the word like he doesn't understand it.

"Can I... Can I tell you what my dream is?"

Nolan quirks his head. "Okay."

I curl my fingers over the railing and take a deep, shaky breath. "I'm going to paint you a picture. My dream is that we climb down off this ledge and call Chris. I tell Chris that the tour is over, canceled. You're not okay. You need time and healing and help. I take you to Clay Springs, where my best friends are, and we get you some help and medicine so your brain can work the way it needs to. And you let me love you even though I'm just some stupid golden retriever. 'Cause I think... I think we could have a great life once you accept some help. And I'll hold your hand every step and cheer you on and to me you're just Nolan, the man who makes me laugh and feel like I'm doing something good in this world that sometimes gets really fucking dark. You're beautiful, Nolan. I wish you were mine, just mine."

Nolan's chest stops moving halfway through my speech as if the breath is caught in his lungs. He looks down at the street below, his fingers curled against the railing right beside mine. My skin tingles when his skin touches mine.

"I can't picture a future when my brain is so cloudy and loud."

"I'll picture it," I tell him firmly.

His gaze returns to me. "I'm not sure I'm good at... at being okay. I haven't been okay for so long. I think the only way out is... for it to end."

"I can't make the decision for you. But if you decide to stay, I'll get you the help you need to stop feeling this way. We'll... we can try to make it better. My mom tried to kill herself when I was little. She tells me all the time that, at the moment, it felt like the only way out, but it wasn't. She just didn't know how to find her way in the dark."

Nolan's gaze is so heavy. "How long ago was that?"

"Seventeen years. She sees a therapist, takes medicine, and lives on the freaky commune with my mama. Life got so much better once she got some help. Do you want to talk to her?"

Nolan raises a shaky hand to his eyes. God, he's so close to falling. I curl my fingers tighter against the railing in case I have to reach out to grab him. He doesn't want to die; he just doesn't see the other option. Not yet.

"She regretted it?"

I nod shakily. "Very much."

"I..." Nolan trails off and looks down. "What's Clay Springs like?"

"Magic. Let me show you."

Nolan takes a deep breath, and for one terrifying, very long second, I ready myself to watch him jump. But he doesn't. He deftly swings his legs over the other side and jumps to the ground. The moment freezes, air caught between us like right before a storm. Right before the lightning strikes. And when I join him on the firm, beautiful ground of the balcony, it feels like lightning strikes, and the thunder echoes between us.

"Nolan," I say quickly, just before the tears start to fall.

He dives into my arms, and I hug him close, breathing in his comforting scent. Sweat and amber and something so promising that it feels like the future suddenly finally fucking exists for us both.

"I still want to die," Nolan admits, voice tender and raw.

"I know, but it'll get better. I won't leave you. It's us now, it's us."

145

Nolan nods, and I pull him close, squeezing him tight until he feels safe in my arms, no longer afloat on whatever ocean of pain that was trying to sweep him out to sea. We stand there for so long that time starts losing any meaning. I just want to hold him in my arms forever, give him comfort, and make him feel safe. That's all.

But time has to move on, and I have things to take care of now.

When I pull away, I hustle Nolan inside and sit him down on the sofa. After a text to Chris, I patiently wait for him to arrive. Nolan's eyes are downcast, caught on where our hands lie tangled over his thin thigh.

The sound of a keycard swiping through the door is the only notice we get before Chris strides into the room. He takes one look at Nolan and pauses, stride caught halfway, eyes flicking between us.

"Okay, so..." I glance at Nolan, then back to Chris. "The tour needs to be over. I'm taking Nolan home. He needs... help."

"Okay," Chris says quietly.

"He's not okay."

Chris swallows loudly. "Did he... did you..."

"No," Nolan mumbles, clearly already over the entire conversation.

"I'll handle the label, don't worry about it. Everything is fine. It's going to be okay. Nolan... Nolan, it'll be okay," Chris says again, voice sounding how it would if he was addressing a small child.

I forget sometimes that outside of this tour, outside of Nolan Hastings, all these people have lives. Chris has mentioned family and children before, and I see it very clearly now in the way he approaches Nolan. Maybe one day

Nolan will be able to see what's right in front of him, that so many people care about him without him even realizing it.

"I want to go home with Benji," Nolan says, lip trembling on the words.

Chris's gaze pings back to me. "Where's home?"

I squeeze Nolan's hand tightly in mine. "Clay Springs."

PART TWO

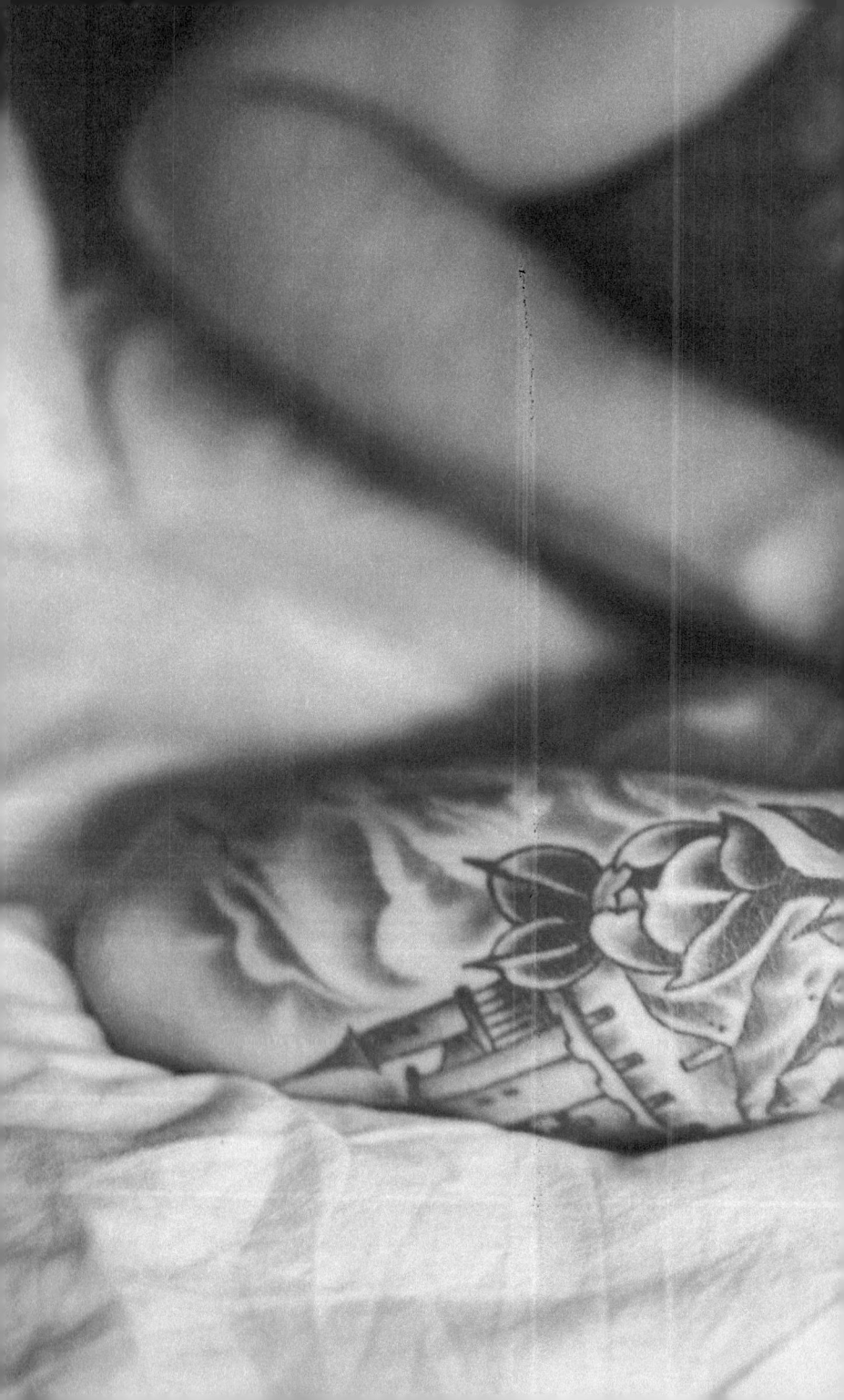

12

NOLAN

JANUARY 2028

I slept for the entire flight. Sleep has always been hard for me, something that doesn't come easy. But when I'm with Benji, it comes as easy as breathing. I blink the sleep from my eyes as we land with a gentle thump. Benji just presses a sweet kiss to my forehead and murmurs, "Shh, it's alright."

If I asked Benji, I think he'd happily carry me off the plane. But I won't. Despite how heavy my entire body feels, how exhausting it is to take a single step. Benji gathers our two suitcases that now contain my entire world. The air is cold and the sky is gray when we disembark the plane. When Benji said Florida, I expected palm trees and sunny skies, not whatever this place has going on.

"Jackson!" Benji calls, relief coloring his voice.

Jackson's lip twitches at one corner as his gaze plays between us. I watch, detached from my body, as Benji and Jackson embrace. They murmur something that's too low for my ears to pick up. But Benji pulls away with a sound in the back of his throat and backs up to tangle his fingers with mine.

"Trevor didn't say you'd be picking us up," Benji comments.

Jackson swings the driver's side door open. "Trevor didn't decide. Get in."

Benji grimaces slightly, but helps me get into the spacious G-Wagon. I slap his hand away with a hiss when he tries to buckle me in. There's sweetness and then there's too fucking far. Benji lets out a frustrated shaky breath, then busses a kiss to the apple of my cheek. I allow the display of affection despite wanting to kick him away. Maybe he feels the need to piss on me in front of Jackson considering we'd fucked once.

The car is full of tense silence as we make our way out of the airport.

"This is awkward," I comment dryly.

Benji pinches his nose in clear annoyance. "Nolan."

Jackson flicks a hard look at me in the rearview mirror. "You're not here to start trouble."

"We're here because I tried to kill myself and Benjamin thinks I'm his soulmate."

Benji's cheeks turn a bright, vivid red at my words. His gaze stays on the road ahead, but I'm pretty sure later I'll get a talking-to about it. I lean forward and tap Benji on the shoulder, holding my hand out when he shifts to look back at me. He sighs and leans down to rustle through the backpack he's been sporting for months. A second later, my headphones are shoved into my hand. I slip them over my ears and pull up a familiar playlist, something full of sad, weepy, rock ballads that makes me feel a little more alive than I do when sitting in the silence.

I lean my head against the window and happily zone out. The murmur of Jackson's and Benji's voices filter in and out, but I can't understand them. I figured Benji needed to talk to his friend without my prying ears. The drive takes a seemingly endless age. My leg shakes, jostling the back of Benji's seat. He reaches back with one hand to curl his palm around the back of my calf until the shaking ceases. His thumb sweeps up and down my leg until my brain does that thing it often does because of Benji, everything just goes static, still, hush-quiet.

When I finally blink my eyes back open, the car is slowing as we approach picturesque farmland. Despite it being January, everything is still green and lush. The land is so alive my breath catches in my chest. Life.

Jackson rolls the car to a careful stop in front of a large farmhouse that would make anyone from a fixer-upper show salivate. The house even has those lovely storybook windows and a wraparound porch with rocking chairs. Jesus. Benji really did bring me to the farm.

A large blond man steps out of the house, hands tucked into his jeans. Benji hops out of the car just as a curly-haired man rushes down the steps. That must be Eli, the only fake boyfriend I've never met. Up on the stairs beside Colby is a ravishing redhead that's staring at the car with lethal daggers in his eyes. And finally there's Trevor standing beside an absolute unit of a man. If any of these guys are possessive, I'm in for a world of hurt.

Benji swings the car door open with a grin that doesn't meet his eyes. That won't do at all. I reach out with my hand, using my thumb to push the side of his mouth up in the mimicry of a smile.

"Like this," I say softly.

Benji turns his head into my palm, placing a sweet, loving kiss to my skin. His eyes dart up to mine and his mouth turns up at the corners, this time his smile is sweet and true.

"Alright, Nolan."

I take a deep breath as I look at the men standing up ahead. "They can't be mean to me. Right?"

Benji reaches up to cover my hand with his own. "They won't be mean. They know... they know we're here to get you some help. Okay?"

"Okay," I whisper softly as I jump out of the car.

Benji wraps a protective arm around my shoulders and guides me toward the large farmhouse. The redhead is still staring daggers at me, but his eyes soften when Jackson rounds us to hurry up the steps. Jackson dips down to kiss the man on the cheek just as the redhead bodily pushes him away. Cute dynamic. Reminds me of someone.

"We've set up the mother-in-law suite for you both. You can stay as long as you need," Eli says, sounding slightly breathless. He worriedly glances from Benji to me. "You know, we all love Benji very much. He's one of us."

"Clearly," I drawl.

Benji's hand squeezes my shoulder. "He doesn't need a shovel talk, Eli. Did you do that research I asked about?"

Eli's face warms. "Yes, Colby emailed you some resources. But first, well, Beau's mom, Cindy, made this huge batch of chicken and dumplings for us. She dropped it off a bit ago, so it's still warm. Are you hungry?"

"Not usually," I bite out.

Benji squeezes my shoulder hard. "Thank you, Eli. A home-cooked meal sounds great. Also, Harper looks like he's going to commit some type of petty crime. It's terrifying."

"Oh." Eli laughs awkwardly and glances behind him toward the redhead. "Don't mind Harper. It's been a long day."

Eli promptly turns around and skips toward the farmhouse, right into the waiting arms of the tall blond man. My nose wrinkles in distaste as Benji guides us forward, there's so much love radiating around here that it's borderline gross. I fight the urge to gag. I lean harder against Benji's side, knowing he'll easily take my weight.

I step onto the weathered stairs and wave. "Hello." I point at Trevor and Jackson. "I know you both, for obvious reasons."

The redhead blinks slowly. "No, please share, what are the obvious reasons?"

Ah, a possessive boyfriend. "Sorry, I fucked your boyfriend."

Everyone stills. Jackson covers his mouth with his hand, but not before I see the smirk tilt his lips up.

The redhead's gaze sharpens. "Surely, he's forgotten all about you by now. What with me being the best he's ever had?"

"You're very beautiful, so I get it."

"I—" The man blinks rapidly and stares at me. "What?"

"Do you top?"

Jackson steps forward with a lethal glare. "Hey."

The redhead slowly smiles before holding out his hand. "I'm Harper."

I give his hand a firm shake. "Nolan."

And then Harper drags me into the house with his small hand wrapped tightly around mine. "They're all acting like the next world war is coming. Cindy's chicken and dumplings are to die for, though. Whenever I have a seizure, they make everything so much less shitty."

"Sorry about the seizures," I mumble as he drags me along.

"Sorry about the depression," Harper shoots back.

Oh, he's my new best friend.

The house is warm and light with the hearty smell of something that makes my stomach growl in hunger. God, it's been forever since I've been hungry. Harper leads me to a beautiful chef's kitchen that overlooks the sprawling fields behind the house. Harper bodily shoves me into a seat and takes the chair beside me. Resting his chin on his upturned palm, he blinks forest-green eyes at me.

Two dogs come skidding into the kitchen. The Irish setter yips at the golden retriever who just slowly makes her way over to Harper to sit beside him. Harper grins and aims his fond gaze down at the dog.

"This is Honey," Harper says with a bright smile. "She's my bullshit meter. If she sneezes, it means you're full of shit. Want to play?"

"Sure."

"You don't *actually* sing your songs. It's some Milli Vanilli situation."

I narrow my eyes. "That's unequivocally false. I can prove it."

Harper makes a disbelieving sound in the back of his throat. "Sure, buddy. After dinner you can sing us a tune but only *after* I check your pockets."

I leer at him just as Benji wanders into the room. "If you want to fuck, you only have to say."

"Jackson wouldn't like that very much," Harper retorts.

Benji steps behind us and dips between us. "Nolan, be good."

"I'm always good," I reply haughtily.

Benji's smile quirks up just a little, that smile that I love so much. When the corners of his eyes wrinkle from a smile, it means I'm being particularly amusing but simultaneously difficult. My favorite smile. The rest of the group wander in with laughter following them in their wake. Colby and Beau head for the kitchen and the clatter of cutlery echoes around us as they prepare our dinner.

Benji kisses my cheek, then takes the seat at the other side of me. His hand wraps around the nape of my neck and squeezes, making everything just a little less anxiety-inducing from his touch alone. Fairy lights twinkle from the back porch as the sun dips lower, just barely hanging on above the horizon.

Beau quietly returns to the table, his big arms laden with plates. I watch as he first lovingly places a plate in front of Trevor, a blush rising on his cheeks when Trevor smirks up at him. Barf city. Kindly placing a plate in front of me, Beau places the next plate down in front of Harper, then ruffles Harper's beautiful red hair with a teasing smile. The man only chuckles when Harper scowls up at him.

Everyone's quiet as they dig in, but I push it around with my spoon for a few moments, instead focusing on watching everyone around the table. Once it appears no one is going to stare at me as they eat, I carefully lean forward and take a small bite. Jesus. The heavenly mixture is warm and thick, and the vegetables and chicken are melt-in-my-mouth soft.

All I can focus on is Benji's hand still a firm weight on my neck and the warmth that pools in my belly with each heaping spoonful. By the time I clear my plate, everyone is staring at me.

"Do you want some more?" Trevor asks quietly, gaze as shrewd as ever.

Feeling outside of my body, I just nod. Trevor leans across the table to grab my plate with a smile, and he squeezes

Beau's shoulder before heading to the kitchen to get me more.

Colby leans back in his chair, crossing his broad arms over his chest. "We've set up the guest suite over the garage for you but there are some conditions."

Benji squeezes my neck hard. "Conditions?"

Trevor sets another heaping plate down in front of me and I heartily dig in as Benji talks shop with Colby.

"I have a friend that's a psychologist in Orlando, Nolan will go to see her weekly. We'll have dinner together every evening. You'll keep and clean the suite." Colby swallows roughly and his gaze pings toward where I'm seated with my head bowed eating. "This is a soft place to land and nobody in this town will tell reporters, if we ask them. But I can't guarantee they won't bother you."

I shrug. "I'm used to it."

Benji's hand squeezes my neck again before his fingers tangle in my hair. "How soon can the psychologist see him?"

"Tomorrow," Colby says with an air of finality. "If Nolan wants."

"I have to do something if I don't want to kill myself," I mumble as I push my plate away.

"Do you want to die?" Trevor asks, voice devoid of all emotion.

I look over at him, hardly able to recognize him since I last saw him over a year ago. There's a healthy glow about him, a slight flush to his cheeks, and he's put on a bit of weight, too. This place has been good to him, and I weirdly wonder if it could be good for me too. If I let it. Suppose I don't let the monsters inside my head win.

"I just want to feel like I belong to myself."

Harper pushes his arm against mine. "I get you. Do you

want dessert while they all plan your life out for you? Jackson got cupcakes." Harper stands from the table with a flourish and points at Jackson. "Stay."

Jackson stays, but grins brightly at Harper's back as he walks toward the kitchen. I tug out of Benji's firm grip and push away from the table, heading in Harper's direction. The man is already leaning over a box full of cupcakes, eyes seemingly set on the sole chocolate one.

"Score." He carefully unwraps it and takes a bite, eyes rolling into his head. "So good. Sorry, the chocolate one is always mine." His gaze flicks over my face for a few moments, before he smirks. "You seem like a red velvet guy anyway."

Okay, fuck him, I do like red velvet. But now I don't want to admit it.

"Definitely more of a carrot cake guy," I say.

Harper rolls his eyes while handing me a red velvet cupcake. "Liar."

"So you and Jackson..."

Harper blushes slightly as he fiddles with his cupcake wrapper, intently focusing on the remaining treat in his hand. He clears his throat slightly. "Yes, for a couple of months now. He says he loves me."

The wording catches my attention. I finish off my own cupcake, licking at my fingers while jumping up to sit on the island. I glance behind me to see Benji intently watching me and I smirk at him before letting my gaze fall back on Harper.

"He seems absolutely besotted," I point out.

The flush on Harper's cheeks pinkens. "Yes, well. He looks at me the way Benji looks at you, I guess."

Oh, good play. I'm definitely not ready to talk about... that.

"What do you do for a living?"

Harper's nose wrinkles. "I'm a data analyst for a marketing firm, like figuring out trends and stuff for their campaigns. It works out well... 'cause I get to work from home."

"The dream," I say honestly. God, I wish I could just stay home and not see people for weeks. I think that would cure me.

Harper glances up at me from under his eyelashes. "You don't like being a rockstar?"

"I fucking hate it."

"Then why do you do it?"

And isn't that the million-dollar question. "I don't know anymore."

Jackson ambles into the kitchen with eyes only for Harper. If Benji looks at me like that, then I'm fucked, because the love radiating from Jackson could power the earth for millennia.

"Time to go home," Jackson says softly.

"You're not the boss of me," Harper quips. The two have a small staredown, before Harper flushes and looks my way. "I'll see you later. Next time you have to sing so I can prove it's actually you that does it on stage."

Harper and Jackson disappear out the door, but not before Jackson wraps an arm around Harper's shoulder, and the other man cuddles into his side. They're cute.

"Ready for some sleep?" Benji asks as he steps between my thighs.

"I slept the entire way here."

Benji cups my face in his palms, thumbs swiping gently under my eyes. "We can sleep some more. Let's go see our new suite for the next few... well, however many weeks or months."

I helplessly lean against his hold until I can press my forehead to his. "I'm scared. They're all going to think I'm weak."

Benji shakes his head. "I think living with your pain shows the opposite. You're being brave by getting help, by staying with me."

I nod gently and turn my head to press a kiss to his palm. Benji lets go of my face to wrap his arms around my middle, giving me a firm, tight hug that releases all those icky feelings from my body.

"Come on," Benji whispers against my ear.

He helps me down from the island, hands hot on my slim hips. Hooking one thumb into my belt loop, he guides me back toward the front door. Trevor and Beau are outside chatting with Colby and Eli as the sun finally dips below the horizon. The land dotted with trees in front of us glows with the dying light and I take a deep breath of the chilled fresh air that smells sweet, like citrus and jasmine blooms.

Benji tugs me toward the three-car garage, the mother-in-law suite waiting for us above it. Thank God. I didn't feel like talking anymore.

The suite is quaint and charming. My heart clenches in my chest with how much it reminds me of my grandmother. A small balcony in the back faces the forest to the other side of Colby's property.

I stand rooted at the back door as Benji pokes around the various rooms. Satisfied with whatever he found, he comes to stand behind me, wrapping his arm around my neck and tugging me against his body.

"Can I be good to you tonight?" Benji whispers, voice small and tired.

I turn around in his arms to face him, our noses barely touching. "Why?"

"I..." He trails off as he raises his hand to cup my face, fingers curling behind my ear. His eyes close tight on a hushed sigh. "I keep thinking about you on that balcony..."

And I feel like shit all over again as tears gather in Benji's eyes. My pulse pounds, and a sinking feeling fills the pit of my stomach. I've hurt him so much. I've scared him, proving that my assholery knows no bounds. I wrap my arms around him and kiss him with every ounce of longing in my bones. He lays me down on the bed and slowly, ever so slowly, takes me apart and puts me back together, and I let him because I feel the most alive under Benji's tender caretaking.

The ghosts don't seem nearly as scary when he holds me as I fall asleep.

———

THE SUN IS UNFAIRLY bright in the sky as Benji drives us downtown. My heart feels like it could beat out of my chest. Fear of the unknown has always been difficult for me. I like predictability, I like order, I like knowing I'm in control. Trying to fix whatever is wrong with my brain is so far out of my control that it feels like my world is spinning too fast and like I might get thrown off despite Benji's harried attempts to keep me chained to the ground.

Sweat dots the back of my neck when Benji parks the borrowed truck in front of a large brick medical building. I lean forward to stare up at the fourth floor, where I know a shrink is waiting for me.

"It'll be fine," Benji reassures me.

I cut a look over at him. "I just tried to kill myself. They might not agree."

Benji sighs softly and hops out of the car, completely

ignoring my comment. He opens my door with that sweet, tender smile that has stopped infuriating me, and started making my heart do this annoying little leap in my chest instead. Fuck me. Benji tugs me out of the car by my hands, then cups my cheeks in his palms, his thumbs sweeping over the bags under my eyes.

"I'll wait right here for you."

I swallow thickly and nod against his grip. "I wish you could go with me," I admit softly.

Benji's eyes turn warm and gooey. "Ah, but you need to keep *some* secrets from me, right? I can't know everything."

I tiredly lean my forehead against his. He smells like he always does, like Benji, like us, like every sweet thing in the world mixed together. The comforting scent radiates through me until all my muscles relax. I wish I could carry that fragrance with me everywhere I go.

As if reading my mind, Benji pulls away and rips his shirt off, then carefully lifts off mine. With a tender, saccharine smile, he pulls his raggedy old T-shirt over my head.

"Now it's like I'm with you, right?"

Holy fuck, I think I love him. I open my mouth to say something, anything, but nothing comes out. Instead I look back over at the building, trying to hype myself up to go in. Best to go and not look back. I push away from Benji and the truck, and make my way toward the front of the building. The farther I get, the more my heart pounds, and I know it's wrong.

I turn back to see Benji leaning against the truck, my shirt clutched in his fingers since it's too small for him. He smiles, big and bright, and I can't help myself. I run back to him, closing the distance between us so quickly that I'm out of breath by the time I reach him.

He wordlessly tugs me close and kisses me, because words will never be enough between us. We speak in fleeting, tender touches and hard kisses and fingers dancing down curved spines as we make love. I pull away from him, gasping, my fingers tangled in his hair. Pressing my cheek to his, I breathe him in one more time, then turn around and walk head-on to face my future.

13

BENJI

JANUARY 2028

I don't know what the hell to do with myself while Nolan's in his appointment. I wish I could've gone with him, held his hand as he faces the unknown with a new doctor. All I can do is wait, I guess. Popping the tailgate on Colby's old truck, I sit and swing my legs. I spend a little while just watching people, but then I realize I'm shirtless and probably look creepy. Oops. Nolan's shirt is a size too small but I tug it on anyway.

A few birds chirp and swoop overhead without a single care in the world. Makes me think of Nolan wishing he could be a bird. My stomach tightens and roils at the idea of him jumping off that balcony. I was so close to losing him. I just want to help him get help. Selfishly, I really want to keep him. I want to see him blooming and carefree. I want to see Nolan when he's his most true self, unshackled by what his brain plays on him. I love him no matter what, and that's the scariest thing for me.

Somewhere along the way I fell in love with Nolan, with his quirky one with the slightly off-beat way he world. When he'd kissed me just before marching into the doctor's office, I thought I saw the glimmer of my own feelings reflected in his eyes. But now isn't the time to go blurting out feelings as big and scary as love. He just needs my support, he needs to know that I'm not leaving no matter how fucking scary things get. And things can't get much scarier than him almost jumping off a hotel balcony, right?

My phone buzzes in my pocket. The relief I feel at seeing Eli's name is second to none. I hadn't realized how much I missed them while being on tour with Nolan. Even just talking to them about *nothing* is enough to settle my nerves.

Eli: How's it going today?

Me: He's been meeting with the psychologist for a while now

Eli: Colby said she's really good.

Eli: She helped Colby's cousin a while ago

Me: How many cousins does Colby have

Eli: A lot

Eli: I asked for a number once, and Colby got this weird, confused, constipated look on his face while he tried to count

Trevor: Beau did the same thing. omg

Eli: There are too many of them

Eli: We're outnumbered

Jackson: I somehow found one of the few only children…

Eli: Not really. Colby and Beau are Harper's brothers.

Jackson: True

Trevor: Harper and Nolan seemed to hit it off

Jackson: YEAH AWESOME

Jackson: Harper keeps saying how he's best friends with Nolan now... his best friend is a rockstar... oh, Nolan, this... Nolan that... brooooooooooo

Eli: LMAO

Trevor: Jackson/Benji endgame is going to make Nolan and Harper happen

Jackson: STFU

Me: SHUT UP

Trevor: Lmao

Eli: Trevor, stop starting shit

Trevor: It's so easy... they're so easy.

Me: Nolan needs a good friend.

Jackson: Harper is a great friend

Jackson: But he's my boyfriend

Jackson: Just pretend he's my husband

Trevor: Oh, here we go

Eli: Jackson, please

Me: Wait, seriously?

Jackson: Yeah, just pretend we got married. Everyone should do that.

Eli: You're ridiculous

Trevor: Harper told me he was excited for college basketball season so he could do March Madness and pick teams by hottest players.

Jackson: WHAT THE FUCK?

Trevor: You should go ask him

Eli: TREVORRRRRR

Me: He's definitely gone now

Trevor: You're okay, Benji?

Me: I will be.

Eli: We love you <3

Me: I know 🙂

"THAT'S A BIG SMILE," a familiar voice calls out.

When I glance up, I find Nolan standing a few feet away, his hands tucked into the pockets of his skinny jeans. His eyes are red-rimmed and his face has that distinct *I've been crying* look. I don't know what to say or do to comfort him, instead I just open my arms and hope. Must've been the right thing to do because Nolan quickly crosses the distance between us and all but falls into my outstretched arms.

"It's okay," I murmur into his wild hair.

His fingers dig into my shoulder blades as he tries to

burrow himself into my body. A cold wind blows over us, forcing Nolan deeper into my arms. In these small moments, I almost think I can protect him from everything bad, mean, and awful. Maybe if I tried hard enough, I could force his brain to be nice to him.

"She wants me in weekly therapy sessions, and she gave me a prescription for a pill," Nolan says, sounding the picture of a defeated man. "She said something about depression and anxiety but I zoned her out because she also used this really big phrase about trauma..."

I take a deep breath and hug him tighter. "Well, now we have a plan, right?"

"I fucking guess," Nolan mumbles sourly into my shirt.

"I'll bring you to therapy every week, and we can get lunch afterward. We'll make it fun, less scary."

Nolan pulls away to stare at me with those haunted, deep brown eyes. "At some point, I'm going to have to answer to the label. Chris can work wonders, but he's not liable... for me."

I run a hand through his hair, smiling when his eyes dip closed at my touch. "We'll figure that out when we get there, okay?"

"Okay," Nolan agrees just a little too easily. He pulls away to run his gaze over my body. A smirk lifts up the corner of his mouth; that small, hidden dimple almost coming out to play. "You look ridiculous in my clothes."

I chuckle. "You look pretty good in mine."

Nolan rolls his eyes while rounding the truck to the passenger side. He leans against the roof to stare hard at me. My blood sizzles and boils as his eyes bore right into me.

"That's because you're a caveman, Benjamin."

"Oh, yeah?"

Nolan nods and rests his chin over his arm. "You like people knowing who I belong to."

"Who do you belong to?" I ask, throat thick with emotion, heart pounding wildly out of my chest.

"You, obviously," Nolan answers as he climbs inside the cab of the truck.

I have to take a minute to gather myself before climbing in myself. The last thing I need is Nolan clocking every emotion I'm feeling just because I can't control the lovestruck look on my face.

"Places to see, people to do!" Nolan calls out from the truck.

I try to wipe away my grin, but it must linger because when I slide into the driver's seat, Nolan rolls his eyes in my direction. Doesn't stop him from reaching over and twining our fingers together over my thigh as we drive.

"Do you feel better?" I ask.

Nolan shrugs slightly, his permanent frown deepening. "Kind of. But just knowing I don't have to perform anymore silences a lot of the worst thoughts in my brain. And having you helps."

"You never have to perform again if you don't want to."

Nolan turns his head so I can't see his face at all and his voice is soft when he says, "I don't know how to make music without performing."

"Is that what you want? To record and release albums but never tour?"

"That's the dream," Nolan quietly admits.

I squeeze his fingers as I maneuver the truck off the highway and onto the small county road that leads into Clay Springs. He's silent the rest of the way, and I don't press him for more. The key to loving Nolan Hastings is to wait him out.

He'll give his small truths when he's ready and not a second sooner. No problem for me. I can wait patiently for a long time, which is probably one of my best qualities.

Nolan eagerly jumps out of the truck the moment it's in park.

"I'm going to take a nap. Leave me alone for a while, stud."

He disappears up the stairs without a backward glance. A moment later, the front door slams shut behind him. I stand still for a while, watching him disappear for the second time today. Glancing behind me, I notice that Colby's Jeep, along with a very beautiful classic Mustang, is parked by the garage.

Well, no better time to bother Eli than now.

I rap my knuckles against the perfectly white front door. The noise of dog claws tapping on wood echoes through the door and a soft bark is let out by Whiskey.

"Damnit, Whiskey. Some guard dog you are. You only tell me someone is here *when* they announce themselves," Eli complains as he hurriedly opens the door.

His hair is a wet mess atop his head, and he looks perfectly adorable. His eyes narrow at the sight of me.

"Aren't you supposed to be downtown at an appointment?"

I brush past him into the house, ignoring the frustrated sound he makes. "Ended a while ago. Nolan is napping."

Eli deflates instantly. "Is he okay? Really?"

I don't really know how to answer that question. Is he okay? I can't tell. He didn't jump from that balcony, but I still feel like he's not yet in my grips. It's terrifying and makes my chest feel tight. Kind of feel like I could cry, really.

"Oh, Benji, love. Come here." Eli tugs me into his arms, swaying us back and forth as I cry silently. Jesus. I never cry. It just feels like the past few days have finally hit me. Everything feels so *big* inside me. "Shhhhhhhh..."

Eli pulls me toward the living room with an arm wrapped around my waist. We fall together onto the plush sofa, and Whiskey climbs into our laps to lie across us. She smells like outside, but it reminds me of being a kid, so I don't mind it so much.

"Tell me what's going on, Benji."

I sniffle and rub at my runny nose. "I just... ugh."

Eli just stares up at me, all doe eyes and sweetness. How the fuck do I just blurt this all out? Whiskey wiggles in our laps as I scratch just behind her ears, the spot all dogs seem to love.

"Nolan tried to kill himself, right in front of me... and I think it broke something inside me. I don't... talk about things much. I know that. My legal name is Sunshine for fuck's sake. I can't be sad or whatever."

"Benji," Eli says softly. I turn my head toward him as I wipe away another tear. He looks so fucking sad that it kills me. "You can tell me or the other boys *anything*. We want to know how you feel and what you think. We want to know anything you'll tell us. Anything! But if you're sad, we want to know so we can try to help."

"I know... I just feel like I have to put on this act all the time. Be what everyone expects. And now Nolan." I stop talking for a moment and take a deep breath. "I have to be strong for him because he's going through so much shit. My mom," I whisper quietly, tearing my gaze from Eli. "She attempted suicide when I was a kid."

Eli gently rests his hand on my arm, but I keep staring at Whiskey. "How old were you?"

"Eight. I grew up on that commune... you know? I think

my mama took Mom there in hopes it would help her depression and mental health issues. It did in a way, like the community was good and they're all weird but they're family. But Mom just... she's built differently. She took a bunch of pills and I found her."

"That must've been hard to see."

"Yeah and then afterward I felt like I was always walking on eggshells to keep her happy, to make sure it never happened again. She's open about her struggles. I keep thinking about," I whisper so low I can barely hear myself, "how I almost saw Nolan jump. I think I love him."

"It's okay to love him, but it's also okay to be scared about what he's going through. It's hard on him *and* you, love." Eli scoots closer until he can rest his head on my shoulder. "I'm so glad you came here. How can I help you? What do you need? Don't tell me what Nolan needs, tell me what Benji needs."

I run my hand through Whiskey's auburn fur as I think over Eli's question. What I really need is just my friends. I need their time and love and to not feel so alone. I need their help in supporting Nolan through whatever this journey is we're now on.

"I just need to know you're there."

"Oh, Benji," Eli says softly, a little sadly. "We're always here. I love you."

"I love you, too."

"Do you want some cookies? Colby made some last night and we have ice cream too, we can have ourselves a little sweet treat."

"I won't say no to dessert..."

Eli stands and looks down at me with a gentle smile. "No, I didn't think so. Up you get."

Whiskey and I follow Eli into the kitchen. Climbing into a chair at the island, I watch Eli scoop ice cream into bowls and then crush some cookies on top. Actually, dessert fixes everything now that I think about it.

"Why's your hair wet?" I ask Eli around a mouthful of ice cream.

Eli flushes. "Trevor's helping me train for a marathon."

"A marathon," I repeat in utter disbelief. I don't think I once saw Eli use the gym at the clubhouse back in Georgia.

Eli shovels ice cream into his mouth until he looks like a chipmunk, cheeks puffed and eyes set firmly over my shoulder. He's definitely avoiding something. I'm too stupid to figure out what it is though.

Eli shrugs. "I just want to be better at running. It's important to be healthy. I want to... I want to be serious about my health for Colby. Take care of myself."

I narrow my eyes at him. "Why?"

Eli bites his lip and pushes some of the ice cream around. "Well, he already lost one man. I don't want him to lose two."

"That's kinda morbid, Eli."

"Well."

"Colby is so lucky to have you. You love him so much, don't you?"

Eli glances behind his shoulder at the fridge where a selfie of them grinning on the beach at sunset hangs. When he turns back to me, his eyes dance with what I can only assume is love. I'm so happy for him and Trevor and Jackson, the happiness they've found here is second to none.

"I love him more than I can ever say." Eli leans forward and rests his hand over mine with a sweet smile. "It's okay to love Nolan like that too. He looks at you like you hung the goddamn moon. That doesn't come around all that often."

"Does he really?"

Eli's grin inches up until his eyes crinkle. "Oh yeah, Benji. I wish you could see how he looks at you. Pay attention next time, when he thinks you're not looking. A million stars at once in his gaze."

———

ARMED WITH A CONTAINER of ice cream and cookies, I push through the front door. The air is chilly as the sun sets, and the heat isn't on. I kick the heat up to lower the chill, then pad my way toward the bedroom. Nolan is still asleep, dressed in one of the hoodies from my suitcase. The sheet only covers his calves since he probably tossed and turned for a while since he was alone.

Quietly placing the containers on the nightstand, I carefully crawl into the bed with him. I curl around him, nuzzling my head into the crook of his warm neck. He makes a surprised sound before tangling his fingers into the hair at the base of my neck.

"Hi," Nolan mumbles, voice thick with sleep.

"Hi." I press my mouth to his warm cheek, tracing the line of his jaw with my lips until I can softly kiss him.

Nolan hums against my lips as I tug him until he's lying halfway over me. He tastes like coffee, which I know he probably drank just before taking his nap because he can somehow drink coffee and immediately fall asleep. I crack my eyes open to watch him as we kiss, only to find him already looking at me.

Nolan pulls away with a frown. "Why were you watching me?"

"Why were you watching me?" I repeat.

A beat goes by, and then Nolan is laughing and falling heavily against me. God, I love the way his laugh sounds. His laughter sounds like he's singing, deep and musical. The best sound I've ever heard. Being the source of his laughter is my greatest accomplishment in life.

"Nice nap?" I ask quietly.

He rubs his face against my stubbled jaw. "Would've been better if you'd been here."

"You wanted to nap alone."

Nolan sighs softly. "Better in my head than in actuality."

Gently moving him off of me, I roll over to grab the now melted container of ice cream and cookies. I hand them over to him with a hesitant smile, but he only looks up at me like he does sometimes, eyes full of wonder.

"I figured you were hungry."

"I wasn't but now I am," Nolan admits, voice so low that I barely hear him.

I push back against the headboard and tug him to sit between my legs. The ice cream is kind of melted, but Nolan doesn't seem to care. He mixes the cookies into the ice cream, breaks them with his spoon, and proceeds to happily and quietly eat the concoction. After a few bites, he lifts the spoon over his shoulder for me to eat some as well. It's good in that comforting sort of way ice cream can sometimes be. Nolan finishes the dessert and bends forward to set the containers at the edge of the bed. I let my hands coast over the breadth of his ribs, then slip back up when he bends back to fall against my chest.

I slip my hands down his arms to tangle our fingers together over his stomach. For a few quiet moments I just count his breaths, feeling his stomach dip and rise with each deep inhale. The soft reminders that he's alive here in my arms, that this isn't all one big dream after he fell.

"Benji," Nolan murmurs.

"Hmm?"

"I'm going to be okay."

I squeeze my eyes tight to stop the tears. "I know."

"Every decision is mine, not yours. You know that, right?"

I nod against his sleep-warm skin. "I know."

"Can we go somewhere tonight? Just you and me?"

"Yes, angel. I'll take you wherever you want to go."

Nolan sighs happily as he snuggles deep into my arms. "I know, Benji."

Nolan falls back asleep while snuggled into my arms, and I let him. I can't explain why it feels so special that he lets his guard down only in my presence. Maybe it's the caveman in me, I don't know, but it feels like he knows I'll protect him the best I can. If I could fight his dreams, I would. The room gets darker as the sun disappears, but Nolan practically glows like some sort of dying star as his eyelashes flutter against his cheeks in his sleep. I lovingly run my fingers through his slightly curled hair.

Careful to not wake him, I tug my phone out of my pocket and text Eli, asking him for help so I can sweep Nolan away once he awakes. Eli is of course eager to help, adding a million smiley faces to his text message.

He shifts awake after only a little while and turns his head so his cheek rests against my chest. A sleepy grin tugs at his lips and that's when I know, deep in the pit of me, that I'm head over heels in love with Nolan. Not with the rockstar, not with the man who challenges and bites at every opportunity, but this soft, gentle man I see glimpses of when he's most vulnerable. Because it is in this vulnerable moment that he shows himself to me so clearly. He's bright and effervescent and I fear the hold he'll have on me for the rest of our lives. He has the power to break me, I can only hope he won't.

"Thought you were going to take me somewhere," Nolan whispers, voice still sleep-rough.

"I am. Thought I'd let you get a little more sleep in though."

"Tired of sleeping."

I chuckle at the irony and he throws a dopey sort of grin up at me. My heart does that dizzy thing again it only does when Nolan smiles at me without a wall of barbed protection. I roll out of bed, carefully tugging him along with me. I leave him standing by the bed for a moment as I tug another hoodie out of my bag for myself, because I need him, and want him to stay cozy inside of my other hoodie. I like when he wears my clothes and I like when he smells like me.

Nolan quietly follows me downstairs toward the truck. Without a word, he climbs into the passenger seat because again he trusts me to take him somewhere safe, to not lead him somewhere that he's too afraid to follow. This weight of responsibility when it comes to Nolan is heavy, but I hope that at some point I'll learn to handle it better.

A happy grin flits across my lips when I notice the pillows and blankets in the bed of the truck. Thank God for Eli. The air is chilly as I climb into the truck, so I flick the heat on as I head away from Colby's land. We both shiver in the cab of the truck, but it only takes ten minutes of driving for it to warm up, and for the windows to fog up slightly.

The pin with directions from Eli leads us even deeper into the country. Stars always twinkle brighter in the winter. Everything gets darker and it reminds me so much of *home* that my heart hurts a little. I don't exactly miss the commune, but I miss that feeling of having somewhere that was home. I've spent so much of my adult life traveling, that my heart has never settled somewhere. Clay Springs oddly feels like a good, solid place to lay a foundation. I glance over at Nolan in the dark of the cab to find him already looking at me.

His eyebrows are slightly furrowed and there's a slight pout on his lips. "You looked sad just then." He reaches out to touch the corner of my mouth just as I turn back to watch the light gray asphalt lit up by the headlights. "Why were you sad?"

"I was just thinking about home... I don't have much of one anymore."

"Not the commune with the moms?"

I shake my head softly. "No. That's more of the *place* kind of home. Not the... not the firm idea of home. Does that make sense?"

Nolan hums in agreement. "I had a home once. My great-grandmother... she felt like home. She died when I was a teen, so I ended up in foster care. Let me tell you, teens don't fare well in the system. People rarely want teens. So I spent the last two years in a group home just waiting it out. Then, well, everyone knows the story, at seventeen I posted the video on YouTube and blah blah blah."

"I didn't know about your grandma," I tell him softly.

Nolan waves his hand around, obviously feeling emotions he doesn't want to talk about. "My parents were young when they had me and had a lot of addiction issues. They dropped me off with my mom's grandma and that was that. My great-grandmother was kind and loving, I had a good decade with her. She was religious and that was hard but... she was never mean."

"Do you remember your parents?"

I can feel Nolan tense despite not even looking at him. Quiet fills the truck as Nolan considers my question.

"Mom was kind," Nolan whispers, sounding oddly defeated. "I don't know why she didn't want me. Grandma never really said. I haven't heard from them since I became famous, so I don't even know." Nolan pauses and takes a deep breath. "They could be dead for all I know."

"And your dad?"

"I don't remember a single interaction with him where he wasn't high."

I'm not a therapist or psychologist or whatever but I feel like that just explained a ton about Nolan's entire personality.

"I'm sorry," I say quietly, meaning every word.

Nolan hums again. "It is what it is. Can't think about the past anymore. I want to think about the future."

"Do you have a lot of thoughts about the future?" I glance over at Nolan, but this time he's looking steadfastly out the window, fingers idly playing with the edge of my hoodie.

"I didn't use to, but now I do," Nolan admits shyly.

I don't push him for more because now's not the time. Life is too volatile right now to make or ask him to envision a future that only a handful of days ago he didn't believe he existed within.

The directions lead me onto a small dirt road with brush on either side. We rumble and ride down the road, the sky getting darker as the trees close in around us. For a moment I'm a little scared that Eli sent us out here to be murdered by some backwoods group of cannibals, but then the trees open up to a clearing. Nolan gasps softly as he leans forward to look up at the sky.

"Look at all those fucking stars," Nolan says, voice full of wonder.

A million stars have nothing on Nolan. We climb out at the same time, but Nolan wanders off toward the sound of water.

"Be careful, there could be snakes," I call out.

Nolan turns around with wide eyes. "Seriously?"

I laugh at him, earning me a scowl from him in return. "There are definitely snakes the closer you get to the water."

Without a single argument, Nolan carefully wanders back toward the truck, eyes scanning carefully over the ground before taking a step. Tugging the tailgate down, I climb into the bed to lay out the blankets and the pillows.

"Benji, this is awfully romantic," Nolan drawls as he watches me move around.

"It's sweet."

"Romantic," Nolan argues.

I freeze and turn back to stare him in the eyes. "Do you have a problem?"

"No." Nolan climbs into the truck with me to help me finish with the blankets.

Once the blankets and pillows are settled, I lie back and Nolan easily falls into my arms. He shivers a little and shifts further into me. The silence between us is easy. I take a deep breath of the fresh, clean night air, smiling at the hint of Nolan's body wash. Well, my body wash that he co-opted somewhere on the tour so that he always smells like me.

"Benji," Nolan says softly.

"Hmm?"

"This is nice and all but kind of boring."

I tug his head up to look at me. He grins a little, so I press a soft kiss to his mouth to taste his smile. "It's not very us, is it?"

Nolan shakes his head, lips softly brushing mine. "No, not really. Nice though. Just feels like someone else's thing."

"What could our thing be?"

Nolan rolls on top of me, straddling my hips with his legs. My heart races and my cock thickens just with the weight of him on top of me. He smiles down at me, cocky and sure, and leans down to brace his elbows on either side of my face.

"You know exactly what our thing is," Nolan says softly, warm breath fanning over my face with each word. His eyes dart between mine as he tangles his fingers in my hair. "Thank you for trying... trying to be sweet to me. But you don't have to try so hard. I like you when you're soft for me, but I like it even better when you tell me what to do, when you make me bend to your will. That's the best part of us, right?"

I stare helplessly up at him, the stars framing his face like a million galaxies brought him to me. Even in the darkness I can see the shine of truth in his eyes, I can see what I feel echoing back to me. We might not be able to say it yet but it's there, so obviously there.

"Yeah, Nolan. You tell me what you need and I'll give it to you."

Nolan leans a little closer to brush his lips over mine. "You know exactly what I need, stud. You always do."

In the middle of the starry field, cold wind whipping over us, I hold Nolan's face between my warm palms and fuck his throat until tears stream down his cheeks. Afterward, I lick the taste of myself from his mouth and hold him close, giving him what he wants and needs, because it's exactly what I need too. Taking from him what he so willfully gives.

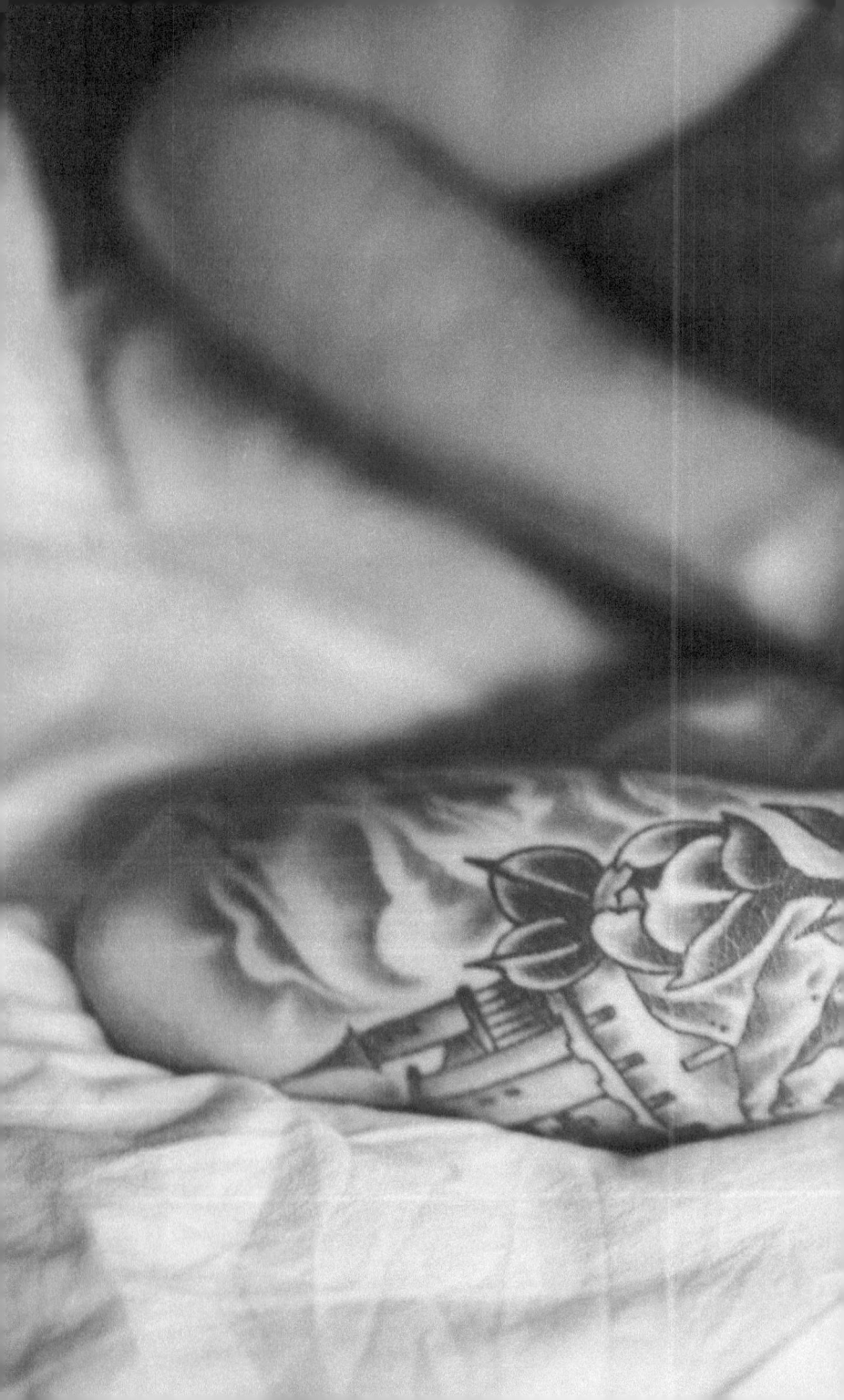

14

NOLAN

JANUARY 2028

So, therapy sucks. The medicine isn't too bad, but I haven't noticed much of a difference yet. Maybe it's because it's only been two weeks. The doctor did say it could take over a month to feel anything. It took everything in me to not laugh because I haven't felt *anything* for years. Whatever this thing is between Benji and me is the first thing that has sparked feelings inside my dead soul for... well, probably my entire life.

Benji drives me into town for each session, then we go out to eat afterward. The guy has this weird fascination with feeding me. Whenever I finish a meal, his grin is the size of the moon, and when I stare back at him in confusion, he just gets this sheepish look and ignores my questions. He's taken to cooking for me in the evenings as well, and I don't know if it's just that I haven't had an appetite in years but he's the best chef I've ever met.

The nicest thing is waking up each day and feeling like there's a two-ton weight on my chest. When I roll over into Benji's sleep-warm body, there's no anxiety.

there's just the comforting feeling of being safe in his arms. Benji usually sighs happily and tugs me into his body, as if he wishes he could absorb me into himself.

I also think his group of friends have oddly taken me under their wings. I've never had friends before. It's kind of weird that I've fucked almost half of them, but oh well, Benji doesn't seem too bothered by it. Probably because the puppy knows that he's the only one I've ever developed real feelings for. Makes him special. Not that I'll ever tell him that.

I'm in the middle of tuning my guitar while Benji's on a run when there's a knock at the door. It's the middle of the day on a weekday, so I'd expected no interruptions while my golden retriever lover was out running off his energy. After gently leaning my guitar against the sofa, I walk over to the front door and swing it open.

"You shouldn't open the door before checking who's on the other side," Harper says with a serious frown. He's dressed in skinny jeans and an over-large dark blue sweater that shows a sliver of his pale collarbone. I can see what Jackson sees in him, the guy is adorable *and* hot, a rare find.

"Nobody here is going to kill me."

Harper tilts his head to the side. "You seem pretty sure about that."

"Well, if you're the hit man they've sent after me, they are bound for failure."

"Hey," Harper whines with a deep, irritated frown. "I might be small but I have a lot of spunk."

"I'm sure you do," I say with a smirk.

"Anyway..." Harper trails off and looks behind me, his eyes widening with barely restrained glee when he notices the guitar. "Are you playing? Sorry. I shouldn't ask that. I was going to have a bonfire at my house tonight... marshmallows and shit. I thought you and Benji might like to come?"

I lean against the doorway. "This isn't some way for us to have a foursome, right? I don't think Benji wants to share."

Harper laughs so loudly it's jarring. "Oh, that's hilarious. I'll mention that to Jackson. You can witness his reaction first-hand when I mention it tonight. You'll come? Jackson will grill dinner. He fucking loves to grill." Harper says all of this with a fond sort of irritation that is quite honestly oddly endearing.

"Yeah, sure," I agree. "We'll come."

"We'll go where?" Benji asks, slightly out of breath as he jogs up the stairs. He's all sweaty and shirtless and *mine*. His freckles pop against the flush that dots his cheeks and I so badly want to kiss him, that I don't deny myself. I grab his wrist and tug him closer until I can press a gentle kiss to his smiling mouth. "Hi."

"Hello," I whisper against his mouth.

"Yuck," Harper says loudly.

"Hi, Harper," Benji says with a genuine smile. "I saw Jackson in the car. Y'all heading somewhere?"

Harper flushes maroon and narrows his eyes at Benji. "No, he drove me over here so I could invite you over later."

Oh. I hold my hand out and wiggle my fingers. "Give me your phone. I'll give you my number so you don't have to drive over next time."

The grin on Harper's face could probably broker world peace. I hurriedly punch my number into his phone and hand it back to him. He looks down at his phone in amazement for a moment before seemingly shaking himself free from the starstruck haze.

"Well, if you want to bring the guitar tonight, that would

be fun. We can sing Hannah Montana together. Do you know 'The Climb'?"

"Of course. It's sacrilege to *not* know that song."

Benji's gaze pings between us, a furrow between his brows. "Not sure what's happening here."

"Shhhh... best friends are communicating," Harper says with his chin in the air. "You're sweaty and you should put a shirt on."

"Don't," I tell Benji with a wicked grin that makes him flush even deeper. "Go on inside and wait for me."

Benji goes inside without a word and Harper leans to the side to watch Benji disappear. "Jackson would kill for him, you know."

I smile blandly. "I'd kill for him even more. I'll see you later. Text me the address."

I slam the door in Harper's face before he can reply, but his laughter echoes through the door. I find Benji in the bathroom, leaning one hip against the counter, still gloriously sweaty from his run. He cocks one eyebrow at me as I slowly approach him.

"You think you can tell me what to do?" Benji asks quietly.

I shrug as I pull my shirt over my head. "It worked."

Benji reaches out to slip his fingers into the waistband of my sweatpants, using his fingers to tug me close until I slam against his sweaty skin. I run my hands up his back, marvelling at the feel of his muscles moving under my palms.

"Hi," Benji says quietly, light blue eyes glistening.

"Hi," I repeat softly.

"Wanna shower with me? Help get me clean?"

"Let me enjoy you all dirty first."

I tuck my head into his shoulder, breathing in the smell of him. Even after running miles he still somehow smells fresh and clean. Maybe it's the cold air from outside lingering on his skin. Benji pulls out of my grip to turn the water on for the giant shower. Steam fills the room as he repeats his favorite process, slowly undressing me. Once I'm shirtless, he slowly kisses down my chest, his eyes peeking up at me as he lowers to his knees. He slowly tugs my sweatpants down to reveal my thighs, planting kisses down my leg as each new inch of skin is revealed.

I follow his direction to step out of my pants and breath stutters out of me when he lifts one foot to ever so softly kiss the tattooed arch. No one has ever been so tender with me, probably because I've never allowed someone the chance. Only ever Benji. Just Benji. He stands slowly and tugs my naked body against his own. I can feel his heartbeat against my chest as I make myself breathe slowly to savor the intimacy of the moment.

His hands cup my hips, thumbs rubbing at the tattooed skin. "I've missed this. I like taking care of you, like when you let me."

"You always take care of me," I whisper like it's a secret.

Benji chuckles softly. "I know, but there's something special about these moments in baths or showers. You open up for me, let me be softer than normal. I like this version of Nolan best."

"How many versions of me are there?"

Benji nuzzles my nose, eyes going half-mast. "A lot, and I like them all, but I have my favorites."

After helping Benji get undressed, we slide into the warm, hazy shower. Benji dips us under the water, and I blink my eyes rapidly so I don't lose sight of him. The way he tips his head back to reveal the long line of his throat as he wets his hair leaves me breathless and wanting. I don't even care about getting off. I just want to... be with him. Hold him. Feel his heartbeat against my cheek as I press close to him.

I grab his face between my palms and tug him to me, eating at his mouth as he gasps in surprise into the kiss. His hands find a home on my hips, pressing tight into my flesh. It's sad that my tattoos will make it hard to ever see the bruises he leaves on my skin, the proof that I am still alive, that blood pulses through my veins. Maybe the bruises he leaves on my heart will have to be enough.

"Nolan," Benji murmurs against my mouth. "Slow. I'm not going anywhere. Like this."

And then he kisses me deeply, like he's drinking a fine wine that needs to be savored. His lips glide over mine as he curls his arms around my back to cup his palms over my shoulders. I melt against his body, feeling hazy and delirious with this odd, new urge. My heart pounds and my ears ring as his soft, slow kiss takes me apart. This is when I feel most alive, when the world feels a little less scary, when Benji treats me not like fine glass that could break, but like the finest china that he wants to admire for how carefully it's been created.

It's only when Benji's thumbs move to swipe across my cheeks that I realize I'm crying. I blink my eyes open to find Benji already watching me.

"Okay?" Benji asks against my slack mouth.

"No, but I'm getting there."

"Better?" Benji asks hopefully.

I nod jerkily. "I think so. Benji... you. You won't leave me, right? I can't do this without you, and I know that's probably shit to say, and I know I hurt you with the balcony stunt, and you probably think I'm insane. I just... I just want you to always stay. Stay with me? Okay? Okay."

I finish talking and realize now I'm really crying, fat tears falling from my eyes. Fuck this man and his ability to make me open up in ways I've never thought possible.

Benji's own eyes glisten as he stares deeply into my eyes. "Nolan, wild horses couldn't drag me away from you. You could ask me to go, and I wouldn't. You're stuck with me, okay? Don't worry about that at all. Let me worry about everything else."

"I want to be better. I want to feel whole," I tell him, my voice shaking on the words.

His smile is tender and quiet, just for me. "You'll get there, angel. We'll get there."

Then he kisses me again before tenderly washing my body. Nothing about it is remotely sexual, yet I don't think I've ever wanted him more. Because in these small moments, Benji shows how much he loves me. Our relationship is terrifying and new, but it's so real that I can almost reach out and touch the emotions. I never thought a love like this was possible, not for someone like me. And yeah, maybe I don't deserve it, but I can spend my life trying to, and I think that would be enough for Benji.

———

"It's cold as balls," I complain as we step out of the car at Harper's place. It's a sweet little farmhouse with white paneling, dark blue shutters, and a wraparound porch. The chatter of voices and laughter floats through the air as we approach.

Benji takes my hand in his, tangling our fingers to keep me warm. "I'll warm you up."

"By shoving me into the fire?"

Benji snorts. "I don't think we're committing a ritual sacrifice tonight, angel."

Well, one never knows. When we round the house, we see a raging bonfire in the backyard. Jackson stands with his hands on his hips as Harper points at the fire, mouth moving a mile a minute.

Harper grins when he notices us. "Hi! I'm arguing with Jackson about if we should start with hot dogs or s'mores."

"Hot dogs," I answer, because who starts with s'mores?

Harper tosses his hands at me with a sort of expression that makes Jackson sigh.

"Fine, I'll go get everything. Don't burn yourself," Jackson says, eyes narrowed in Harper's direction as if it's a real possibility.

"I'm not going to get close," Harper whines.

Jackson keeps his eyes on Harper even as he disappears into the house. A moment later, a loud truck rumbles down the gravel driveway; I assume it's one of the other escorts with their sugar daddies. Benji wanders over to help Harper set up some camping chairs out of the direction of the smoke. I step a little closer to the fire, hugging my arms around myself to enjoy the warmth. The heat bleeds through Benji's hoodie that I stole for the evening. Well. For life, maybe. Dipping my head down, I can smell the warm summer scent of Benji on the toasty material, and my heart does this scary little skip and flip in my chest.

I glance over at Benji to watch him help Harper, watch his muscles flex under the tight, long-sleeve shirt he put on for the evening. He must feel my gaze because he looks over his shoulder and catches my eyes. One corner of his mouth kicks up in a soft smile that I know is only ever just for me. Despite the bonfire, I feel the heat of a flush creep up my neck, so I tear my gaze away to stare back into the jumping orange flames.

The murmur of voices behind me reaches my ears, but I ignore it. Sticking my hands out, I let myself enjoy the fire's warmth against my skin, feeling it bleed into my always-cold bones. A firm hand wraps around my neck and squeezes.

"Alright?" Benji asks softly.

I close my eyes just to bask in the moment. "Hmmm."

Benji presses a distracted, soft kiss to my left temple. "You smell like bonfire."

I tilt my head to look over at him. "Is that good?"

"Makes you smell wild," Benji notes, eyes sparkling as he teases me.

"Better than drenched in sweat from a four-hour show."

Benji's cheeks flush crimson, and his eyes flit away. "Didn't mind that so much."

"Silly boy." I kiss his red cheek, feeling the glowing skin under my lips.

Glancing over my shoulder, I spot Trevor and Eli heading toward us with their sugar daddies in tow. Trevor sends a smirk my way while Eli smiles softly, and that weird feeling in my chest erupts again. That odd feeling of belonging, despite many years of not feeling anything remotely close to it. Benji's hand squeezes my neck once more before slipping under the hoodie to rest against the skin of my back. I lean into him as everyone gathers around the bonfire, teasing one another and having fun, and I feel oddly at home.

Benji hustles me into one of the camping chairs and supplies me with a wire hanger so that I can roast hot dogs. I glance over at the others to see how they do it, holding back a laugh when Trevor looks at Beau with a mixture of fond confusion and disgust as Beau readies his hot dog. Beau promptly thrusts it into the fire with a bashful grin.

I glance over at Benji to find him watching me, so I mimic what I just watched Beau do and feel delighted when I earn a happy little grin from Benji. A cold breeze blows over us, sending the heat of the fire away for a moment and leaving my bones cold, but I warm back up as Benji continues to stare at me with hearts in his eyes as I roast the hot dog.

"It's just a hot dog," I snap at him.

"You're enjoying yourself," Benji remarks.

He's right, but I don't feel like admitting it. "Who doesn't enjoy hot dogs?"

"Me!" Eli pipes up. "They're the leftover parts of the pig."

Colby chuckles and rolls his eyes. "Baby, so is sausage."

"What?" Eli asks, voice full of heartbreak.

"Just pretend no one said anything, Eli. It's okay." Trevor reaches over to fondly pat Eli's head as Eli stares into the fire with a sort of glazed, terrified look in his eyes. "You broke him," Trevor says to Colby.

Colby's smile is bittersweet. "Sorry, baby."

I pull the hot dog from the fire when it just starts to burn slightly, crinkled and gnarled around the edges. It's hot, and my mouth fills with saliva from the rich flavor. God. It's been forever since food just... tasted good. For so long, nothing had flavor, and everything was miserable. And I don't think I realized just how sick my brain was until that fateful day on the balcony. The day I almost stole myself from the world, from Benji.

When I look over at Benji, he's staring into the flames, a contented grin tugging at his lips, and there's warmth splashed across his cheeks. He's so effortlessly beautiful, so kind, and so very mine. If I can keep him. I want to tell him I love him, I want to scream it, I want to clutch his cheeks between my palms and tell him I'll try my best to never hurt him again, but I can't promise that I won't. And the beautiful thing about Benji is that it would be more than enough for him; just the fact that I promised I would *try* is enough to make him think rainbows come out of my ass. If that's not love, I don't know what is.

I'll be damned if I tell the man I love him at a fucking redneck bonfire, though.

With two men I've previously fucked sitting beside us, no less.

Benji speaks softly with Jackson beside him as he busies himself, roasting a marshmallow. Without even asking me or looking at me, he makes a s'more and then hands it to me. My fingers graze his as I take it, and he glances at me out of the side of his eyes, then returns to Jackson with that little, soft smile on his lips.

Okay, the s'more is way fucking better than the damn hot dog. Jesus Christ. I all but moan as I eat it, licking my fingers clean.

"Oh," Harper says quietly. When I glance over at him, his cheeks are flushed as he stares at me. "That was pornographic."

I wink at him. "It was a good s'more."

"You should say the thing about the foursome to Jackson," Harper whispers, an edge of trouble to his voice. He sits back in his chair hard as he eats his own hot dog. "I'd like to see it."

"You're trouble."

Harper shrugs. "Maybe so. Do it."

"Jackson?" I call out.

Jackson leans forward in his chair to look at me, one eyebrow raised. "Yeah?"

"We should have a foursome, me, Harper, Benji, and you."

Jackson stares at me blankly for one long moment, jaw clenched, before he leans forward even more to look past me and straight at Harper. "Stop starting shit, punk."

Harper grins at him. "I didn't do anything."

"Nolan," Benji says with a laugh. "You guys are bad influences on each other."

Benji leans over to kiss me, sighing softly at the taste of the s'more on my tongue, and I don't think it's too bad if that's the response I get by starting something.

"So," Harper asks as he leans over into my space. "Do you know any hot athletes?"

"Uhm."

Harper groans. "Give me something."

"Well, a few hockey guys came to one of my shows. Big fans I guess? This big guy Grayson, I wanted to climb him like a tree. I even hit on him, he just flushed and ignored me."

"I'll google him when I get home. When you say big, how big?"

I take a look over at Jackson, considering him. "Bigger than Jackson I think."

Harper gasps and his eyes widen. "Really?"

I really like this guy. "For sure. Hockey players are a different breed."

Harper smiles softly as his gaze flicks over to Jackson. "It's okay, I like my basketball player."

When the fire burns to embers, everyone disperses back to their homes. That night, when Benji curls around me as we fall asleep, I think I finally know what home is.

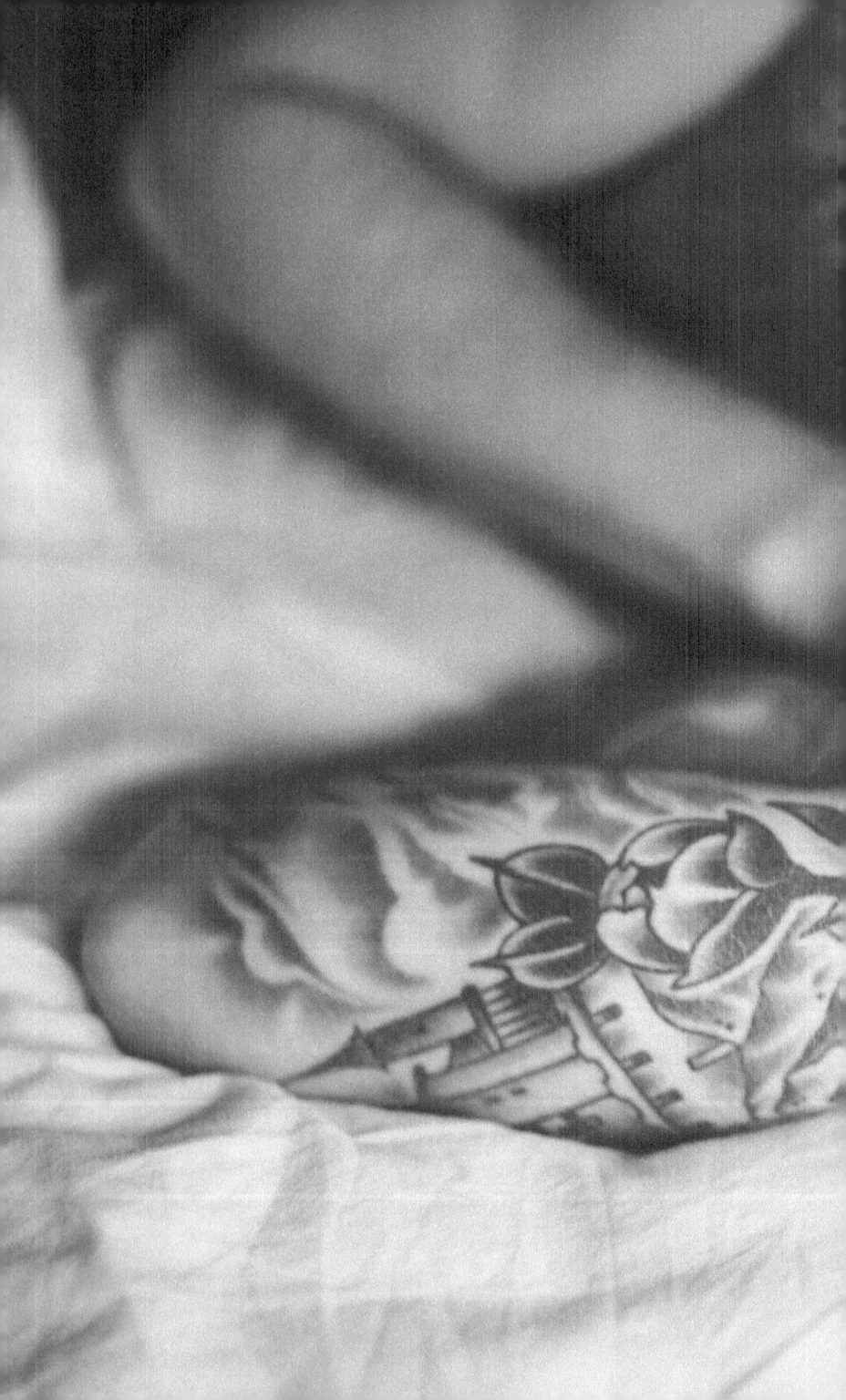

15

BENJI

FEBRUARY 2028

Everything cannot be perfect forever. After four weeks in Clay Springs, Nolan has made so much progress. Medicine and therapy and not pushing me away. But I know more than anyone that bad days come with good days, especially after seeing how much my mom has struggled with depression over the past twenty-something years.

So when Nolan can't get out of bed one day, I know all I can do is try to take care of him. There's no cure-all fix to depression and anxiety, there's no pill that'll fix it so every day is perfect and cloud-free. But the bad days come far less frequently and are easier to handle when the good days outweigh the bad.

I busy myself making bland toast and a cup of peppermint tea in the kitchen, knowing that Nolan would drink it if I brought it to him. My phone buzzes in my pocket. It must be my mama because I texted her to update her on everything.

"Hi, Mama," I say into the phone, tucking it between my cheek and shoulder.

"He just won't get out of bed?" Mama asks without any sort of greeting.

"Nope."

"Just feed him."

"I know. Toast and peppermint tea."

Mama updates me on a few of the people at the commune, all but begging me to come for a visit. Now isn't the time, and when I tell her so, she's understanding as always. I do want to take Nolan to visit them; I think meeting my mom would help him a lot. But right now isn't the time, and it has to be *the* right time for that scenario. I don't want to scare him away with my mother's stories about me streaking across the lawn at five years old because I'd decided clothes were not for me.

"Are you taking care of yourself too?" Mama asks quietly, in the most gentle way only she can.

I pause as I touch the hot side of the mug. "As best I can."

"It's important to take care of yourself, too, to allow others to care for you. Can I send you one of my care packages? I'll make those cookies you like."

"Snickerdoodles?" I ask hopefully.

"Yes, mijo."

"Okay."

Mama sighs softly, sounding oddly lonely. "I'll get it to you this weekend. Enough for Nolan, too. We love you, you know that, right?"

"Yes, always."

"Alright. Go take care of him, lie with him, kiss his forehead. Leave him alone if he asks you to. Okay?"

"Yes, Mama."

"Good boy." Then we say goodbye, and I carry the toast and tea back into the bedroom where Nolan lies frozen on the bed. I only know he's even there by the black tufts of hair appearing from underneath the quilts against the pillow. After placing the toast and tea on the bedside table, I crawl under the quilts beside him, pulling the blanket over my head so we're cocooned together in the warmth Nolan's body has created.

"Hi," I whisper.

Nolan blinks slowly and licks his lips. "Hi."

"I brought you toast and tea."

"Okay."

"Can I do anything else?"

Nolan slowly reaches his hand out to tangle his fingers with my own against the cool of the pillow under my head. His fingers are so warm, so alive that my heart settles just a little at the reminder of life.

"Just be here. I'm sorry... I felt so much better..."

"It's okay. It's normal. You'll have good days and bad days. Life."

"Do you have bad days?" Nolan asks seriously.

"Probably... I just guess they're so far and few between that I don't notice them much. Usually, when I have a bad day, I work out or go for a hike or do something, anything to get my mind off of it."

Nolan's eyebrows furrow, and he moves closer, slipping his thigh over my hip. I drop my hand down to cup his thigh. His hand comes up to rest against my face, his thumb rubbing under my eye.

"I wanna tell you something very badly, but now isn't the right time."

"Okay," I say softly, even though my heart could fly out of my chest.

His dark brown eyes bore into mine, and that's when I

know he doesn't even need to say it. Just like I don't need to say it. It's just there, just known. I love him, and he loves me. For now, that's enough.

"It's okay, Nolan. I know."

Nolan closes his eyes with a soft sigh and dips his head forward to press his forehead against mine. He rocks his head back and forth a few times, breath ghosting over my face. It's stale and awful, but I don't care because it's just another reminder that he's so very real in my arms.

"Will you eat the toast and drink the tea for me? Then maybe I can just hold you for a while, until it gets to be too much?"

Nolan answers by sitting up, my T-shirt hanging off of his thin frame, dipping to reveal his jutting collarbone. I lean over to grab his tea and toast, and when I return I press a warm kiss to that collarbone that's always so distracting. Nolan dutifully eats and sips until he's had enough and shoves it back into my waiting hands. Then I cuddle him back down into the bed, holding him as closely as I can. Just doing my best to let him know that I'm here and this is just where I want to be.

"Talk to me?" Nolan asks, voice soft and vulnerable.

Gently dancing my hand up and down his spine, I smile when he shivers and moves in closer against my body. "The first time I saw you in that hotel room, my heart skipped about ten beats. I thought you were the most beautiful thing I've ever seen."

"And then I opened my mouth," Nolan says tiredly.

"Nah," I quickly disagree. "You just got more beautiful. I like it when you argue with me, when you bite back, when you tell me what you want. I like giving you what you want."

"I know, stud." Nolan's warm breath ghosts over my neck

and his fingers dig into the small of my back. "I knew I was in trouble when I saw you. That you were different."

God. The vulnerability in his voice still shakes me to my core. All these months and I think he's still worried that I'll hurt him, that he can't trust me with his most inner thoughts.

"Well, it ended up pretty okay, right?" I bury my face in his messy hair, breathing in the still somehow smoky scent of him.

"Yeah, I think maybe it did."

"Mmm."

"Did you ever fuck Jackson?"

The laughter is so hard and immediate that Nolan pulls away slightly to aim his bleary dark brown eyes up at me. I can't help but dip down to kiss him, a closed-mouth kind of kiss that echoes intimacy more than anything else. Tenderness and softness are two things I never thought I'd have with Nolan.

I press my forehead against Nolan's. "We tried once. Didn't work."

"'Cause you're both tops?"

This time, the laughter hurts. "Yeah, I guess. That and well... we're just too similar I think. What do you call me? A golden retriever? It's just two golden retrievers running in circles, and I piss him off, and then he riles me up... we're better off as friends." I pause as I run my hand through Nolan's messy hair, thinking about Jackson and my other friends. "I kept them at a distance for a really long time. Can't really say why. I love them, and they love me, but I think I've always felt like the odd one out. I never really belonged growing up... at the commune. I've always had trouble finding a place to belong."

Nolan stares at me so hard, his gaze unblinking, that for

one long moment I'm worried maybe this is the thing that does us in. But all Nolan does is reach up and delicately run his fingers over my cheek.

"You belong with me," Nolan says firmly.

I swallow against the sudden lump in my throat. "I know."

"Enough talking now," Nolan says as he closes his eyes and snuggles back against me. "Hold me as I sleep away all the bad thoughts. You always make them go away."

"Alright, angel."

Nolan sighs happily at the nickname, and in moments, he's back asleep in my embrace, and I feel beyond sure that I hold my entire universe on this small cedar-scented bed in Clay Springs.

———

NOLAN and I spent two days in bed. I left him alone for the length of a solitary run, only to come back to try to ply him with food. I've always found joy in cooking, but cooking for Nolan brings me a sort of peace that's hard to explain. Maybe it's because making food for him is the easiest way for me to pour my love into him without frightening him away. Other times, all he wanted was to be held, for me to talk to him, and I was more than happy to comply. Finally, on the third day, he woke up, took a shower, and grabbed his guitar before fleeing to the living room. It felt like some huge weight fell off my shoulders just at the sight of him out of the bed.

And, of course over the two days, my friends dropped care baskets off at the door. My favorite was the basket from Harper, which was full of freshly baked muffins in a bunch of different flavors and a book full of crude jokes that Nolan still refuses to let me read. I think Jackson and I are in a load of trouble when it comes to Nolan and Harper, because some of the few times I've seen something resembling a smile is when Nolan is seemingly texting with Harper.

"You're doing that thing," Nolan says from the passenger seat. I glance over at him to find his eyebrows furrowed, lips tugged down in a thoughtful frown. "You're thinking very hard about something."

"Thinking about you."

Nolan huffs a small laugh. "About how much you wish you could get rid of me."

I almost veer off the road. What the hell? "No, Nolan, I never think that."

Nolan just hums and leans back harder in the seat. When he angles his head away from me, I can clearly see the hard bob of his throat as he swallows. There's something he's not telling me, something he's not asking me, but I don't know what. Mind reading has never been my strongest ability, that's more Trevor's style. His therapy session today was long, and he'd returned to me a little more mellow than normal. But I know how that goes.

"Nolan, do you need me to say it? I'll say it. I'll say it first, I don't care."

His head pings toward me so fast I'm afraid he's given himself whiplash. Tears line his eyes, and he looks so fucking raw that my heart cracks wide open. Not like the day on the balcony, but maybe the days before, when he was so haunted by something he didn't know how to tell me.

The county road leading to Clay Springs spans in front of us, empty and desolate, so I do the only thing I can do. I pull over onto the side of the road. A farmhouse dots the horizon, and a few horses roam free, suddenly paying attention to the vehicle on the side of the road. Nolan's frozen, eyes wide, as I hop out of the car to come over to his side.

But suddenly, all I care about is making sure, without a doubt, that Nolan knows how I feel.

Ripping the car door open, I grab his hands in mine and dip my head until he's forced to meet my gaze.

"What happened in therapy today?"

Nolan's jaw tightens, and he shakes his head. "Benji..."

"Talk to me."

He sighs softly as I hold his gaze. "Nothing, I just... I feel like I'm hurting you. I feel like... I don't know, Benji. I don't want to be like your mom."

"You're nothing like my mom," I say, hoping desperately to reassure him. All he does is roll his eyes. "I love my mom so much, and her depression and her struggles are a part of her. I can't pick or choose parts of people to love. And... and..." I take a deep breath and puff out my cheeks because really, on the side of the road after a therapy session is when I tell fucking Nolan Hastings that I'd burn the world down for him. "I love every single part of you. Okay? Okay. Don't say it back. I don't want to hear it yet. Not until you want to say it, but I needed you to know. So you don't... don't question things anymore. Just, I fucking love you. Every part. Every version. Okay?"

Nolan's jaw clenches hard for one long moment, before he releases a sound that's a mix between a cry and some sort of sigh of relief. He wraps his thin arms around my shoulders and tugs me in until my cheek is squished against the warm material of his hoodie. The hoodie that smells like me and him. Like us.

"I'm a piece of shit," Nolan says with a shaky voice.

"Don't say that about the man I love."

"I'm scared about when the real world comes back," Nolan admits into my hair, voice wrecked and terrified. "When... when the label makes me make a decision. When people find out I'm here. I don't want to leave the bubble. I don't want people to know I'm fucked up."

My heart cracks in half at the shake in his voice, the fear making his body tremble. I tighten my arms around him and try to meld our bodies together so I can make him feel safe, even just for a moment.

"We'll tackle it together when we need to. You're not alone anymore. And Chris will do anything for you."

Nolan's ribs expand with a large sigh. "I have to talk to Chris... I've been ignoring his calls."

"Don't do that."

"I know, Benji." Nolan presses a kiss to my temple, lips lingering in the way he often does. "Take me home now, please?"

I pull out of his grip, take his cheeks between my palms, and tug him to me to kiss him soft and slow. He tastes like peppermints, and I know it's because therapy makes him nauseous, and the mints help. But he still tastes just like my Nolan, like something soft and spicy. My man. His eyes stay closed when I pull away. I try to capture the moment to remember forever, the moment I told him I loved him, and he didn't fight me back.

LIKE USUAL, Nolan curls up in bed to sleep after a therapy session. I sit beside him for a while, brushing my fingers through his hair that desperately needs a cut. When it's short, it curls ever so slightly and he tucks it behind his ears when plucking at the guitar. But when it's this length, it hides his eyes that are the window to his soul. No matter the length, the strands are baby-soft and fine, easily slipping through my fingers on each stroke.

His phone vibrates on the bed between us and I hurriedly pick it up before it can wake him. I sit still, waiting for him to move because sleep is so hard for him to come by, but his eyes stay closed, fingers curled gently into the pocket of my sweatpants. Eyelashes fluttering softly, he lets out a soft sigh in his sleep, then rolls over onto his stomach to starfish out on the bed.

I carefully climb out of the bed, and swipe the screen on his phone to see twenty missed calls from Chris. Jesus. No one else has reached out to him over the past few weeks, just notification upon notification from Chris. I should've called him sooner.

Pocketing Nolan's phone, I grab my own and head out to the living room. After closing the door softly behind me, I curl up on the sofa under a blanket and dial Chris.

"Is he okay?" Chris asks urgently.

"As okay as he can be," I admit, picking at a loose thread on the blanket. "He's doing better. Therapy exhausts him though, and it's a lot of work. I don't want to violate his privacy, but, Chris, you have to find a way for the tour to be done."

Chris huffs an annoyed grunt. "What do you think I've been doing since New Year's, kid? I don't give a fuck about the label. I don't even really give a shit about the fans. I care about that boy who's now solely under your protection."

"Chris—"

"Listen," Chris says slowly, making me freeze on the sofa. "I have a kid in college and a kid currently in high school. I'm old enough to be Nolan's father. I love him like one of my own. Telling him that is out of the fucking cards though because he wouldn't believe it even if I said it. You know that though, right?"

Yeah, I do fucking know that. I'm still not sure Nolan believed a single word of my love declaration on the side of the road. I know how he is, but I'm starting to think maybe he just needs people to say it even if they're scared of his reaction.

"I told him I loved him," I admit quietly.

Chris goes quiet for a few moments before asking, "Really?"

"Yeah."

"And he... he was fine?"

"He hugged me after," I say with a small shrug. "I think he's at the point where telling him these things might help more than hurt. But also actions speak louder than words with him, right? You got him here with me, maybe that tells him more than anything."

"I wish he'd speak to me," Chris mumbles into the phone.

"Maybe he's worried about the label. I can't speak for him. But just back off a little and give him time, I've got him."

"You're a good kid."

I laugh lightly, because sure. "I try. Also, the contract is null and void now. You know that, right?"

Chris lets out a large sigh. "I figured. You don't want any payment?"

I look toward the bedroom, toward where my future is sound asleep. "Nah. I've got my payment."

We both sit quietly for a while as Chris thinks over everything I've said. No noise comes from the bedroom, so I'm pretty sure Nolan is still fast asleep, thank God because he'd definitely go into a fit of rage if he knew the conversation we were having right now. But Nolan's entrusted his care to me, so I've got to let Chris know everything is fine.

"I'll show up in town once I've got news from the label. I'll want to see him," Chris whispers into the phone. Jesus, the man sounds like he's crying. "You won't tell him we spoke?"

"And risk his wrath? I think not," I say around a laugh.

"Touché."

And then Chris hangs up, and I sit quietly for a while, before rejoining Nolan in the bedroom. When I lie down beside him, he shuffles closer out of instinct and burrows himself into my arms, and somehow even further into my already gone heart.

———

"HARPER IS TAKING ME INTO TOWN," Nolan says the next day, out of the blue.

I blink slowly at him. "Okay. Now?"

Nolan tugs on one of my sweatshirts, nodding when his head pops through. "Yes, now. I want to do some things. Without you."

"Okay, that's fine. You can do anything without me. That's cool. That's chill."

Nolan walks back over to where I sit on the couch and pats my head like I'm a scorned puppy. "Benji, I'll be fine without you for a few hours. Go run around or go bother one of the boys."

"Yeah, sure."

He obviously doesn't believe me because he dips down to kiss me soft and slow, lips gliding gently over mine in an affirmation that words can never give.

"Better?" Nolan asks against my mouth.

I nod slowly. "Yes. You'll call me if you need me. Who's driving you?"

Nolan slips his hand into my pocket and tugs out the car keys. The wink he gives me makes my heart skip in my chest, my gut tightening with want. I watch him go, feeling less worried and more anxious that we'll be apart. We haven't really done that... not since the balcony. But this is good for us. Plus, he'll be with Harper; what can they possibly get up to?

It's freezing outside, so I change into workout clothes and decide to go for a run. When Nolan gets back, he won't want to deal with me and my boundless energy. I can't help but smile when I think of him calling me his golden retriever, though. Guess that's what I am.

Running through the area around Colby's house always kind of reminds me of home back in Georgia. I get lost for a little while on the oak tree–lined concrete roads. Despite the cold air, the sun shines bright as ever, slashing through the trees. Not a cloud in sight. Clay Springs really is something special. Almost like the place is its own little bubble, an oasis away from real life. It sure has been that for Nolan and me.

For some stupid reason, my brain leads me to Jackson and Harper's house, even though I know Harper isn't there. I have to assume Jackson is, if only by the sight of his precious G-Wagon parked out front.

Jackson swings the door wide open after one knock. He stares at me hard, one eyebrow raised, and I feel the usual urge to squirm. After a moment he steps aside to let me walk through. Harper's house is beautiful, with a lot of natural light flowing from the back of the house and into the front. It makes sense for Jackson, this house.

"Harper took Nolan somewhere," I say as Jackson hands me a cold bottle of water.

Jackson leans against the counter, and crosses his broad arms over his chest. "Yes, downtown. Nolan needed to get out."

"Away from me," I point out.

"You're smothering him, but he likes it." Jackson laughs and rubs at his slightly stubbled cheek. "I've got one just like him. It's a careful tightrope you have to balance."

I take a careful gulp of the water as I think over what I want to say next, what I need to say next. What Jackson deserves to hear.

"I don't know how I'll be able to thank all of you... for everything." I swallow hard as the urge to cry once again wells up inside me. "When he... well... it was a lot. And the first place I wanted to come was here."

"It took you five weeks to say that to me? Jesus, Benji. We're family at this point."

I wince at his words, but he's right. I've spent so long keeping them all at a careful distance. Not wanting to let them in so they could hurt me. No clue why; I've just always kept people at arm's length.

"I don't want to argue."

"I'm not trying to argue with you. I love you."

For some reason, the words hit me like a blow to the chest, right between my ribs. I rub at the warm skin over my heart, wondering if I'm going to have a heart attack. The sound of Jackson moving closer makes me lift my head, only to find him looking at me in a way he never has before. Not pity, but something much worse. Worry.

"Are you okay? Really? What can I do for you?"

I wipe my suddenly hot nose against my sweatshirt,

curling my fingers into the ends as the urge to cry over-whelms me.

"It's so fucking hard, Jackson. I have to stay strong all the time for him. I can't... can't let him see I'm afraid or worried. Not right now. Not like this. I love my mom so much, and I don't hate her for being who she is, but I never imagined falling in love with someone who has her same fucking struggles because sometimes I feel so alone even when I'm in the same room as him. And it's getting better every day with therapy and the medicine... but sometimes I look at him and worry the balcony event isn't the last time. If he killed himself, a part of me would die too. I'd die, too. I would. I love him so fucking much." Tears are falling down my face now, and I claw at my chest as Jackson stares at me in profound loss of words. "I love him so fucking much, and if something happens to him, I will fucking die."

Jackson grabs me by the arms and tugs me against his body, wrapping me in his strong arms so tightly that I can't help but just let go. All the tears I've been holding in for months finally fall. Time crawls by as he holds me while I weep, his hand wound in my hair as he murmurs words I can't even understand. Finally, my breathing calms and the tears slow, but I don't feel stupid like I normally would. I just feel held and safe by one of my very best friends, a brother.

"Oh, Benji," Jackson whispers into my hair. "You are so loved by all of us. When you were gone, we thought about you every day; we worried for you. Now that you're here, let us help you, not just Nolan. It's okay to need your friends, okay?" Jackson pulls away to dip down and look into my eyes. "It's okay to let us see you like this."

"I know... I was just so scared on the tour that if I told you guys, if you knew... especially Trevor because he knew Nolan... you'd make me leave him."

Jackson's jaw firms up, and he glances away. "Yes, I would've tried to get you to come back here. With or without him, I can't say."

I make a *see* gesture with my hands. "We all made mistakes. I just... I need you guys now. I see a future with Nolan, a beautiful one, if I can get him there. If he can see it too."

Jackson squeezes his eyes shut, pinching his nose. "He sees it. I can't betray trust because then I'd be a massive fucking asshole, and Harper would seriously punish me, but Nolan knows. He feels the same way you feel."

I swallow hard because I knew that. I know that. "You're pretty whipped by Harper."

"Jesus Christ, that's an understatement." Jackson laughs, deep and low, before pinching my cheek. "You're gonna be alright, Sunshine. Everything's going to be alright."

For the first time in a long time, I believe him.

"I like Harper, he's funny."

"Nolan's funny, too."

We smile at one another, some weird sort of truce developing between us. Jackson's always been my secret favorite, even though half the time I want to murder him. We're too alike, too headstrong, too focused on protecting to be anything more to each other than brothers. But I think at the end of the day, if I needed someone to kill for me, I could call Jackson and know I was safe.

Jackson hustles me back out onto the porch, where we chat about not-life-or-death topics for a few hours. It's kind of nice to just not worry about anything for a little while. Just be normal.

"You need something just for you, Benji," Jackson says with a sigh. "Putting all your focus on Nolan for now is fine, but not for the future. What about all the traveling you love to do? All the cooking? Your huge social media following? You haven't updated your socials in forever."

I splay my hands wide and shrug. "Hard to do that the past few months without people figuring out somehow that I was on tour with Nolan."

"I get that," Jackson agrees, face still thoughtful. "Cooking? You could go back to school. I know you dropped out but look at you, you're not made for a business degree in stuffy classrooms. Maybe culinary school? You'll constantly be moving in a kitchen."

Oh. I hadn't ever thought of that. "You're kind of smart, Jackson."

Jackson rolls his eyes deeply. "Here we go."

"Genius over here," I tease some more, before getting serious again. "Cooking would be fun. I love to cook for Nolan and I like providing for people."

"I'll have Harper see if Beau or Colby know anyone." Jackson reaches over to pat my cheek. "I'm afraid if we push it, we'll end up killing each other. Wanna talk sports?"

"Thank God, neutral territory," I say with a grin, feeling full and happy when Jackson's booming laugh fills the space around us.

When Harper and Nolan wander into the house a while later, laughter echoing off the walls, my heart does that scary jump again that reminds me just how far deep I'm in.

And it does a crazy dive when they step through the back door.

Harper stands with his hands on his hips as he glares at us. "What's going on here?"

"Planning a coup," Jackson replies with a smirk. He pats his leg and Harper happily wanders over to perch himself on Jackson's lap. They share an easy smile, but my attention can't stay on them because I'm captivated by Nolan.

He's had his hair trimmed, making it just barely longer than it was a year or so ago, with tight black curls that've been his signature look for years. His nails are painted, too, a deep midnight blue. I stand from the chair and cross the distance between us. I want to tangle my fingers in his hair like usual, but I also don't want to fuck it up because it looks way too damn good. Nolan grins at me, small and soft, because, of course, he knows the effect he has on me.

"You look good," I say, voice thick.

"Do I?"

"Yes."

Nolan swallows hard. "Wanna take me back to the apartment?"

"Yeah, I kind of really do."

"Bye," Nolan says loudly without tearing his gaze from mine.

I aim a lazy wave over my shoulder. Grabbing Nolan's hand, I tug him after me until we're climbing into the car we've been borrowing for weeks. I keep Nolan's hand in mine the entire drive back, my heart pounding in my chest with each mile it takes to get us back home, back to our bedroom.

I always thought the movies were full of shit when they painted people as unable to keep their hands off of each other, clothes falling off as they climb stairs, hands roving bodies just to touch bare skin. But it is real when you love someone. I can't stop touching Nolan even as I back him toward the bedroom. I can't stop mapping his tattooed skin with the warm palms of my hands, feeling the vibrantly alive lines of his body. His lips are warm and supple against mine, like drinking ambrosia of the gods. His kisses make me feverish and they make me ache.

"Benji?" Nolan asks quietly.

"Have you ever topped?"

Nolan pulls back enough to stare at me, eyes wide. "No."

"Would you?"

Nolan looks nervous but not scared as he continues to stare at me. His throat bobs a few times, fingers tightening against my ribs as he holds me close.

"If you want to, I would. Only with you. Have you ever..."

I shake my head quickly. "No, never. But I want to, I think, with you."

Nolan surges to kiss me again, less of a kiss and more of a branding. His lips say I belong to him, that I'm his, and he's mine, and that I can trust him with my body, just like he trusts me with his.

I fall back onto the bed, and Nolan follows me down, blanketing me with his warm body. His kiss slows until it feels like his mouth is making love to mine. I feel heat all over just from his touch, from his closeness. Nolan leans back on his knees to peel off his shirt and sweater and he gently helps me out of my own.

"Wait!"

Nolan freezes like a deer in headlights. "What?"

"Well... I was jogging... and stuff and I don't know. Can I shower first? This is kind of a big deal and I want..."

Nolan kisses me again, this time hard, tongue dipping into my mouth. He pulls away to pant harshly against my neck. "You can take a fucking shower, Jesus, Benji. Go on. I can't come with you or I'll eat you alive."

"Okay! Okay." I run to the bathroom and take the fastest,

most thorough shower of my life. When I return back into the bedroom, damp and nude, my breath catches in my lungs at the sight of Nolan, gloriously naked on the bed, laid out before me. Miles and miles of skin that I know just as well as the back of my own hand.

Nolan tilts his head to the side, his hand circling his dick as he licks his lips. "Well, get on the bed, stud."

Jesus fuck. I'd expected to be more nervous, but there's no room for nerves in the bedroom with Nolan. We've tried everything and been through so much that somewhere in my head, this just felt like the natural progression. We're safe with one another. I lie down on the bed beside him, and he leans over me to kiss me softly, just the hint of a kiss. But I want and need so much more. Finally giving in to the impulse from earlier, I tangle my fingers in his hair and tug him closer, eating at his mouth until he's feeding me his moans.

Nolan breaks from my lips to kiss down my chest, tongue licking over my skin and making me squirm. Without any warning, he swallows my cock down, and I arch off the bed in surprise. Fuck, he has an incredible mouth. When a lubed finger swipes across my entrance, I instinctively clench and glance down at Nolan.

Nolan pops off my cock, lips shiny, eyes bright. "Trust me, Benji."

I nod rapidly and lean back again, closing my eyes with a sigh when he takes me back into his mouth. My gut tightens and pleasure curls at the base of my spine as Nolan licks around my head. I don't even notice that he's added a finger; it just feels full, feels like—

"Oh my God!" I shout as he finds my prostate. Holy fuck.

Nolan grins around my cock and continues to take me

apart. Sweat dots my hairline as I tangle my fingers in the messy blankets between us. I bend my knees so I can fuck against his hand, needing more, needing something I don't know how to ask for. Finally, just when I'm about to come, Nolan pulls off my cock to slide up my body. His fingers are still curled inside me, just now gently pressing against my prostate, making my toes curl and feet tingle. Fuck.

He gently kisses my temple, nose nudging against my sweaty hair. "I'm scared I won't do it right."

I wrap my arms around his middle, holding him close, feeling his heartbeat against my chest. We lie there, joined together, as Nolan gathers his courage. I don't know what to say or how to tell him that he could do it *all* wrong, and it would probably still be the most beautiful experience of my life.

"It's just us, Nolan. It's us."

Nolan nods against my head and pulls away to lean back on his haunches between my spread thighs. He stares at my hole as he covers his cock with lube, his fingers swiping over the swollen head. When he lies back down over me, flushed skin so hot against mine, it feels like some sort of benediction. I see forever in his eyes when our gazes meet. His palm slides down my thigh to lift my leg higher up to rest over his shoulder.

I feel so splayed open and vulnerable that, for a moment, my head spins. Is this how Nolan feels every time I fuck him? Nolan's other hand comes up to cup my face, his gaze staring straight through me.

"It's us, Benji." Nolan notches his cock against my entrance, just barely pushing the tip in. I breathe through it, staring so deeply into Nolan's eyes that I wonder if he can see every single one of my inner thoughts. He slides in slowly, waiting for me to adjust, giving me the time to accept all of him.

Once inside, his elbows fall to the bed, and he pants above me, pupils so wide that his eyes look like the night sky in winter. For a few long minutes, we just stare at one another, the special moment between us frozen, suspended precariously in time. Then he moves, and we both groan at the dual sensations. I reverently run my hands over his back, finally letting my fingers tangle in the sweaty curls at the nape of Nolan's neck.

"Is it good? Okay?" Nolan asks, out of breath.

I pull his head down to press our foreheads together. "It's good, Nolan. Now make love to me."

He kisses me then, soft and slow, and I gasp into his mouth when he makes a particularly hard thrust. I don't think we'll be switching it up all that often, but for now, it feels important to have this with Nolan. Have this closeness that promises something I'm not sure words from me will ever say. Nolan curls an arm behind my neck and reaches the other hand between us to take my cock in hand. I try to tip my head back at the perfect feeling but Nolan lifts his arm so that I have to hold his gaze.

Our eyes stay locked as he fucks into me over and over, his hand working magic on my cock, until pleasure blossoms in my stomach, my toes curl, and my release shoots out of me as I gasp with pleasure. Nolan groans deep and low, and I feel him come inside me, warmth spilling out of me. Fuck. He falls on top of me and lazily lifts his head to kiss me with every ounce of love he can muster.

"Benji," Nolan murmurs reverently against my lips. "I'm gonna play you a song right now, and don't be fucking weird about it."

"While you're still inside me?" I ask, just a little concerned.

Nolan chuckles against my neck, planting a sweet, warm kiss to where my pulse pounds. "No, I'm gonna stay here for a minute. Wanna remember this forever."

I press my face into his curls, inhaling the scent of him. He feels different in my arms. The weight he's been carrying for a year doesn't seem to be there anymore, but it's been replaced with something else. Maybe healing is just as heavy as pain. But if I can help him work through it and come out the other side, then maybe we can have a chance to grab the life I can so easily envision for us. A nice house on a few acres where we can watch the sunset as Nolan plays a new song for me. More laughter lines will fill his face because I'll make him laugh every chance I get, every moment, every single second of our life together.

Nolan pulls out of me slowly, and I fight a wince, but he sees it, because he knows, just like I always know. I lie still and let him care for me, just like he always lets me care for him. There's a catharsis in allowing him to care for me and repeat the motions that I always so tenderly go through for him. His eyes are warm and loving as he traces a towel over my skin, his fingers following the path. Once I'm clean to his satisfaction, he leans down to kiss me again, his fingers cupped behind my ear in a way that makes goose bumps break out over my skin.

"Thank you, Benji," Nolan whispers against my mouth. The thing is, I don't think he's thanking me for the fuck, I think he's thanking me for more than I can ever really know.

"It's okay, Nolan."

Nolan nods once, then rolls to a stand. He holds his hand out for me to take, and he pulls me up, then tenderly dresses me in a clean pair of discarded gym shorts from the floor. He hustles me into the living room and firmly presses me down to sit on the couch. I watch as he moves around the room, a pair of sweatpants slung low on his slim hips. That damn Grim Reaper stares back at me, but the meaning of it feels a little different now. Maybe instead of the Grim Reaper reaching for Nolan, he's pushing everyone away because he knows it's not Nolan's time. It's my time now, my time with Nolan.

A few seconds later, Nolan's sitting cross-legged on the floor in front of me, guitar in his lap, and eyes steadfastly caught on the neck of the guitar as he plays a few chords. He still has one of the most beautiful voices I've ever heard in my life. Angels weep when he opens his mouth. Nolan might not be able to look at me, might not be able to say the words, but he's saying them in song. My heart catches in my chest as he gets to the end, the chords slow and steady as his gorgeous voice just slightly trembles. It's a love song for *me*.

Nolan trails off slowly, throat bobbing as he swallows. His fingers slowly unfurl from the neck of the guitar as he lifts his gaze to mine, his eyes full of so much longing that my own heart echoes it back.

I fall to my knees from the couch and crawl toward him. His gaze is so fucking dark, cheeks slightly flushed with embarrassment, or maybe want, but I have to let him know it's okay. I carefully take the guitar from his grip because I know he loves it more than he'll ever love me. Once the guitar is safely nestled against the sofa, I place my hand on his crossed legs and lean into his face.

"Thank you, Nolan," I tell him firmly, squeezing his thighs hard. "I love you. I'm not going anywhere, okay? I won't leave you. Not unless you want me to leave."

Nolan closes his eyes tight, and a tear slips out. "I don't think I'll ever want you to leave. You're"—he presses his hand to his chest with a grimace—"in here now... you're in here, and I want to keep you forever."

"You can keep me. I'm yours."

He opens his eyes back up to stare at me with those deep black eyes. "I don't want to hurt you, Benji."

"We'll hurt one another. But I want to keep you, want you to keep me, and I want to make you laugh and hold you on bad days. Okay?"

Nolan sighs, bone-weary and exhausted, and he slumps against me as I wrap my arms around him.

"Okay, Benji. We can keep each other."

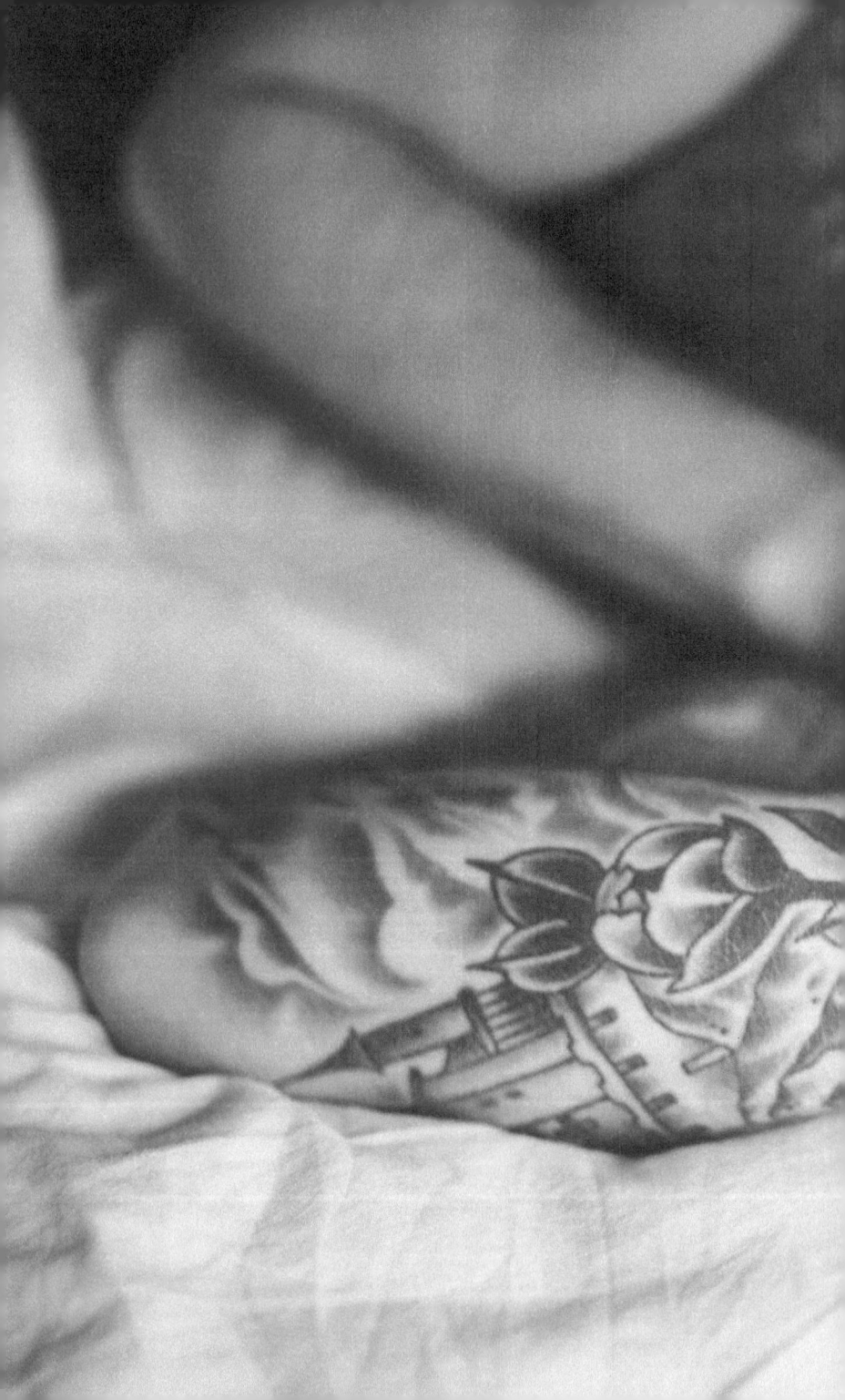

16

NOLAN

FEBRUARY 2028

"So when you're out on the stage, you disassociate?" Maggie, my therapist, asks as if we have not gone over this a million fucking times already.

"Yes," I say through gritted teeth.

She smiles benignly at me. "Nolan, when else do you disassociate?"

I clench and unclench my hands to contain the rage. "Only on stage."

"Never any time else?"

I stare at her for a few moments before flushing and looking away. "Sometimes during sex, that's why... That's why I liked the pain element. Because it would stop me from doing that so much and keep me in the moment. And then, of course when someone gives me negative feedback... there's this loop in my head sometimes that if someone hates something I've created, or if they have a suggestion, it feels like they're telling me I'm a useless piece of shit, I should kill myself."

"And the loop in your head, you disassociate..."

I nod even though it annoys me. "Yes, sometimes."

"We haven't talked much about your childhood yet. I know that in your own words, your parents dropped you off at your grandma's as a child and then left. They never came back?"

"No," I say firmly because I hate my parents. "Not even when Grandma died."

"But you know they're alive?"

I shrug. "I assume so. I've never checked. Both of them were addicts, and I think my mom took pills while pregnant... it was a fucking mess. Grandma loved me; she tried her best, but she was already retired and on a fixed income, and she had another mouth to feed. Then she died when I was a teen."

"What sort of memories do you have of your parents?"

I try to rack my brain of memories, but truly, there aren't many. Even as a kid, I could tell my mother never really wanted me, she wanted the drugs more. She kept me clothed and fed, but that was about it. I remember being home alone when I was six years old because I was scared shitless when it rained that night. I told Grandma about it a few days later, and she argued with my mother; then, a week later, I'd been dropped off like a sack of potatoes because I was too annoying to care for. Remembering my father is a little more difficult. I remember dark curls like mine and his hand shaking when he was asleep on the trailer's ratty couch.

"Not many. She wasn't around much, even when I lived with her."

"Was she nice?"

I shrug again. "I don't remember."

"And the homes you were in from sixteen to eighteen, what were they like?"

"Group homes," I answer.

"And were they healthy?"

"Well," I drawl as I cross my legs and lean back on the sofa. "The older boys didn't take too well to a gay kid that preferred to play guitar suddenly being added to the home. They liked to jump me when I was asleep."

"That sounds awful. Were you hurt?"

I shrug because it doesn't matter anymore. "I'm here, aren't I?"

Maggie smiles sweetly, I scrunch my nose up as I stare at her. "Being here now doesn't negate old pain."

This is all old news. "You could just google all of this, you know. It's out there for everyone to know."

Maggie blinks slowly at me again. "Why would I google my client? You're here in front of me, in that seat; I want to learn about you from you."

"No one ever wants to learn about me from me."

"Is that true for Benji? Harper? Trevor?"

Ugh. She's so annoying. "No, Maggie. Obviously, it's not true for them," I snipe at her.

"Do you think you've got a solid group of friends now that care about you and your well-being? And Chris, obviously, he cares for you."

"I acknowledge that they care for me. Does that make you happy?"

"Does it make you happy?"

My eye twitches at her question. Letting Benji in, letting him really *see* me has been one of the hardest things I'll ever do. Now that he's told me he loves me, and I serenaded him like a total fucking goof, I don't think there's any going back. Why does he want me? I'll never know and I'll never understand, but for some weird reason, he does. He makes me feel happy and safe, and makes me feel alive. After so many years of feeling dead, it's a huge change for me.

"It makes me happy that they think I'm worth all this, that Benji's pure, joyful self sees something in me worth loving."

"What do you think he sees that's worth loving?"

I close my eyes tight as my heart almost pounds out of my chest. "I think he just sees me."

———

THE SUN IS bright as hell when I step out of the therapist's office. As always, Benji's leaning against the borrowed truck, waiting for me to return to him. His smile goes loopy and warm when he spots me, and he opens his arms to let me walk right into them.

"Wanna have lunch with the guys?" Benji asks where his face is buried in my hair.

"Where?"

"Trevor and Beau's. It's Wednesday and I guess Beau is off, so Trevor said Beau's grilling some fish he caught with Lee over the weekend."

"So many words," I tease.

Benji's chuckle is warm and vibrates through me as I clutch him tighter. "Up for it?"

"Mmmm, I guess. I want to go back to the apartment first and change."

Benji's hands sneak under my hoodie, well, his hoodie actually, and rest against the cold skin at the small of my back. "I like it when you wear my hoodie."

"'Cause you're a caveman."

"'Cause you're mine."

I sigh against his cheek, pulling away with a teasing smile. "Take me home."

The drive back to the apartment is quiet, but Benji keeps his hand firmly on my thigh, squeezing every now and then to remind me that I'm not alone. He doesn't need to reassure me though. I know in my bones, because he's a part of me now, buried so deep that I think if we tried to extricate ourselves from one another, the entire universe might implode. Stardust and all that shit, that's what Benji and I are made of.

There's a new car parked in front of Colby and Eli's house when we roll by toward the mother-in-law suite. I crane my neck to look behind Benji toward the house, this weird, sinking feeling like lead in the pit of my stomach. Hopping out of the truck, I walk toward Colby and Eli's house slowly, with Benji following along behind me.

The front door opens and Chris walks out, hand held to his eyes to blink at me in the bright sun. "Hey, kid."

My heart falls out of my chest. "I'm fucked, aren't I?"

Chris smiles slightly, but it's off. "Let's talk." He glances behind me at Benji, I presume. "Bring Benji. Colby and Eli said we can sit out on their back porch for a while."

"I was supposed to have lunch... with friends."

Eli pops out around Chris with a pitying smile. "I'll bring some fish back for you! Don't worry about it!"

I turn around to glance at Benji to find him mouthing *thank you* toward Eli. Benji lifts his hand and I tangle our fingers together, needing the strength of him more than ever right now. When I turn back, I stare at Chris, hoping maybe I can parse the reason he's here just by the odd slant of his mouth, or even the absence of the glint in his eyes.

Eli bounds down the steps past us, squeezing my arm

gently as he goes by to hop into the Jeep in the driveway. The crunch of gravel reaches my ears, but my gaze is caught on Chris as he walks back into the house. Everything feels heavy and slow as I follow him. We all sit down in the chairs on the raised back porch that overlooks the gentle hills beyond, but tension fills the air.

Chris sighs deeply, his salt-and-pepper beard the thickest I've ever seen. "I've been trying real hard the past few weeks, Nolan, to try to work out a deal that will be best for you."

"They want me back on tour?"

Chris winces. "They want *a* tour."

I rub at my chest. "I can't go back on stage. It's... what's killing me. I can't. I want to make music, I want to share it with the world, but I can't tour. I just can't. I own my songs, they can't make me."

Chris leans forward a little, eyebrows furrowed. "You'd still make music? You just don't want to tour?"

I shake my head furiously, nauseous just at the idea. "I never want to tour again. I'll make a million albums, I just can't commit to a tour. Unless... they let me do dive bars. But the arenas and stadiums? Those days are long over. I want a quieter life. I want to *live*."

Benji squeezes my fingers tight and I turn my head to look at him. My favorite smile is tugging at his lips, and his cheeks have a splash of crimson on them. Maybe everything I said was more profound to him than any *I love you* could ever be. Just the acknowledgment that I want the life we're building together, just us. Well. I can give him that, I think.

"I want to stay here with Benji. I'll record music at a studio here, but that's my line. No more tours. I don't care if they sue me... if they say I'm a piece of shit. I don't care, Chris. I can't..." My throat itches with the urge to cry. I lean forward to brace my elbows against my knees as I cover my face. "Chris, I have to fucking stand up for myself one time in my life. You have to help me do this. I can't go back, it'll kill me. You know how much it kills me. I can't, please."

It's not Benji's arms that wrap around me, but Chris's. Warm and solid and he smells like every good memory I've ever had since I started this terrifying journey. The only person who's ever stuck up for me has been Chris. The only person who's ever worried for me before Benji and my newfound family was Chris. I hold on to him as hard as I can, crying into his neck as he shushes me like he probably does his own children.

Once I stop sobbing, Chris pulls away to clutch my face hard. "I'll make your dreams come true. I always do, don't I? They can demand a tour all they want, but I'll make it happen for you. Make you happy. I want to see you happy, so much. Nolan, I..." Chris clears his throat awkwardly as tears gather in his eyes. "You're like one of my own. Seeing you... like that always killed me. And you look so happy here, you're healing. I won't let them take that away from you. I'll get the lawyers involved and we'll draw something new up. You'll start a new life here, and you'll be happy. Promise me you'll be happy?"

I wipe my runny nose against my arm and give him a trembling smile. "I'm going to fucking try so hard, Chris."

Chris clears his throat again before pressing a hard kiss to my forehead. "Let me call the label. I'm going to stay in town until I figure this shit out. But I'll stay out of your hair."

"Wait!" I yell as he stands up. He looks down at me in confusion, glancing between me and Benji. "Maybe... maybe the three of us can get dinner sometime. Just, no work shit. Just... us."

Chris's lips turn up in a beaming smile. "I'd love that, kid." He pats my head once, then sighs softly. "I'm staying at a hotel in Orlando. I'll see what I can do over the next few days. But now that I know what you really want, I have something to work with." He starts to walk away, then pauses, turning to look back at me. "They wanted to force you back on tour with a therapist and shit. I told them to go fuck themselves, that's what I came here to tell you."

The minute Chris is out of sight, I fucking lose my shit. Like always, Benji's there to hold me together when I feel like I'm going to fall the fuck apart. I can't say how long we sit there with me sobbing and Benji cradling me against his chest, murmuring things I can't even make out, but know they're probably the most comforting words in the entire world. Everything about Benji is a comfort. Strong and solid, the wall that holds me up when the entire world tries to beat me down.

"Benji," I say, voice shaking.

"Yeah, angel?"

"I'm in love with you."

Benji pulls away to cup my cheeks between his palms, his thumbs sliding under my eyes to wipe away my years. His eyes are so vivid and bright that it's like looking into a perfectly cloudless sky, or the lightest Caribbean water in the world.

"I'm in love with you too. Deeply and darkly." He brushes a soft kiss to my mouth that holds more weight than any word he could ever say. "Two halves of the same whole, you and I. Just us."

"Just us," I repeat as I lean hard against his body again.

The sun hangs low in the sky by the time Eli returns, but this time he isn't alone. Trevor, Beau, Jackson, and Harper follow along behind him out onto the porch. Eli smiles shyly at me as he sets a covered plate of food down on the table in front of us.

"We thought maybe you could use some friends," Eli says sweetly. "So we brought food and ourselves."

I'm going to fucking cry again. Jesus. Benji squeezes my neck hard as I dip my head so that they all can't see how much it means to me.

"So, about that foursome," Jackson says awkwardly, breaking a loud laugh out of me. I laugh so hard that I snort, covering my mouth with my hand as the giggles erupt out of me. Soon everyone is laughing, even stoic, usually quiet Beau.

"Benji?" I ask quietly.

"Yeah?"

I lean forward to kiss his cheek. "Will you go grab my guitar?"

Benji's grin is wide and warm, without a word he disappears around the house like the doting lover he is for me. Harper takes the empty seat vacated by Benji.

"On a scale of wanting to die to life is grand, what are we feeling today?" Harper asks, eyes glinting with mischief.

"A warm hot dog at a baseball game," I answer honestly.

Harper whistles happily and elbows me in the ribs. "You're feeling good!" Harper leans forward to grab the plate off the table, removing the tin foil from the top. Crispy fish, some sort of mixed rice, and the biggest-looking cupcake I've ever seen. "Beau grills the best fish. The cupcake is from Bee's, my favorite, the double chocolate."

I swallow hard at the sight of the offering. "Thank you."

Harper waves off my gratitude. "I know what it's like to

need help, but fucking hating to ask for it. Also, it was mostly Eli."

Benji returns with my guitar case in tow and stows it behind the couch. He dips down to kiss my forehead, before heading over to sit beside Jackson. I dig into the still warm food, letting it settle in my belly and in my bones. It's nice to be cared for, even if I'm not quite used to it.

Once I'm finished with the food, I set the plate on the table, and sit back on the couch with Harper beside me. I busy myself with getting my guitar out of the case for a little while, ignoring the fact that the others are more than likely watching me.

"Still wanna sing some Hannah Montana?"

Harper's grin could power entire cities. "Nah. Let's sing one of your favorites."

"You probably won't know it."

"I probably will," Harper promises as he shifts closer to me.

Honey settles at his feet, lies down, and rests her head on my foot. When I glance up, Jackson is staring at us with some weird emotion in his eyes that I can't name. Benji practically has hearts in his eyes and I fight the urge to scowl at him. Instead, I smile softly and glance back down to the guitar. The chords are as easy as breathing, I've played this song so many times.

It takes Harper a few moments, but surprisingly he does know the song. That earns him a lot of points in my book. Through the first chorus, I glance up to find Benji singing along as well. And soon everyone is singing along to "Times Like These" by the Foo Fighters. Something inside me clicks into place as we all finish the song. Life is about finding your people, finding your home, and somehow I totally lucked out with this group of men who have accepted me as their own. And I've somehow lucked out with Benji.

Maybe luck has nothing to do with it. For once in my life, maybe the universe took pity on me and gave me something good to hold on to for myself.

As we all finish, Jackson cups his hands around his mouth and shouts. "'Free Bird!'"

Benji shoves Jackson's head so hard it looks painful. "Fucking idiot."

"It's a good song!"

"My boyfriend isn't playing 'Free Bird.'"

"How about 'Landslide'?" I call out, and everyone grins and smiles.

———

It's full dark by the time we head back to the garage apartment. Benji flips some of the lights on and stows my guitar back in the living room. I watch the long, strong line of his back move under his shirt, watch the way his shoulders bunch as he stands to turn around, to watch me in the soft, warm light of the lamps.

He slowly crosses the space between us to stand in front of me, like a gift from the gods. I reach for him and he tugs me into his arms, where I'm held and safe and no longer so very alone.

He smells like he always does, like sunshine, strength, and like maybe he stole a spray of my cologne this morning. Maybe his caveman tendencies are wearing off on me because I like that he smells like me. I like that I'm a part of him and that he'll never shake me loose, never be free of me.

"I want to build a life here with you," I tell him quietly, my voice so soft that even I barely hear it.

"Angel, what do you think we've been doing since we came here? We've already started."

"Yeah?"

Benji nods and presses a kiss to my temple. "Yeah. Wanna build a home with me too? Maybe get a dog that'll go on runs with me and keep me out of your hair when you need to write a song?"

Warmth fills my chest as I picture it. A farmhouse on a couple of acres with a fire pit out back. A house full of love and photos of Benji and me from our escapades around the world when we get the urge and decide to travel somewhere new. Waking up every morning tangled with Benji, being kissed by him whenever he wants. Breakfast in bed as I write a new song from the comfort of our messy sheets that smell like *us*.

"Yeah, Benji, I want all of that."

Benji squeezes me tighter as he says, "I'll give you the world, angel."

And I know without a doubt that he's telling the truth.

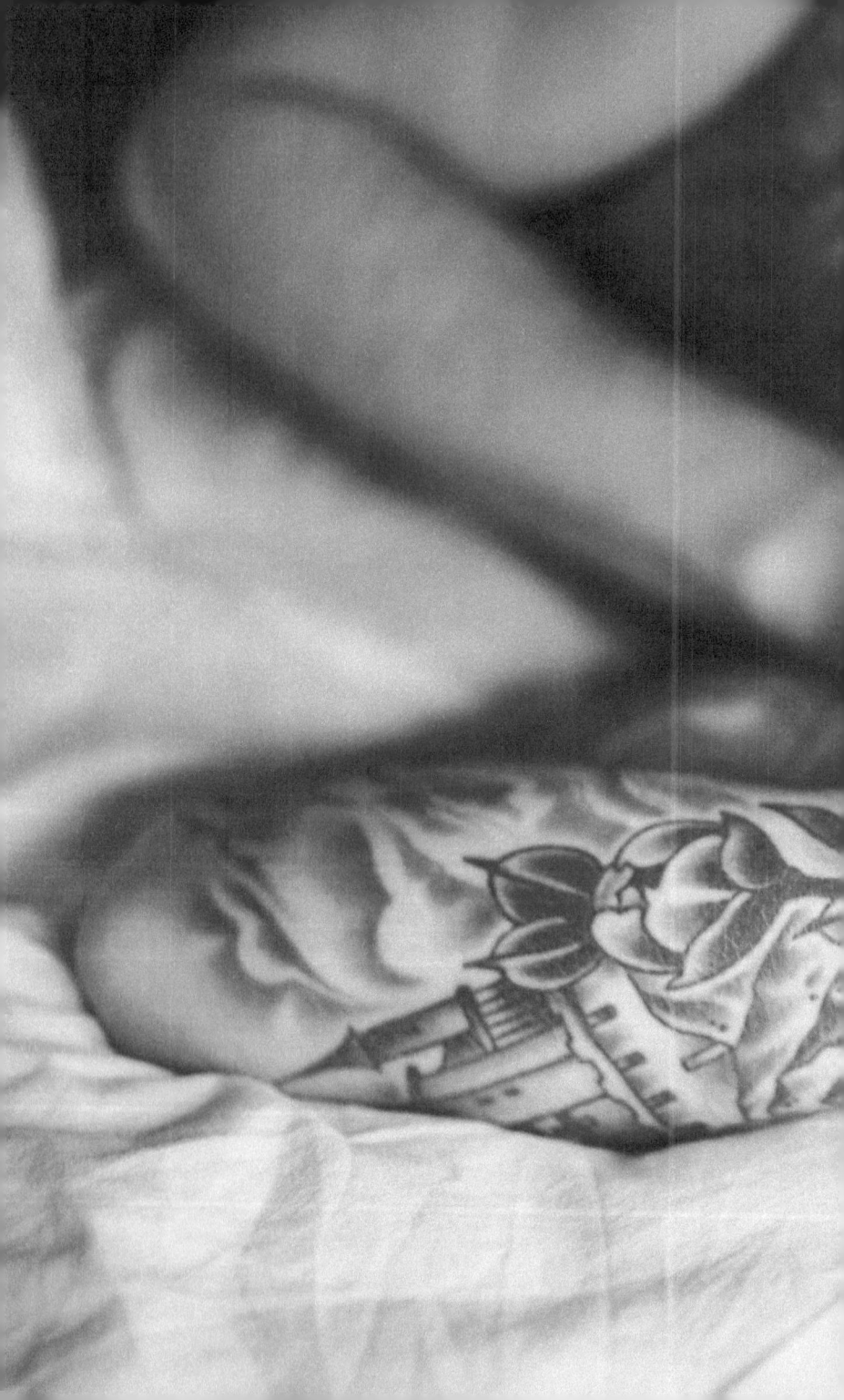

17

BENJI

FEBRUARY 2028

I should've known a care package from my moms wouldn't just show up at the front door in a nice little box with a bow. Nolan is still sleeping at noon on a Saturday when a knock comes at the door. I tug on the hoodie that was tossed across the island last night after Nolan gave me the greatest blowjob of my life, my hands gripping the granite like a man possessed.

And all thoughts of the most amazing blowjob of my life disappear in a wisp of smoke when I open the door to find my moms on the other side. Mama is standing with her hand over her eyes surveying the scenery and Mom is chattering about *perfect soil for citrus, oh my*.

"Moms?"

Mama spins around with one of her warm, affectionate grins. "Mijo! Sweetheart. Hi. We just..." She pauses, looks over to Mom with a soft smile. "We just really wanted to see you."

"You drove six hours to hug me?"

"We'd fly to the moon to hug you," Mom says seriously as she steps forward to do just that.

Her hug feels like safety, and warmth, and bandages on bruised knees. I breathe the scent of her in, the same perfume she's worn since I can remember, and the incense she's always burning when she meditates. She smells like home. Well, halfway like home. The rockstar still sleeping soundly in my bed smells more like home these days than anything else.

But no matter how big I get, I still feel like a child held in her arms.

Mama joins the hug and suddenly the universe doesn't feel so big or scary anymore. They whisper soothing words into my hair as they hold me close. I realize then that I'm crying and I pull away with a small laugh.

Wiping at my tears, I stare at both of them in confusion. "I don't have anywhere for you to stay..."

"Nonsense," Mama says with a wave of her elegant hand. "We've got a hotel in Orlando. Mom wants to go to the theme parks."

That stops me. "You want to go to a theme park? My anti-capitalist mom?"

Mom sniffs delicately. "I just figured while we're here, we might as well."

A noise behind me has me turning around to find Nolan standing awkwardly at the edge of the living room, my extra-large sweatshirt hanging off his thin frame. He looks so unsure, so off-footed, that I can't help but cross the room to tug him against my side.

"Moms, this is Nolan." I turn my head to look at Nolan with a tender smile that he tries very hard to match. "He's my..." I pause and stare down at Nolan. There's no word that really describes him. Nothing is enough, everything is too little. "He's mine."

My hopeless romantic mom sighs and steps forward to take Nolan in a tight hug. Nolan stands frozen, his arms hanging loose at his sides, until finally his brain kicks in and he tentatively returns the embrace. She whispers something in his ear that I can't make out. I watch as Mom tugs Nolan into the living room, her fingers tightly holding on to his own. My heart does this weird drop and roll in my chest at the sight of them together.

"I think maybe they're kindred souls," Mama says quietly from beside me.

I tip my head to look over at her. "I think so too, Mama. I think the universe wanted me and him to meet very badly."

"The universe is very magical in that way. It knows what we need more than what we want."

"I agree." I clear my throat softly as I turn to look at her fully. "I think I'm going to stay here. It's good for him. When he needs to travel somewhere, I'll go with him. But I spent so long looking for my place, needing to know where I belong, and I think all along I belonged with him. Is that crazy?"

Mama cups my cheek and presses a soft kiss to my temple. "No, love. He's the other half of your soul, just like Mom is for me. When you find that missing piece, you grab on and never let go. Do you think he'll lead you anywhere good?"

My throat dries and my heart races at her question. "I think he'll lead me somewhere great."

Her smile is simmering and kind, and her hug is like the sun. By the time they leave to go back to their hotel, I think Mama was right, and that Nolan and my mom were also made to find each other. Nolan and I stand on the balcony and watch their car peel away to Orlando, with promises of a dinner before they return home to Georgia in a week.

"That's what it's like?" Nolan asks quietly, voice small and frail.

"What?"

Nolan reaches out to grip the edge of my hoodie, the tops of his fingers trailing over the warm skin of my hips. "That's what it's like to have parents?"

"Yeah, angel. They're yours now too."

A tear slips down his cheek when his eyes shut tight, so I tug him close to hold him against my chest.

———

NOLAN IS OFF WITH HARPER, so I do the only thing I know to do. I go for a run. February in Florida is either freezing cold or almost spring. Luckily, today the air is just cool enough to keep me comfortable as I jog along the back roads of Clay Springs. My feet pound the pavement and my heart races as I run, run, and *run* until all the thoughts in my head are silent. Just me and the road. I run for long enough that my muscles ache and I know it's time to slow down. Instead of taking the turn back to the apartment, I turn down the gravel driveway that leads toward Beau and Trevor's place.

Beau's work truck sits outside, alerting me to the fact they're both home. Laughter from the backyard has me walking slowly that way, huffing and puffing as I do my best to catch my breath. I must look a total sight because Trevor sits up from the hammock with a slightly frightened look.

"Jesus! Are you okay?" Trevor calls out.

"Oh." I wince awkwardly. "I was just jogging."

"Christ," Trevor swears again and presses the heel of his

palm to his forehead. "I thought maybe... God." He turns toward Beau with a high-pitched laugh.

I watch awkwardly as Beau smiles softly and rubs at Trevor's back. Oh. He probably thought...

"Sorry," I apologize quickly, taking an awkward step closer. "Nolan's fine."

"Right," Trevor says quickly. He stands from the hammock, pats Beau's stomach, then heads inside without a backward glance.

"I fucked up."

Beau grunts and lies back down in the hammock, his big body swaying it dangerously. "Nah, he's just had a busy day. What brought you over?"

"Oh, I was just jogging and turned this way instead of going home..."

Beau raises one eyebrow. "Do you need a job? I can put you to work."

I toss myself down on the plush grass. Picking some of the green strands from the earth, I tear them apart in my hands as I continue to cool down from my run. Maybe I do need a job. Maybe I need to go back to school. It's hard to focus on myself when I'm still so worried about Nolan.

"I dropped out of college," I tell Beau without looking up. He's silent, so I keep picking at the grass. "I wasn't ever really good at learning. I'm not the smart kind, you know? I'm funny and good looking and steady, but that's about it. But Jackson mentioned maybe cooking school would be good for me? I think maybe that's a good idea. But I want a job too. A real one, not that sex work isn't real, it is, but I just..." I trail off and finally look up at Beau. He's staring at me like I imagine he'd stare at a pacing lion, slightly worried, but wondering what the hell I'm thinking.

"You're allowed to start over too," Beau says matter-of-factly. "Not just Nolan."

Well. He's right. "I've always taken care of someone else."

"You're no good to Nolan unless you take care of yourself too. There's a culinary school in Orlando, Joey can probably get you in pretty quickly. And if you want a job while you're in school, Joey always needs more help at the truck."

"Oh, the guy in the food truck?"

Beau sits up slightly to fix me with a hard gaze. "I'm thinking of opening a restaurant on the property. Joey doesn't know that yet though. If you're gonna stay here, gonna make a living that way, you could have a place at the farm. If you wanted it."

"I want!" I yell and sit up on my knees. "I want," I repeat slowly when Beau looks slightly frightened. "I want it a lot. Please."

Beau situates himself back in the hammock with a sigh. "I'll talk to Joey. Go inside and check on Trevor for me, would you?"

Beau promptly tangles his fingers atop his chest, closes his eyes, and seems to fall asleep. Alright. I stand from the ground, dusting the dirt and grass off my legs, then meander toward the house. Trevor's standing just inside with a mug of tea between his palms. His smile is tremulous and small, but I try to settle him with a grin of my own.

"Do we need to have a talk now, too? You're the last one I haven't had a talk with," I tell Trevor as I take a seat at the dining table.

Trevor quietly joins me, then stares down at the table. "I care about Nolan."

"I know."

Trevor takes shaky breaths as he rubs his finger around

the rim of the tea. I wait him out, not wanting to rush him, but knowing we've been needing to have this conversation for a while.

"He and I... I wish I could've seen what you see in him. Not romantically. But I feel like shit that he was hurting so badly and I didn't see... I was hurting so badly too." Trevor pauses and squeezes his eyes shut tightly, before lifting his head to stare at me. "He needed you, I'm glad you gave him what he needed to feel safe."

I reach out to take his hand in mine. "You didn't do anything wrong with him. You gave him what he asked for, right? I gave him what he needed, he just didn't know *what* he needed."

Trevor hums thoughtfully. "You're happy?"

I grin. "Very, when he lets me love him. How's Claire?"

Trevor sighs loudly. "She's fine." Trevor flips his hand over to cup my palm in his own. "She's got no boys to do their jobs anymore. She's out of business."

"Eh, she should become a realtor."

Trevor laughs and leans forward to envelop me in his arms. I bury my face in his blond waves, smiling when I realize he smells different, like outside and engine grease. We've all changed more than we'll ever know thanks to Clay Springs.

"Beau just told me he'll get me a job at the farm," I whisper into Trevor's hair.

Trevor's laughter echoes through me. "He's been trying to put my friends to work for a while, so you probably just made his day."

———

BECAUSE THE WORLD continues to work in mysterious ways, Chris calls us and asks us to meet him at a restaurant a few days later to discuss the final deal he's made with the label. Nolan is restless, radiating nervous energy beside me in the truck. I need to buy us our own car since we've decided to settle here. Actually, doesn't Nolan have one back in Los Angeles?

"Nolan."

"Benjamin," Nolan says with a curl of his lip.

"Can we get your car brought here? And what do you want to do about your house in LA?"

Nolan wrinkles his nose up as he thinks. I have to curl my hands tight against the steering wheel to resist the urge to pinch his cheeks. He'd probably punch me in the jaw if I did.

"Yeah, I'll mention the car to Chris. He kind of handles everything about my life. I haven't done much for myself in a long time."

Doesn't surprise me. "The house?"

"I kind of want to keep it. It was the first thing I bought myself... means something to me." Nolah sighs loudly and rolls his eyes. "Plus, I assume sometimes we'll have to go to LA for meetings with the label. Even just to have it out there for us, is nice."

"Good with me."

"But a house here is what I want... Harper said Beau's family has some spare land that butts up to the river that they'll sell us for cheap. We could wake up every morning with a view of the water. But Harper also said that means maybe gators... I don't know."

"Whatever you want, Nolan. We'll do whatever makes you happy."

Nolan turns in the seat to face me fully, eyes calculating and hard. "I want what you want too. What do you want?"

I shrug as I pull off the expressway heading toward downtown. "I'm a simple guy. I want you, a bed, a roof over my head, and a fucking golden retriever that you name something stupid like Izzy or Slash."

"Slash is a shepherd name, how dare you."

"Izzy?"

He considers it for a moment before nodding. "Could work."

"So house first? Then dog?"

"Dog first," Nolan admits quietly, sounding awfully shy. "I think a dog would be good for me."

"I think so too. I mean, I'm basically a dog and I'm great for you."

"You're an idiot."

"You love me."

Nolan swallows loudly and looks away before quietly murmuring, "God help me, but I do."

"I think I'm going to go to culinary school," I say without looking over at Nolan.

It's silent for a little while before Nolan reaches over to tangle his fingers with mine. "Good, I think that would be great for you. Is Beau going to put you to work at the farm?"

I snort. "Obviously."

"I'm proud of you, Benji. You tell me what you need, and I'll do my best to give it to you, okay? This works both ways."

I stay quiet as I park in the parking garage downtown, only speaking once we've stopped.

"I love you."

Nolan smiles gently. "I know. I love you too."

"Everything's going to be alright, no matter what Chris says. Okay?"

Nolan's eye twitches at the corner, but he nods in agreement. If I say it enough, maybe he'll believe it.

Nolan keeps his head ducked down as we pass by strangers on the street. I curl my arm around his shoulders, splaying my palm over his racing heart. Every time he leans against me, accepting my strength, it feels like the biggest win in the book.

The restaurant is quiet, with wood accents, and steampunk lights along the ceiling. Chris is already seated in a private booth in the back, and the hostess leads us to him, all while sneaking surreptitious glances at Nolan. This is why I love Clay Springs, because no one there blinks twice at Nolan, not like in the cities.

Chris stands to hug Nolan, and I shake his hand with a grateful smile.

Once we're all seated, Chris smiles across the table and curls one hand around his ice water that's dripping with condensation.

"Good news or bad news first?"

"Bad," Nolan replies instantly.

Chris lifts his other hand to thoughtfully scratch his now full beard. "They won't commit to no tour forever, but they have for the next three years. No tour. They'll let you release an album without a tour, limited promo, to see if it's worth it for them."

"Alright," Nolan says, sounding unsure.

"Good news is that they won't sue you for dropping out of this tour. Insurance covers it and they had a lot on you considering... everything." Chris doesn't have to say it, all of us know. He sits forward a little. "But I also got them to agree to let you record here, instead of in LA."

Nolan's mouth falls open in surprise. "What?"

Chris raps the table with his knuckles. "Whatever house you build here, better include a studio. You'll need to hire engineers and we'll have to get Tyler out here for production, but you're clear to record the next album here."

"And what did they think about small venue tours? When I'm ready?" Nolan pauses and looks over at me. "If I'm ever ready."

"We'll consider it at that time."

"When's the next album due? I mean, I've already got one out there that's just maybe six months old."

Chris stares at Nolan for a heavy moment before leaning forward. "Kid. This is on your timeline. Do you understand what I'm telling you? You're free. Make music when you want. They're being stupid about the three-year timeline and nothing will come of it. Plain and simple, make music, and you never have to tour again if you don't want to. Get it now?"

Nolan falls back against the booth, hand pressed to his chest. I rest my hand against his thigh, squeezing just hard enough for him to know I'm here. That I've got his back. His eyes dip to the table for a moment before lifting back to Chris.

"I've never been free."

Chris smiles slowly as he reaches across the table to take Nolan's hand. "You are now."

———

NOLAN IS SOMEHOW EVEN MORE quiet as we drive back home. I can't imagine how he's feeling, to finally be able to do whatever he wants with his life. Not answering to anyone. Not being forced out on a stage for a horse and pony show. All he has to do is wake up, kiss me good morning, then decide what he wants to do for the day. What a life.

An odd sort of tension radiates from Nolan as he climbs the stairs into the apartment. The feeling follows us into the apartment, and eats away at me as I follow him into the bedroom. I stand at the edge of the bedroom, watching him turn in a dizzy circle, before coming to a stop to let his eyes land on me. His hands shake as he lifts them to run through his hair. Fuck.

Nolan lifts his chin to meet my eyes. "I need you to be rough with me tonight."

"Okay," I reply instantly, not wanting him to think for even a second that I'll say no.

"I know you like a softer dynamic... That we don't do it that way anymore. But I think sometimes I'll need it. It helps me... helps my brain. And I talked about it with Maggie and she said as long as we talked it through, that we both consent, that it's okay. Because we're adults, in a healthy relationship."

I blink slowly because those were a lot of words. "Nolan, you know I'll give you anything you need. It's always been that way." I step toward him, and loop my hands around his neck to squeeze. His pulse pounds against my skin, and desire shoots through me. He'll always be everything I want. "Sometimes I'll want to give it to you soft, slow, make you beg for it. Make you feel cherished and loved because you are." I lean forward to breathe the next words into his ear. "But sometimes I'll make it hurt for you because I think some-times we'll both need that too. Huh, angel?"

"Benji," Nolan whimpers.

"It's okay. If we both want it, it's okay."

I try my best to hide my nervousness, to be steady for both of us at this moment. Lifting his hoodie off, then his shirt, I shove him back onto the bed. When I tug my own shirt off, I find his gaze locked on me, heavy and hard like a smack to my face. His stare always carries the weight of a touch. I slowly unbuckle my jeans, watching as his throat bobs the more of me that I reveal. When my cock bobs free after shoving down my jeans and boxers, his gaze lifts back to mine.

"Make me feel it," Nolan demands, voice low and rough.

"Don't I always?"

Nolan nods rapidly as I roughly tug him out of his jeans, making him slide down to the edge of the bed. I lift his legs to my shoulders, running my fingers across the warm skin of his tattooed thighs. Turning my head, I kiss the inside of his knee, then bite down hard until he writhes and moans against me. Yeah, soft is nice, but I fucking love him like this for me. I let my other hand fall to his ass, cupping his cheek for a moment before landing a hard smack.

Nolan basically goes supernova. Head tilted back against the bed, eyes squeezed tightly shut, he's everything beautiful and perfect in this world. At least to me. When I dip my thumb between his crease, my heart pounds, and my jaw clenches to find him already prepped.

"Nolan," I say roughly. "Did you plan this?"

Nolan shakes his head furiously. "I thought maybe I'd need you to fuck me in the bathroom. If the news was bad. I wanted..." He swallows loudly when I dip my thumb inside him. "Wanted to be ready for you to fuck me against the bathroom door. Make me scream and cry."

Jesus Christ. I drop his legs from my shoulders and roughly flip him over. The lube is where it always is these days, under one of our pillows. Nolan pants into the sheets as I lube myself up, barely resisting from just jacking myself until I come all over his back because fuck that Grim Reaper. Nolan is mine. I climb onto the bed behind him and tug him up until he's kneeling too, this way I can wrap my hand around his throat as I fuck him from behind.

He gasps when I notch against his entrance and just push right in, past the resistance, past everything, until I'm almost all the way inside him. Our thighs brush and desire dances right down my spine at the closeness of our bodies. Will he never not make me feel this way? Not make me need so badly I could go mad? Even when I'm fucking him like this, it feels like making love, because no matter how hard I fuck him, it's what we both want, what we need. Every version of fucking with Nolan means more than I can ever say.

Nolan lifts his hand to grip my waist, tugging me closer as his nails dig into my skin. I squeeze his throat and grin against the salty skin of his shoulder as he moans when I thrust all the way in.

"Nolan Hastings, rockstar, known around the world by millions, but he's only ever on his knees for me, only known by me." I turn his head so that I can look into his starry-eyed gaze. "I fucking own you, Nolan. You're mine and no one else's. You belong to me, forever. Right?"

Nolan's grin is terrifying. My toes curl as he leans his forehead against my cheek. "Shut the fuck up and fuck me, Benji. You've owned me for a year now."

Isn't that a kick in the head? I take his mouth in a kiss that steals both of our breaths as I pummel into him. He gasps against my mouth, fingers digging into my side, begging for more, wanting all of me. And I'll give him everything just like I've been giving him everything for months, for almost a goddamn year. I curl my arm around his chest to lay my palm over his heart, letting the hard beat of it course right through me as if we were one person.

My orgasm sneaks up on me, starting at the base of my spine, and coursing all the way down to the tips of my toes. I have just enough presence of mind to sneak my hand down to Nolan's cock. Just as my release rockets through me, painting his insides as *mine*, Nolan comes with a shout, warm all over my hand. We collapse on the bed together in a sweaty heap of tangled limbs.

Nolan pats my cheek fondly, eyes closed with the force of his orgasm. "You've still got it, stud."

Because traditions can't be broken, I carefully help him out of the bed and guide him into the bathroom. As I ready the bath with the lavender bath salts I know he's come to love, I look over my shoulder to find him staring at himself in the mirror. My heart pounds in my chest as he reaches out to touch his reflection. A small smile tugs at his lip for just a moment before he turns to look at me.

"That's me. The real Nolan."

"Yeah, angel. That's you."

Nolan hums softly, then walks over to join me in the tub. I pull him between my legs, letting his back come to rest against my chest. Burying my face in his neck, I breathe him in, settled in the knowledge that he's mine forever, and that we belong to one another.

18

NOLAN

MARCH 2028

"You're really going to stay here? In Clay Springs?" Harper asks with one of his serious little frowns. He's so cute.

"Why not? I like it here. Benji is happy here. I'll probably take him on vacation whenever he wants, wherever he wants, but this is home now." I push my foot on the ground so that the hammock Harper and I are lying in swings a little harder. "You don't want me to stay?"

"Uhm, pause, I didn't say that." Harper reaches down to absentmindedly pat Honey's head. Her vest is off, so I'd given her a few pats earlier, but otherwise she usually just stays hanging out with us wherever we go. "Just weird that a rockstar would choose to stay in my hometown. I've spent so many years thinking of escaping, hard to imagine someone choosing it."

"You want to leave?"

Harper tilts his head down to look at me. "Everywhere with you makes it better."

"Everywhere, huh?"

"So crazy," Harper says around a laugh. "How's therapy?"

"Same old, same old. It's nice to not wake up and want to kill myself."

"Well, that is a positive. Have you thought more about the land offer from Beau? They've got so many acres they can stand to lose a few. And I'm sure you and Benji would like a place of your own."

I guess now's the time to tell Harper. I'm shit at secrets anyway, at least when it comes to him. Who would've thought the redhead from that first night would become one of my best friends? But Harper is Harper. He makes me laugh in a simple way that I can't explain. He makes me forget sometimes that I am who I am. Isn't that what friends are supposed to do?

"I bought the land from Beau," I admit, just waiting for Harper's reaction.

"What!" Harper sits up so quickly in the hammock that we almost fall to the ground.

"Jesus, Harper."

"Sorry," Harper says shamefully as we return to a slow rock. "What?"

"Yeah, I bought it. Gave him a two-million-dollar check even though he only asked for five hundred thousand. The guy seriously needs to consult his accountant before just doing things. The land is valued at three million... I felt bad even giving him just two."

Harper blinks slowly. "I forget you're rich."

"You forget I'm a rockstar," I remind him with a leer.

Harper waves his hand at me in this weird flourish. "Well, it's easy to forget when you just lie in the hammock all chill."

"So chill," I mock as I poke him with my foot.

"Dinner's ready!" Jackson shouts from the porch. "Stop touching. Leave room for Jesus."

Just for that I lean forward, and tug Harper by the shirt until he's lying on top of me in the hammock. I can all but hear Jackson's furious whispering up on the raised porch. But I focus more on Benji's ecstatic laughter. See, my man gets it. Harper kisses my cheek, then pushes out of the hammock to wander up toward his man. I watch as Harper lifts up onto his toes to kiss Jackson's cheek.

Benji stands on the porch, leaning against the railing, eyes focused only on me. The weight of his attention always feels just a little undeserved to me. But I have to hope that with years and patience, maybe that feeling will go away. I feel a blush creep down my neck as I make my way toward him. The moment I'm within reach, he wraps his palm around my neck and tugs me close to kiss me softly on the mouth.

"You taste like cupcakes," Benji murmurs against my lips.

"Shared one with Harper."

Benji hums softly, face scrunched in thought. "Carrot cake?"

I snort. "That's terrifying."

Benji fondly shakes his head as he pulls away. "I know what you taste like, and what good carrot cake tastes like. Not that hard to discern."

"What do I taste like?"

Crimson splashes across Benji's face as he runs a palm over his own neck. "Like mine."

And there goes my heart again. I hope Benji can always tear me down to the studs with one shyly muttered sentence. I step into his arms to hug him tight, letting my cheek rest against his own. I love him so fucking much. I don't think I really lived before Benji. He made life so vivid and colorful, splashing hues across the dull pages that used to haunt my every waking moment. He's the sunshine in my sometimes very dark mind.

We sit down at the table outside, with Eli and Trevor also in attendance.

"Where're Beau and Colby?" Jackson asks as he sets the grilled chicken thighs in the middle of the table.

"Work trip," Eli says morosely. "Sucks."

"You could've gone with him," Trevor points out.

Eli shakes his head. "I'm too distracting. He needs to focus sometimes."

Jackson snorts in clear disagreement and rolls his eyes. "That man can't focus if you're within five yards of him. I doubt it's easier when you're *away* from him."

Eli's eyebrows furrow as he thinks it over. "I hadn't thought of it like that. Maybe next time... I'll go with him."

Trevor affectionately pats Eli's cheek, earning him a glare. "You get it now. Beau's just running a little late." Trevor turns to look at me and winks when he notices Benji isn't watching. Great.

I can't help but look around the table at the group of people who have decided I'm worth pulling into their circle. This group of friends that have Benji's back without blinking an eye. The same people that took me under their wings, somehow made this entire situation brighter than it ever could've been. My heart aches in my chest just at the very thought. I lift my hand to rub it and turn my head to find Benji staring at me like he often does. A year ago his eyes terrified me, how they looked right into me, seeing something that I couldn't. But now when he looks at me, I know he sees Nolan. The real Nolan. The Nolan I always wished that I could be.

And suddenly I don't think I can really make it through this dinner without falling apart.

I stand abruptly from the table, my chair skidding across the wooden planks of the porch. Everyone turns to look at me with confused eyes, everyone except for Trevor who wears a self-satisfied smirk. He nods ever so slightly at me and my heart swells again with what I can only assume is love. I grab Benji by the bicep, tugging him up even as he stares at me in concern.

"I have to show you something. Come with me?"

Benji grips my wrist tight, eyes flitting between mine. "Everything okay?"

"Yes, yes. I just—" I pause and blow a raspberry, wishing everyone wasn't listening with bated breath. "I have to show you something."

"Alright."

Benji holds on to my wrist as I tug him away from the table, back toward where our truck is parked in front of the apartment. Just as we round the corner, Beau pulls up in front of the house. He hops out of his work truck and swipes a hand over his forehead.

"Hey! I was just looking for you." Beau tosses me a pair of keys with a warm, crooked kind of grin. "See you later."

I catch the keys in my palm, feeling the heat of them burning through me. Benji looks between us, confusion etched across his face. I take his hand and tug him toward the truck without a word. Because Benji is Benji, he follows without asking any sort of questions. Just blindly trusting that I'm not going to drag him into the woods to kill him.

My hands shake as I get behind the wheel, even as we

head toward the property I bought from Beau. It's only about fifteen minutes down the road, but every mile feels like a million. Even the sound of Benji's soft breaths has me on edge, my teeth gritted as I worry that maybe this isn't what he wanted. What he pictured. I just want to give him what he wants. Everything he wants. After all, Benji gave me life. Can't I at least repay him this way?

The gate is right where Beau told me it would be. The wooden fence wraps the property full of scrub brush and tall oak trees full of moss. Even in the winter, everything is so green that I can't help but feel like this place is bringing me back to life as much as Benji has been. I hop out and unlock the gate with the keys Beau gave me.

When I return to the truck, Benji looks so impossibly confused that I can't help but laugh. "You'll see in a second."

Benji grabs on to the oh-shit handle as I pull through the gate. I feel silly as I hop back out to close the gate behind us, but a little silliness won't kill me. The sun is sinking below the trees as we continue down the heavily wooded dirt road. Orange and pink tinge the sky, while all the trees are deep green. Even the air smells more alive out here. Everything in my soul just settles. Everything is right for the first fucking time in my life.

I come to a stop in the middle of a clearing with flags dotted around it. The cascade of the river moving in the distance reaches my ears, along with the sound of the wind whipping through the trees. Even an owl hoots in the distance. I can see everything clearly, now I just have to paint the picture for Benji.

I come around the side of the car and open the door for him. His eyebrows rise into his hairline, but he takes my hand when I hold it out for him. Our fingers tangle together as I lead him toward the land that the contractor cleared just earlier this week.

"I brought you here to kill you," I tease.

Benji's laugh is warm and so familiar. "Well, have it at."

I clear my throat awkwardly as I squeeze his fingers. "I bought this property from Beau."

Benji's eyes go wide. "Yeah?"

I nod slowly as I take a deep breath. "I bought it, hired contractors, and they're going to start building our house next week." I tug him along behind me to stand where our front door is going to be. "This is the front door." I step through it and wave my arm around like the biggest fool on earth. "The entryway. Beyond is the living room that'll face the river behind us. The elevation is high enough that during hurricanes we shouldn't worry about flooding too much. But the insurance will be high anyway. And our bedroom will be in that corner." I walk him over to the far corner. "It'll have floor-to-ceiling windows so we can always see the trees and the sky. A bathroom with a clawfoot tub so you can bite me to bits, then soak me with your love afterward. And there will be five bedrooms, plus a music studio separate from the house."

"Nolan..."

I squeeze my eyes shut hard. "Let me finish. Please."

"Okay," Benji whispers.

"I thought a guest room would be nice so that Chris can visit, along with your moms. But I also thought maybe a study would be nice too so that we could have books and maybe a piano. I also thought maybe... I don't know. Maybe a spare room if one day we need a nursery. Just, thought it might be a good precaution."

"A nursery," Benji says, sounding oddly out of breath. "Nolan, look at me."

I shake my head hard. "Can't."

"Nolan." Benji grabs my face in his warm palms and squeezes. "Look at me."

When I open my eyes, I find Benji's gaze so warm, so steady, that my heart skips a few beats in my chest. His love is so visible to me now, so healing, so true. I tip forward to press my forehead against his, needing to share my breath with him in this too-emotional moment. Everything we've been through to this point got us here. Gave me him.

"Oh, Nolan. I want the life you've painted so badly. I want everything with you. I'm so glad you see it now, angel. I'm so glad you see it. Can I kiss you?"

"Please," I whimper.

And then Benji kisses me. The weight of his lips is as big of a promise as the house will be. He curls his arms around my body, tugging me close against the strong line of him. His heart beats against my chest, strong and real. Benji kisses me with such care and tenderness that I fall apart all over again in his arms, just to be remade when he pulls away to softly whisper in my ear, "Just us, angel."

I breathe in deeply, living in the glowing, beautiful knowledge that my life is finally mine. Belonging somewhere never seemed possible, yet here I am now. The future spans before me with all the promise of Benji's lips moving tenderly against mine. With Benji, I'm myself. Always just us.

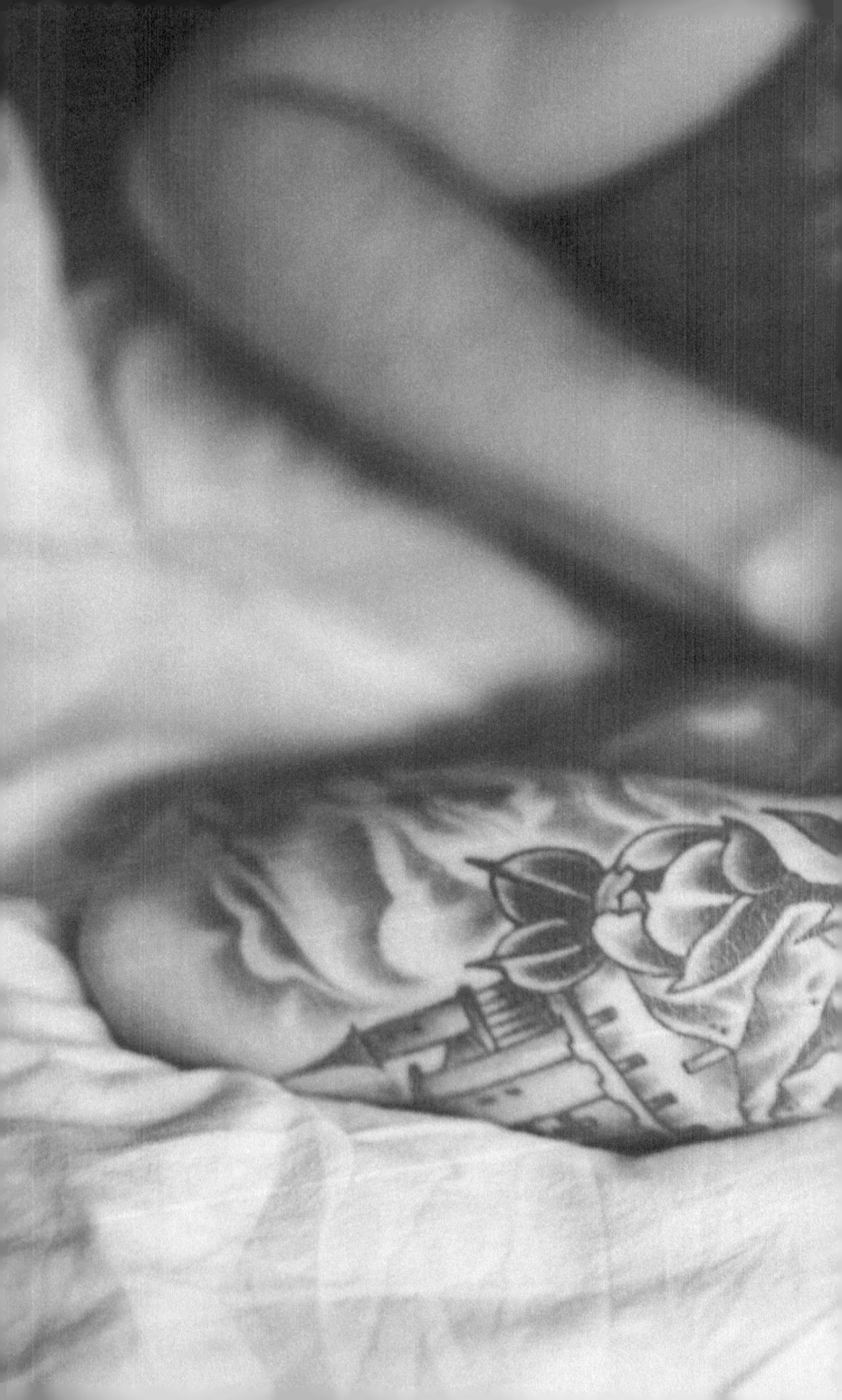

EPILOGUE
NOLAN

Three Years Later

Benji is sound asleep beside me. Sometimes, I still get caught up in staring at him as he sleeps. Just the very fact I'm lucky enough to call him mine is an astonishing fact that I'll never fucking take for granted.

A small snore escapes Benji just before he rolls over onto his stomach. The little hand-scrawled *just us* tattoo on his rib cage still makes my lips twitch in a hesitant smile because a full-blown grin is trying so badly to break loose. Just us. Ironically my matching tattoo is on the only piece of bare skin we'd been able to find, on my ass, of course.

Izzy shakes out her fur and paws her way toward me, all puppy eyes despite being five years old. giving her a few good morning scratches. I

put on Benji's hoodie, and take Izzy outside for her

Early spring in Florida is still my favorite. The air has just a slight chill to it as I step onto the raised back porch to let Izzy out. As predicted, she runs out into the expansive backyard and does a million loops before doing her business. I lean against the porch railing to look out at the river.

Sometimes I still can't believe this life with Benji is mine. Lifting my hand, I rub at my throat as the emotions I spent so many years pushing down rise to the surface. Letting myself feel things is somehow still foreign, even after so many years of therapy. Gets better each year, but still a shock to the system to feel the urge to cry and not push the tears down.

Izzy barks her happy little bark that she only ever aims at Benji. Turning my head, I grin brightly when I notice a sleepy Benji walking out to join us. His eyes are squinted from the early morning sun and he's so beautiful my heart aches with it. I reach out to grab his wrist and tug him close.

"Morning," Benji grunts before kissing the corner of my eye.

"Morning, stud."

Benji grumbles again before spinning me around to face the river and pressing his naked chest against my back. He wraps his arms around me to tuck his face into the crook of my neck with a satisfied hum. My body goes liquid and soft at his touch as always.

"Good sunrise," I point out.

Benji hums again. "Love you."

"Of course."

Benji bites my neck and grips my hips tight. "And?"

I fight a smile as I reach down to pat Izzy, who jumps at our legs. She's not the dog we imagined getting, but I'll take our rescued border collie over any other dog, any day. She's the perfect girl. She travels with us, knows when I need love, and is basically the dog version of Benji.

"Wanna take a trip?"

Benji pauses with his hands over my stomach before pressing even closer. I can practically feel his smile against my neck. "Finished the new album, did you?"

"Nope."

I get why he'd think that, though. Usually we celebrate a new album with a fun trip, just us, always just us. But I think maybe it's time for a different kind of trip. I spin around in the cage of Benji's arms and kiss his cheek when he's grumpy at the cuddle change. He's somehow even clingier all these years later.

"I'm thinking somewhere to see the northern lights. You've never seen them, right?"

Benji's smile is so warm it melts me to my bones. "Yeah, angel. Another one just for us."

Another thing we like to do is go places or see things neither of us has ever done. We are joint explorers, as Benji likes to call us.

Reaching up, I trace his eyebrows and nose, then lean forward to give him a soft good morning kiss. As usual, the kiss goes from *good morning* to *oh hello* to *uh-oh, let's get inside*, but I pull away because I'm not ready for that, yet.

"Think you can get a few weeks away from the restaurant?" I ask coyly, looking at Benji from under my eyelashes.

Benji chuckles and pushes closer until our bodies line up. "Let me see if the owner will allow it."

"And?"

"He allows it," Benji murmurs with a laugh.

A year ago, he'd bought into the restaurant he and Joey co-run at the farm. A little piece of paradise for us both had been found in Clay Springs. A beautiful little life. Every day is my happily ever after since I spent so many years expecting to die. But I kind of want to give Benji a permanent happily ever after.

"Marry me."

It's a statement, not a question. I watch as the orange and pink from the sunrise play over Benji's face. Watch as his eyes go from surprised to ecstatic to full of love.

"Are you asking or telling me, angel?"

"Telling," I whisper just before leaning close to kiss him again. His fingers tangle in my hair to tilt my head at the exact angle he wants.

After a few minutes of kissing, he pulls away to leave me breathless and wanting, which is pretty standard nowadays. His smile is so big that I see a million stars in his gaze. He swipes his thumb along my bottom lip, then laughs softly.

"I'll marry you every day if you want. Tell me when and where, whatever you want, angel."

"Marry me every day for forever?" I ask, my heart still somehow in my chest despite pounding away.

"As long as you'll marry me back," Benji argues.

I wrinkle my nose. "I don't think there are one-sided marriages."

Benji looks so fucking excited as he pulls away. "Let's go to the courthouse and do it now. Then you can sweep me away somewhere, all romantic-like, know how much you love that."

"If you tell anyone it was my idea, I'll kill you."

Benji's laughter is the last thing I hear before he tugs me inside and smothers me with his love.

ACKNOWLEDGMENTS

I'll keep this one simple. If you are loved by me, this is my love story to you. Benji is every person that has ever looked at me and found me worthy of love, of life.

Kristen, Lauren, Amber, Lexi, Devin, Hannah, JJ, Jenni and Gabi. Thank you for believing in this story and in me even when I made it hard to champion. Thank you for telling me Nolan is worthy of love and for calling him brave. Each time someone loves Nolan, a little crack inside myself is glued back together.

ABOUT THE AUTHOR

Maya spends most of her time imagining happily ever afters for the characters that live in her head. If she's not plotting how to heal broken hearts for her characters, then she's spending time with her precocious daughter. She loves baking competitions, listening to the same song on repeat for months, and discussing the latest pop culture event in a group chat with her best friends.